How
Snowball Stole
Christmas

Books by Kristen McKanagh

SNOWBALL'S CHRISTMAS

THE TWELVE DAYS OF SNOWBALL

HOW SNOWBALL STOLE CHRISTMAS

Published by Kensington Publishing Corp.

HOW
SNOWBALL STOLE
CHRISTMAS

Kristen McKanagh

KENSINGTON
PUBLISHING CORP.

www.kensingtonbooks.com

ISBN: 978-1-4967-3695-6 (ebook)

ISBN: 978-1-4967-3694-9

First Kensington Trade Paperback Printing: October 2022

10 9 8 7 6 5 4 3 2 1

Printed in the United States of America

To Courtney

Chapter 1

The fluffy blanket in this cushy leather chair is definitely my favorite place in Peter Diemer's house. After all, he put this here for me specially while I'm staying with him. Temporarily, of course. I like Peter, but he's not my forever family. Peter claims to not be a cat person, but I secretly think he is. I could snuggle into this cushy goodness all of December, especially now that the weather has turned cold and blustery.

Not that I *want* to stay. I miss my own home.

My owners, Emily, Lukas, and Miss Tilly, left me here with Emily's brother, Peter. I didn't pay attention to why. At the time, I might have been miffed about being abandoned. Again. However, this time they were smiling when they left, so I've decided not to worry about the why and I'm sure they'll be back.

They love me.

Besides which, this is the busiest season at Weber Haus— the Victorian inn they run, recently converted into a larger hotel and shops.

In the meantime, I'm taking advantage of this chair. Stretching all four paws out straight, I luxuriate. All I need is for Peter to come home and light the fire and feed me.

Pure bliss.

The slam of a car door has me perking my ears, but not lifting my head. Peter is late, as usual. The man seems to spend all his time at his job and leaves me here all alone. All day long. He doesn't deserve to be greeted at the door when my belly is this growly and I've been lonely.

But a second car pulling to a stop, headlights flashing across the ceiling, is new. Did Peter bring someone home with him?

Do I care enough to go look?

With a sigh I drop to the ground and pad silently across the carpeted floor to leap to the windowsill facing the street. Peter lives in what he calls a townhome. As far as I can tell, this is just a bunch of homes all squished together with a tiny garden in the back. Hardly a patch. I can hear people on the other sides of the walls, but I can't get into the other units. People are weird.

This is an interesting development, though. . . .

Someone is parked in front of the unit next door. Until a few days ago no one lived there that I've been able to tell. Until Christmas lights went up. I can see the side of Peter's dark head turned slightly toward me as he's looking over at what appears to be a woman buried up to her waist in the trunk of the car parked there.

What's interesting isn't her . . . it's him. The fact that he's bothering to look. Peter doesn't bother with anyone these days.

My, my, my.

Visions of happy humans falling in love dance in my head.

After all, I have a gift for matchmaking. Those silly creatures just can't see happiness staring them in the face until I show the way. And Peter, despite being a bit of a grump lately, is one of the good ones. He deserves happiness.

Since he's moved back home, he seems sort of . . . I don't know. Restless. What Peter needs is to fall in love and settle down. That would fix everything.

He takes a step off the porch and my ears prick and my whiskers twitch in anticipation.

Except, instead of going over to nicely introduce himself, he stomps in her direction. I frown. What is he doing?

"Hey!" He doesn't shout it, but with his low voice, it's close enough.

With a screech to wake the ghosts of Christmas past, the woman jerks up, banging her head into the top of the trunk with enough force that I can hear it through the window.

Hand to her chest, she scrambles away from Peter, her expression a picture of fright.

Good job, Peter. I give a little kitty huff. He's going to mess everything up before I can even get them started.

All he wanted was to get his new neighbor to take down the blasted Christmas lights that she'd put up partly on his side of the roof, not scare the bejeezus out of her.

"Sorry." Peter held up both hands in a gesture meant to ease nerves.

Of course, he'd scared her—a woman alone, at night, in a strange neighborhood, and a man appears out of nowhere. Not his best moment. He scowled. He'd been having a lot of "not his best" moments since his accident last year. Apparently, comas, like the one he'd been in after the accident, could lead to a change in a person's personality. It turns out he was one of those "lucky" few, and easily irritated was now one of his top traits.

"I didn't mean to frighten you." He tried to not sound angry. When she relaxed a tiny bit, he slowly lowered his hands. "I'm your neighbor next door."

He pointed.

She looked in that direction, then back at him, a slow smile blooming. "Nice to meet you. I'm—"

He wasn't here for chitchat. "I'm afraid that you put some of your Christmas lights up on my side of the roof."

The woman, whose face was still mostly in shadow, blinked. That much he could see. "Sorry?" she asked.

Did her voice waver with humor?

"Your lights." He pointed again. "I'm in the condo next to you on the left. Your lights are on part of my roof line."

She looked over his shoulder and seemed to study the lights, which were glowing a bright rainbow of colors. "I don't understand."

What wasn't to understand? "I don't want them on my part of the roof."

"It's only one little area," she countered in a reasonable tone that only set his teeth on edge. He got that tone from his mother and sister a lot lately.

He crossed his arms. Why was she arguing with him? His roof. His rules. "But it's right under my bedroom window and it's making it hard to sleep."

"Oh." She bit her lip. "Don't you have curtains?"

Peter gritted his teeth. The man he'd been even a year ago would have probably laughed it off and not even brought it up. But him these days, and after two sleepless nights in a row . . . "I have blinds. It shows through."

"Oh," she said again. "But it's Christmas."

"And?"

"The lights won't be up more than a month, and it would really throw the whole look off if I took them down. Do you think you could maybe handle it for that long?"

"No."

The slump of disappointment was almost comical, then she suddenly straightened. "What if I get you a sleep mask?"

"No."

Then she suddenly grinned and huffed at the same time, hands landing on her hips. "Do you not like Christmas or something?"

Only she said it with such charm, that a tiny bit of his irritation trickled away. Not enough to give in, though. "I like it fine. Just not when it's shining in my bedroom window."

A flash of white teeth in the shadow and her husky chuckle reached out through the cold and the dark and maybe even warmed him up a tiny bit.

Who was this woman? Most people these days didn't argue with him. They just agreed or left him alone. His sister, Emily, said he could be intimidating when he wanted. So why was his neighbor laughing?

"Fine, fine," she said. "I'll take down that strip."

About time. "That's all I ask." He gave a brusque nod, then turned to head inside his own home.

"Hey," she called after him. "Isn't your name Peter?"

He pulled up sharply at that, swinging around to stare at her with a small pit of dread in his gut widening by the second. "How do you know that?"

The woman stepped out from behind the raised trunk of her car and the lights from her townhome illuminated her features. "We met a few years ago at Weber Haus. My name is Lara Wolfe."

Recognition hit. Two years ago, he, and several other single men, had flirted with her for a single night. Then he'd left to return to duty and oddly she'd stuck in his head for months after. Hard to forget a face like that, though, or her soft gray eyes, or the air of fragility that had hung over her, tugging at every protective instinct he'd had.

Peter hid a wince. Because the man she met two Christmases ago was not the same guy standing in front of her now.

Lara moved closer and held out a hand, which he reluctantly took. Tiny in his. The woman was tall, at least five-seven, yet still petite. She should really be wearing gloves. It was cold out. But if he said that out loud, he'd sound just like the overly caring neighbor on his other side, Mrs. Steinz.

"So, you've moved to Braunfels?" He managed to find a relatively polite question to ask.

If he recalled correctly, when they met, Lara had just been passing through the area, alone at Christmas and staying at Weber Haus. However, if she was moving in next door, it had to be permanent. Peter had seen the "For Sale" sign on the unit next to his come down a month ago, but he'd assumed his new neighbor would probably be another elderly person like Mrs. Steinz on the other side—well-meaning, kindly, a tad nosy with not much else to do beyond pay attention to the neighbors, and at least fifty years too old for him.

But Lara didn't look anything like Mrs. Steinz. She was, however, also out of his league.

She wasn't in-your-face beautiful. He'd had experience with that type and had the scorch marks to prove it. Instead he thought of her more like the sugar plum fairy in *The Nutcracker*. Kind of ethereal. Lara was dressed uber-casual in jeans and a pullover, chin-length white-blond hair peeping out from under a white knit hat pulled down to cover her ears, framing a pixie face. Something about her just radiated something good and true.

He should probably keep his distance. After all, he wasn't in the best headspace lately. Clearly.

"Yes," she said, then waved at boxes in her trunk. "I'm still getting settled."

And yet had found time to put Christmas all over the front of her townhome and part of his.

"Well . . ." He tried to dredge up what old Peter would have said. "Getting around town all right?'

What a dumb thing to say.

"Yes." The smile flashed again, shooting star bright.

Another flash of unwanted attraction kicked in. Because when she was serious, she was girl-next-door pretty, but when she smiled, she was next level. Something he decided not to notice.

"Everyone has been so nice," she said.

"I bet," he muttered. Especially the single men.

Surprisingly dark eyebrows, given her hair color, lifted slowly, amusement twinkling in her eyes. "Should I take that as a compliment?"

Peter huffed a laugh, the unused sound rusty, like his vocal cords needed to shake off the dust and crank into gear. He hadn't flirted with a woman in a while. Not even with the nurses in the hospital last year when he'd been recovering from the injuries that had changed the trajectory of his life. "Pretty girls don't stay single for long around here."

Slim hands landed on her hips, her lips tipping into a grin. "From re-acquaintance to proposal in less than five minutes. That might be a record."

Unaccustomed heat flushed up his neck into his cheeks. "I didn't mean—"

"I'm teasing," she assured him.

Oh. "Well, what can I say . . ." He shrugged.

Then winced because what kind of comeback was that? A lame one, that was what. He used to be smoother. Probably better if he left now.

For a flash of a second Peter considered stepping up his game—not that he'd had any game so far—and asking her out before anyone else had the chance.

Better to leave it. Given how the last date he had gone on went, he wasn't fit company for anyone these days. Besides, he was busy with the family bookstore, and she'd just moved in.

"Is that your cat?" she asked suddenly. "I seem to remember her at Weber Haus when I was there."

Peter jerked his gaze over his shoulder to frantically search the area around them, looking for a puff of white fur among the bushes or down the street. Snowball was the Houdini of all cats. A true escape artist, but he hadn't lost her yet. His sister got home from her trip soon, and he had zero intention of losing that darn cat before then.

"Where?" he demanded, the word coming out like a shot.

"Um . . ." Lara lifted her hand to point. "In the window."

Oh. He should seriously walk away now. No doubt he'd just looked like a panicky mother hen, barking like that about a cat after yelling at her about Christmas lights, which he was already starting to regret.

This just kept getting worse and worse.

Snowball sat primly in the windowsill, watching them with apparent interest, ears pricked. The cat even lifted a paw, pressing it against the glass as though waving at them now that they'd appropriately acknowledged her presence.

He'd have to explain. What kind of self-respecting single man, over a certain age and living alone, owned a fluffy white cat? "Snowball is my sister's. I'm watching her while Emily and her husband, Lukas, are out of town for the weekend for his photography stuff."

"That's nice of you."

Was that a hidden chuckle in Lara's voice? "Yeah, well, she's probably hungry. I'd better go." He glanced at her car. "Do you need any help?"

She shook her head. "I can handle it. Thanks."

Right. "Well . . . it's nice to see you again." His mother's voice in his head told him to add something polite. "Errrr . . . welcome to Braunfels."

"Thanks." The way her eyes crinkled, he was pretty sure she caught that.

With a nod, he turned and left her there. When he walked in his door, Snowball was sitting in the foyer looking extremely unimpressed with that performance.

Peter took off the beanie he was wearing to keep his short-shorn head warm and ran a hand over the burr of his hair. "I know. You don't have to say it."

The tiny white cat—the runt of the litter abandoned by her mother a few years back in the woods near Weber Haus— appeared to shrug as though saying, *As long as you know that wasn't smooth, who am I to harp on it.*

* * *

Lara turned away from Peter's closed door with a chuckle and perhaps a lighter step than when she'd gotten out of her car earlier.

What were the odds that she would be living next door to one of the few people she'd met that one night visiting here? At the time, she'd just lost Granny, and her older brother and his wife had been out of the country for the holiday, leaving her completely and utterly alone. So she had not really been in the right frame of mind for flirting. But she remembered Peter. Might have even thought of him a little bit when she decided to move to the area.

Peter Diemer had been . . . adorable, in a Scroogey sort of way.

Though she doubted he appreciate the descriptor.

Dark hair under a beanie that made him look like a sailor. She remembered from before that he wore it cropped short, slightly longer now on the top and standing up as though he'd been running his hands through it all day. Broad shoulders and, though it was difficult to tell under thick jeans and a winter parka, she also remembered the muscles. Capable. That had been her first impression two years ago. The same impression still stood now.

She didn't remember him being so grouchy back then, but maybe she would be, too, if her sleep had been affected.

"Too bad I probably won't see much of him," she told herself as she went back to work carrying her boxes inside.

It was tempting to do something about that. Ask him out, maybe. But the timing was bad. She was beyond busy trying to move and open her brand-new toy shop.

Lara was a small business owner now, and that needed *all* her focus. Because if she failed at this . . .

She pulled her shoulders back. *Nope. Failure is not an option.*

Her new mantra.

This was her dream and had been since she'd dropped out

of college to pursue it. Yes, she'd made mistakes—some she was still paying for, even. Those mistakes just made her want to do this right even more.

Prove herself.

After making handcrafted toys and selling them from her home for years, as well as running crafting events for kids and adults, she'd decided to expand her business into a brick-and-mortar shop . . . and she'd snagged a prime location. Granted, the bidding war she'd got into over the spot had stretched her budget even thinner, but the location was worth the risk. No matter what her brother said.

The last of a series of small shops located in a renovated barn behind the Victorian inn in the mountains called Weber Haus. Right next door to a bakery, no less.

Prime. Great foot traffic. Guaranteed business. At least it would be as soon as she opened.

Three more trips to the car and she finally closed and locked the front door behind her. All the while, the small cat next door—Snowball, an apt name for an all-white puff of fur like that—had watched with interest from her windowsill perch where she'd returned after Lara assumed she'd greeted Peter. No sign of her neighbor, though.

With a thump, Lara set the last box on her kitchen table, the thin sheets of wood inside rattling against each other, and glanced at the clock. Not as late as yesterday.

I shouldn't be this tired at nine o'clock.

She hadn't realized, when she'd started all this, exactly how much work would be involved. Sleep and food were no longer had with any regularity in her life, snatched somewhere between planning, deciding, moving, stocking, contacting contractors, still making her own toys, way more than she had to when her business was mostly online, and a gazillion other things.

The question right now was, did she have dinner before or

after she worked on packaging the wood airplane assembly kits that she'd already cut?

"Dinner first." Talking to herself was becoming a thing. Granny used to be who she talked to about everything, and even though Granny was in heaven now she couldn't quite kick the habit.

Lara could picture her silver-haired head bobbing in agreement. Her grandmother, who'd raised her, had always been trying to get her to eat.

"I could snap you like a twig," she would say, pinching Lara's arm playfully.

Granny probably wouldn't approve of the microwave macaroni and cheese Lara decided to dish up, but it was fast, hot, and cheap. And she could eat it while going over a few things on her computer.

In less than ten minutes she was all set up and staring with dismay at her screen. Her own personal Scrooge had struck again.

On the Braunfels' town forum, a person going by the tag "Right Rudolph" had posted yet another comment about her shop and it hadn't even opened yet.

> You know you're dealing with an outsider when they bid an outrageous price to lease space for the store. No doubt the new toy store coming to the Weber Haus shops is part of a corporate franchise. A poorly run one, based on that one business decision. How are they going to turn any profit with a rent that high? We've seen these franchises come and go—StyleMart, Diamond District, Francine's. We also know that when these stores fail, it doesn't look good. Is this really what Braunfels needs?

He sounded just like Lance. Her brother picked at her nonstop. He saw it as protecting her from herself, because he'd never understood. Dropping out of college to make toys was a horrible decision, he'd said. Running her business out of Granny's was taking their grandmother's generosity too far, he'd said. Brick-and-mortar stores were almost guaranteed to fail, he'd said. Moving so far away was idiotic, he'd said.

Which was why she hadn't told him about the bidding war she'd won for the space at the Weber Haus shops.

This guy was just another doubter like Lance.

"Who doesn't love toy shops, anyway?" she mumbled.

The universe did not answer.

With a sigh, Lara stared at his words—which poked a hole right in the center of her hopes and dreams—and debated what she should do. She hadn't responded to any of Right Rudolph's bah-humbug comments yet. What a handle, too. Did he think he was lighting the way, somehow? Still, attacking one of the townspeople didn't seem like the way to win friends and customers here, and it was plain as the nose on Pinocchio's face that she wouldn't change this man's mind. Assuming he was a man.

But she could at least address the false assumptions he'd made. And since he could post anonymously, so could she. Quickly she created a handle of "Nutcracker" and formed a brief, mostly professional-sounding post.

> It is good to see citizens concerned about their town. Let me put a few of your worries to rest. I believe The Elf Shop is not part of a large corporate franchise, but a sole proprietorship. They have a strong business plan and built-in customer base from previous online business to support this transition. They also have their own professional business advisors. Thank you for your input, but there is no need for concern. This shop will fit in perfectly with the Weber Haus shops and the town of Braunfels.

The part about the business advisors was maybe pushing the truth a little. She was her own advisor, and she had a lawyer to check all legal paperwork. But she'd learned about owning and operating a small business from her grandmother, so her practical experience counted.

She'd done her market research. In addition to tourism, especially around the holidays and winter months with a ski slope fairly nearby, there were plenty of young families with children. And her crafts workshops were geared for all ages. She knew this was the right place for her.

Now . . . no more posting. She would bide her time and just have to prove to everyone that a toy shop was exactly what the town had been missing all along.

What if he ruins everything before I even get started?

"If I ever figure out who this guy is, I might be tempted to risk Santa's naughty list to bop him on the nose."

No way was she going to get any more work done tonight. Not after that. Besides, she had to take down that strip of lights.

Thinking of those, a sudden spark of mischief lit her up. After dealing with Right Rudolph, she was in a feisty mood, and she knew exactly what to do with those lights.

Chapter 2

———————

Heading to work a few days later, Peter locked his front door behind him, then turned around and stopped dead in his tracks, staring at a sign in the small yard in front of Lara's townhome.

Two wooden signs that had been painted. One was cut to look like Ebenezer Scrooge. Beside it, a sign decorated in Victorian Christmas style. The strand of lights she'd taken off his part of the roof wasn't off completely and had obviously found a new home. She'd draped the tail of them in old Ebenezer's hand, making it look as though he was yanking them down.

And the sign beside him, so beautifully decorated, read, "Bah humbug."

Peter stood and stared, and stared some more, because he was pretty sure Scrooge's face looked a lot like . . . him. He let his head fall forward until his chin hit his chest. The thing was, he should be irritated. Even pre-accident Peter would have been. Maybe. He sometimes found it hard to tell how he might have reacted to certain situations before. But right this second, instead of anger, he found his lips twitching. Enough that he pressed them together hard.

She was calling him a Scrooge. In front of *everyone*. Subtly. Because most people driving by and glancing quickly would just think she was calling herself a Scrooge. But *his* was the only townhome without decorations, and it looked like Scrooge had started there to take the lights down and kept going. It really shouldn't be making him laugh.

But it was just . . . well . . . funny.

Plus, he had to admit to being a little impressed that he hadn't scared her off with his grumpy ways.

The sound of another door opening caught his attention. Without meaning to, he raised his head to look and paused. Then shook his head.

Clearly Lara Wolfe was his exact opposite when it came to waking up and starting the day. One of that incomprehensibly cheerful breed . . . a morning person. The woman practically bounced out of the house, despite hefting another large box. She hummed to herself as she moved. He almost expected to see birds and mice dancing around her and humming along. Thanks to his previous occupation, he would always be an early riser, but he didn't have to like it.

As soon as she saw him, she beamed a smile in his direction, and probably would have waved if she could.

Meanwhile his stomach clenched. He knew what it was. He'd been attracted two years ago, the other night, and was again right now. Didn't mean he had to do anything about it. No woman deserved the bad mood he was perpetually in these days.

Try not to bite her head off.

"Nice sign," he called out before thinking through the words.

She paused, balancing the box on top of her knee, and blinked like she had to think about it. The grin that spread across her features stopped his breathing for at least five seconds. "You like it?" she teased.

"Like is a bit strong." He shrugged. "But I'm sleeping much better."

She chuckled.

"Can I help?" He tipped his head at the heavy—based on the way she leaned back to heft it—box she carried.

"That would be great."

He moved closer, only to have her plop the box in his arms. Whatever ton-of-bricks she was disposing of inside, it gave a rattle. While he held the thing, she unlocked her car and popped the trunk.

"Old books or something?" he asked as he deposited it inside.

She shook her head. "Stuff for work."

Only with the way she gave a little frown, he got the impression she didn't want to talk about it. When she closed the trunk and shot him a quick smile and a final sounding, "Thanks. See you later," he didn't bother to push.

Only she paused as she was getting into her car. "Where are you off to so early?"

The street was as dark as it had been when they'd met the other night, the winter sun not yet rising at this hour. Even in summer, though, this would still qualify as early.

"I moved home recently to take over my family's bookshop." Now why had he chosen to say it like that? He could have just said "work" or "I run a bookshop."

"Huh." She nodded.

Peter cocked his head. "What does that mean?"

More than one person had told him he could be intimidating, or at least intense. But once again, did Lara act like she found that to be true? Nope. Instead she laughed. "I just didn't have you down as the bookshop type."

She wasn't wrong. "What type did I strike you as?"

"I don't know." She narrowed her eyes and studied him, as though giving it serious consideration. "Motorcycle racer? Police captain? Forest ranger?"

Not bad. She wasn't far off on the police force guess.

"I was ready to be home." Those words felt as awkward out loud as they had in his head. "My parents aren't far off from retiring and offered for me to take over. If I didn't, then Mom and Dad would eventually have sold it, since my siblings' interests went in other directions."

"Do you enjoy it?" Something in her tone told him this wasn't just idle curiosity. As if his answer meant something to her. Though he couldn't begin to guess what or why.

Peter tapped his thumb against his nicest pair of jeans. "After a year of learning how things are run, it's still . . . hit and miss. I like the business side of it at least."

Books weren't really his thing, and while most people who came into the store were nice enough, people really weren't his thing, either. Besides which, some were pushy, or rude, or downright odd. But as jobs went, this was a good one and already established, so he was determined to make it work.

"Where is it located?"

"Just off Main Street right behind Morrison's Mountain Shop."

The location wasn't great. They didn't get enough foot traffic from downtown because they weren't on the main strip, which was why he'd wanted to move the store to the shops at Weber Haus, the same location where Emily's highly successful bakery was doing so well.

Unfortunately, someone else had outbid him for the last open storefront. They'd offered an exorbitant rent that went well beyond what Peter knew was good business sense. At that rate, they'd be out of business faster than Jack Frost could nip at their noses. Peter had had to let them have it. Didn't make him less bitter, though. Now he had to wait for them to fail.

"Maybe I'll swing in and check it out if I get done with work early enough tonight," she said.

She wanted to check out the bookstore. Why? Probably just being nice. Paying lip service to her new neighbor.

Before he could say anything, Lara waved and closed the door, driving cheerfully away a second later, leaving him feeling out of sorts. Nothing new. Nothing that he seemed to be able to control, either, which only upped the frustration. The grumbling going on in his head lasted all the way to the bookshop, which wasn't far.

He let himself in the back door only to find his father already in the building. Andrew Diemer was tall and lanky with salt-and-pepper hair and a distinguished beard, which was a more recent addition. He'd given his height and his blue eyes to all four of his sons, including Peter, but not his only daughter. Emily looked like their mother.

"You don't have to come in so early, Dad," Peter said. Then winced at how bossy he sounded. Clearing his throat, he tried again. "I told you I'd be here."

"I wanted to adjust the window display."

The one his father had adjusted at least three times this week. The new holiday display highlighted seasonal books along with some cute decorations, which was usually his mother's department. When his parents finally retired, which was supposed to be soon, he would definitely need to pawn the buying and displaying of what he silently labeled "cutesy stuff" off on one of his clerks.

"I thought we'd got it right this last time." Peter tried not to let the frustration leak into his voice.

His dad shrugged, studiously ignoring Peter's tone. "Our foot traffic didn't increase this past week, so one more try couldn't hurt."

A new location was what couldn't hurt, but the best one had been stolen from him. It would have been so perfect. Right next to Emily, with her husband Lukas's photography gallery on the other side of her, and all located with the inn run by Lukas's great-aunt Tilly with the help of her manager, Sophie, who had just this summer married Peter's best friend, Daniel.

Nothing he could do about it right now, though, so he pushed the tide of frustration down, as much as he could.

Peter strode into what had been his dad's office for almost three decades and was now his. Taking a seat, he started his computer. Since the location situation was on his mind, he hopped over to the Braunfels town forum and turned slightly smug with what he read there.

He wasn't the only one who didn't want the new toy shop that was going in at the location he'd bid for.

"Are they picking on that poor toy shop owner again?"

Peter jumped at the sound of his mother's voice right behind him but didn't turn around. "Picking on" was a strong way to word it anyway. People were just voicing opinions and concerns. Perfectly valid.

He cleared his throat. "Multiple commenters are agreeing that expensive, handmade toys aren't going to sell well. Not with a big box store that offers reasonably priced toys just down the road."

Okay, down the mountain in another town, but not that far away.

"Hmmm . . ." His mother leaned closer, her still mostly dark brown hair pinned up in an elegant bun, dark brown eyes perusing the various comments. "Actually, it's not a franchise," she said.

"What?"

"Yes. Someone else posted about it." She leaned over him and scrolled to a comment he hadn't seen yet, posted several days before, too. "See."

Peter frowned over the words. A sole proprietorship? Was that true? A faceless corporation was one thing, but a small business owner was different.

"I don't understand why people make such a fuss," his mother murmured. "I think a toy shop is delightful, and if it fails, then that will be too bad, but really the owner's problem."

"But the town's problem too, Mom," Peter insisted. "And

Weber Haus's. After all, it impacts their reputation if stores start not thriving there."

"I doubt that," she returned idly, as she stood up and leafed through a stack of mail. "With the new hotel addition for extra rooms, as well as event space, the various community activities, including the Christmas Market, and the shops that are in there now, which are all doing well, it's a very popular location."

He was more than aware. Which was why he'd wanted to move the bookstore there. Peter's hand curled into a fist.

"Oh, it looks as though the toy store has announced their opening day." Now Mom sounded excited. "They're going to have a Santa for the children and ice cream. That's a good idea."

Peter sat straighter in the chair, looking at where his mother was pointing. Sure enough, the grand opening was announced for a week from tomorrow. A Saturday and Saint Nicholas Day.

His mother was right. The toy shop owner was smart, and clearly aiming to be here to stay. But ice cream? In winter? Sounded like a bad idea to him.

Maybe it was time for another "Right Rudolph" post on the forum. Except guilt wormed its way through the frustration he'd been dealing with since losing the space. If this was a single owner at that toy shop, and not a corporation, maybe he should just back off.

He and his family were lucky that they'd inherited a business already well established, but that didn't make it easy. To be going it alone starting from scratch . . .

Still, the business decisions they were making weren't a good sign. He logged in to the forum and typed a quick response to Nutcracker's reply. The last he'd post. He was out of it now.

Good luck to them.

* * *

Walking into her shop, Lara deeply inhaled the scents of fresh-cut wood and paint, excitement fizzing through her like Pop Rocks candies. It was finally coming together. After all this time. Years of trying not to listen to her brother. More years building her craft and her business. And now these last months setting up the store.

There'd been days when she thought her dream wasn't going to happen. But here she was!

"It's turned out well," a male voice sounded from the back of the shop, and she glanced over at Daniel Aarons, tall and broad shouldered with a beard. That combined with the plaid work shirt and jeans, he always put her in mind of a lumberjack.

When she'd bought the space, she'd been informed that Daniel was the person all Weber Haus properties worked with for all things construction, interior and exterior. She'd met him once before that, when she'd stayed here last time. That one brief visit was why she'd set her heart on the shops at Weber Haus in the first place.

And Daniel, happily married now to the woman who managed the inn, had turned out to be a gem.

She glanced around, her cheeks stretching with her happy grin, because the place looked exactly like she'd hoped. "There were days I didn't think it would be finished."

Daniel chuckled. "I have days like that on every project I take on."

Sounded awful to her. Lara couldn't wait to finally be settled. Moving to Braunfels had been a huge leap of faith, and if this store failed, she'd be wiped out financially. No way was she proving her brother's doubts about this endeavor right, but she had only one shot to make it work. One shot held together with Christmas wishes, helpful elves, and more than a sprinkle of hard work and determination.

"Ready for the walk-through?" Daniel asked.

Today was supposed to be the final day of construction-related items, focused on details and cleanup. Tomorrow, she would start filling the shelves. That was entirely on her and she could not wait. She set down her bag and the box with a thud and nodded, heart thumping. A huge step closer to her dream today.

Daniel handed her a roll of blue painter's tape. "Put a small strip next to anything that needs fixing or changing and tell me what you want done."

"I'm sure it's fine—"

"I don't just do fine."

"He really doesn't," a feminine voice sounded from behind her.

Lara made a mental note that she needed a bell for the front door. Daniel had done his job too well and the thing was silent. Turning, she found a young woman with long dark hair pulled back in a ponytail, a kind smile, and a familiar face.

Last time Lara was here, Emily was helping run the inn and cooking for the guests. The other woman had been kind to her over that previous visit, when her heart had been hurting so badly after losing Granny. The question was, would Emily remember?

"Hi." Emily tipped her head, frowning with vague recognition as she moved into the shop. "I'm Emily Weber, but I think we've met before."

Lara grinned on a small whoosh of relief. "We have. I stayed at Weber Haus a few Christmases ago."

"That's right!" Emily's smile broadened. "And are you the new tenant?" She waved around the shop.

"I am!" That came out a little too bubbly, but she didn't take it back.

"Good for you. And I'm your neighbor." Emily pointed to the location to the left of The Elf Shop.

"The bakery is yours?" Lara asked, perking up. Having a

familiar face, especially such a nice one, nearby would make things feel a tad less lonely.

"It is. Miss Tilly hired a new cook for the inn and a manager last year as well, so I was able to focus solely on my business."

"Well, the bakery is terrific. I've been in there every day. You're going to be dangerous for my thighs."

Emily chuckled. "Thanks. It's a lot of work, but following a dream makes it all worth it."

Lara glanced around her. "I can relate to that."

Another smile from Emily. "My husband, Lukas—who you might remember from Christmas as well?"

Lara nodded.

"Well, he owns the photography studio and gallery on the other side of me. We've been on a trip for his work and got back just now. I wanted to introduce myself and welcome you to the Weber Haus shops."

"Thank you so much." At least one person in this town seemed happy about her bringing the toy shop here. Right Rudolph could just stuff it.

"Out of curiosity . . ." Emily cocked her head. "Why did you choose Braunfels for your shop? Is this an expansion perhaps?"

No one had asked her that except the people who had denied her loan. Not that she'd really spoken to more than her Realtor and lawyer, as well as Daniel and the workers so far.

"This is my first store," she said. Expansion wasn't remotely in her sights yet. "I've been working out of my home, primarily with online orders and classes held in my workshop, until now. I came into a little money a few years ago and decided to go for it."

Her inheritance from her grandmother, actually. She'd rather still have Granny, but her beloved grandmother had been so proud to give Lara this opportunity.

"But why not start a shop in the town where you were?"

Too close to her brother, for one thing. "I fell in love with Weber Haus and the whole area when I was here. When I found out about the new shops attached, I just knew it would be perfect."

What she hadn't realized was the tornado of decisions and activities to make the transition and get started. She'd had to handle a lot of the negotiations, construction, and decorating long distance as she moved at the same time.

Emily grinned. "It is perfect," she assured Lara. "I'm sure your shop will fit right in and I hope we'll be friends."

"I would like that."

"Right," Daniel said beside her, clearly antsy to continue. "Very nice, but we have things to do, Em."

Emily wrinkled her nose good-naturedly at Lara's construction manager. Though, of course, Daniel had been at that same Christmas celebration, so clearly they knew each other. Even so, Lara raised her eyebrows at Daniel, who shrugged. "Her brother is my best friend."

"Peter?" she asked. Emily had more than one brother, she knew from before.

Daniel chuckled. "You remember him?"

"Of course." Wait. Did that sound too eager?

Apparently not, because Daniel was still talking. "You'll find that when you remove the tourists from the equation, Braunfels is a pretty small community."

"I'm starting to learn that."

"We're taking Tilly out to lunch, so I'd better get going," Emily said. With a friendly wave she left.

An hour later, Lara and Daniel were done with marking the various spots that needed fixing or changing. Luckily all small things that Daniel assured her would be finished by the end of the day. The shop was . . . perfect.

A long, skinny space, she'd set it up with three separate

sections. At the front of the store in the larger section were all the toys, arranged not only on tall shelves along the walls, but on oblong tables with more shelves throughout the middle of the floor. The cash register was on a counter tucked against one wall toward the back of the space, forcing customers to walk deeper into the store to check out.

A dividing wall led to a smaller area in the middle, which was set up with long, communal tables, where she could hold her toy-making and crafts classes for both children and adults. In addition, when not in use for her workshops, the tables could be used to sit at and enjoy the handmade ice cream set up in a refrigerated glass display to one side, along with old-fashioned candy chutes along one wall and a few more shelves of toys. Finally, in the back behind another dividing wall was her office and storage area.

And all decorated with a Santa's workshop theme. All exactly how she'd pictured it.

She'd quit college for this. Worked hours and hours for this . . . for years. Despite everything Lance said, she was going to make it. Or bankrupt herself trying. She bit her lip, trying hard to hold back the worries that wanted to bury her.

No time for worries, though. Too much to do.

Daniel had also given her the green light to start stocking the shelves. Immediately she headed to her car, then on to the storage unit where she'd been holding most of the goods as they'd arrived or she'd finished making them. Her previous business had been only her handmade items, but now she'd be bringing in stock from other fellow toy makers. All custom items like her own, sold on consignment.

She tossed her purse on the front seat of the car.

Mrrrow . . .

Lara froze at the tiny sound of a cat meow.

"What on earth?" Lara wondered aloud with a frown.

Mrrrow . . .

Cocking her head as she slowly got back out of the car, she checked underneath and all around, worried she'd run over the cat if she tried to drive away, but found nothing.

Mrrrow . . .

That had been muffled, but definite.

She stopped and listened hard. When the sound came again, she moved in the direction of it. Toward the back of her car.

Mrrrow . . .

"No way," she muttered.

But she pulled out her keys anyway and popped the trunk, only to look into a white fluffy face and two frightened crystal-blue eyes.

"Snowball?" she asked. The cat Peter had been watching?

The beautiful, tiny animal was shaking so hard her white fur appeared to vibrate. "You poor thing." Lara scooped her right up, cuddling her against her chest and running a soothing hand over her soft, slight body. "How in heaven's name did you get into my trunk?"

And when? Lara had been here for several hours now, so at least that long. Peter would probably be out of his mind with worry if he'd already realized she was missing.

Since she didn't have Peter's number, she figured she had two options. She could take the cat to Emily, except the other woman had just said she was off to lunch somewhere. Or she could take her to Peter. Let him figure it out.

Clicking her tongue, she got back into the car, settling the still-trembling cat on her lap. Probably not the safest spot, but she couldn't let her shake on the car seat. Besides, Snowball curled right up, staying perfectly still, except for the quiver of her muscles.

"I guess we better get you back to Peter," Lara decided. Good thing she knew where he lived and worked.

It shouldn't take too long to add the stop to her list. Although, it all depended on that four-way stop on the way into town. The only road available from Weber Haus to town, that intersection had a tendency to turn into a parking lot from all four sides, with people politely trying to wave other people through, or being too confused about who would go next. Hopefully that wouldn't slow her down today.

I am never, ever sneaking into a human's bag ever again. Not ever.

It's never gone so horribly wrong before. After all, when I've done this with Emily, she always puts her purse in the back seat of her car. Not the trunk.

The *pitch-black* trunk with no way to get out.

Not only that, but while Peter and the neighbor woman were talking, the bag I got in wasn't her purse, I guess. Because when we got to where she was going, she turned off the car and didn't get anything out of where I was hiding.

She left me there.

For forever.

Even with my cat eyes, I could hardly see. And I was in there so long. What if something had happened? A thousand what-ifs had occurred to me in the hours—hours, I tell you—that I was stuck in there.

I've never been so terrified in my life. Lesson learned. No more sneaking into human bags.

Emily will be happy about that, at least.

I can't stop shaking, but thankfully this lady is nice, letting me snuggle with her as she drives.

Also . . . I perk up as her warmth penetrates my fur coat . . . she's taking me to Peter. Which is exactly what I was hoping would happen.

The job of a kitty matchmaker is to bring the couple together as often as possible.

Chapter 3

The bell over the door chimed, and Peter could hear his mother greeting whoever came in. Then suddenly . . . "Oh my gracious." Followed by, "Peter!"

He was out of his seat in the office faster than Santa shot back up a chimney, reacting to the tone in his mother's voice. Not panic or alarm. More like exasperation.

"What is it?" he asked, coming into the store from the back only to slow at the sight of pale blond hair and amused gray eyes.

Lara.

Why would his mother be exasperated by his beautiful neighbor showing up? She'd said she might check the bookstore out. He just hadn't expected it so soon.

A small kernel of warmth—he didn't want to identify it, but smugness probably came closest—settled in the center of his chest. One that he should probably ignore. Too complicated.

"I didn't expect you to visit the shop *today*," he said around a frown, sounding gruffer than he intended.

"Peter—"

Lara's laugh cut his mother's warning off. "I didn't expect to, either," she confessed. Which slowed him down slightly, mostly with confusion.

Then she turned to face him more fully and, in her arms, she was cradling a fluffy white cat who looked back at him with guileless, wide blue eyes.

Peter came to a dead stop, still a few feet away. "Snowball."

How did Lara have his sister's cat? The one who was supposed to be happily locked up in his house right this second. "Where did you find her?"

"I'm afraid she somehow stowed away in the trunk of my car. Poor thing has been stuck in there for hours. I just found her."

Peter mentally smacked his forehead. Lara wasn't here because she was interested. She was here for the darn cat.

Of course she is, a small voice poked at him. *You're not exactly pleasant to be around lately.* Though, given the teasing sign in her yard, he thought she hadn't minded that much about the light thing.

Frustration started to sizzle just under the surface. Peter bent a glare on the cat. "I thought we had a deal, runt."

They had, and Snowball had kept up her no escaping side of the bargain . . . until today.

"A deal?" Lara's voice wavered with a new layer of amusement, lips twitching.

He grunted. "Snowball here is an escape artist. They let her get away with it at Weber Haus, but I told her quite clearly that if she escaped my house, I'd bathe her every day for a week."

The way Lara's lips pinched together, he knew she was laughing. Not at him, but sort of alongside him.

Slightly behind her, Peter's mother raised her gaze to the heavens as though praying for help for him.

He ignored his mother and shrugged, not about to explain how this particular cat acted more human than feline. "She hates baths."

"I'm fairly certain," his mother said, "that I raised you well enough to understand that cats don't speak human."

"This one does." He was sure of it.

With a sigh, he crossed the rest of the distance to Lara and scooped Snowball out of her arms, doing his level best not to brush against anything off-limits. Difficult when the cat promptly latched her claws into Lara's soft pink sweater.

"Eek," she squeaked. "Hold on. She's got skin."

Working together, they carefully detached each little claw. Wow, Lara smelled good. Something sweet. Not cookies or bread like Emily often smelled of after working all day in her bakery. This was different . . . like cotton candy maybe. Or candy canes. That was closer. More peppermint-y.

Peter loved peppermint. Would her lips taste like that, too?

With a jerk he stepped back, ignoring the way Lara's eyes widened at the abrupt move. She'd given no indication that she thought of him as anything but the moody neighbor who hated Christmas lights and whose cat had messed up her day. Kisses should be the furthest thing from his mind.

"Thank you for bringing her to us," his mother said to Lara in her patient mom voice.

Peter winced. He should have said that.

"It was no problem," Lara assured her, gaze flicking to him, then away. "The shop is along my way, anyway, and I told Peter this morning that I wanted to see the bookstore."

"This morning?" his mother asked, glancing between them.

Adorable color surged into Lara's cheeks. He was too busy staring, though, and she glanced at him suddenly, obviously expecting him to have jumped in already.

"Lara is my new neighbor, Mom," Peter tossed at his parent abruptly.

"Your neighbor." His mother straightened suddenly. "The one with the 'Bah Humbug' sign in the yard?"

Lara choked off a laugh. "I get a little creative sometimes."

At least she didn't tell his mother about the lights.

Peter ignored them both. "I bumped into her this morning as we were both leaving for work, which must be when Snowball got in her car." He lifted the little cat—her body so slight in his big hands he had to be extra gentle—to look her in the face. "Because I know I left you in my kitchen right before that."

He swore the darned animal grinned at him, which only made him scowl harder.

"I think you're right . . ." Lara was definitely hiding laughter again and doing a bad job of it. "She really does understand human."

Peter shot his mother a triumphant look and got a doubtful snort for his trouble.

"Why don't you give your nice new neighbor a tour of the shop before she goes," she said.

Wince.

His mother could not have been any more obvious. Scooping Snowball out of his arms, she smiled at Lara. "Welcome to the area, dear."

"Thank you," Lara called after his mother's retreating back. Then smiled at him. "I'd really better be going."

The disappointment that settled in his gut, as though the day had suddenly turned a little less bright, was followed by an immediate brush of surprise. Because while this woman was just his type, he'd hardly said more than hello and goodbye to her. Why should he be this level of disappointed?

"Things to do?" he asked, stalling.

"Millions." But her tone of voice said she enjoyed doing whatever those millions of things were.

"I guess you'd better hurry up, then." Hell. Even when he meant to tease it came out snarly.

Except rather than take offense, she chuckled. The husky sound struck the opposite chord as her leaving did, but in the same disproportionate way. Day suddenly brighter again.

What is going on with me today? Maybe he should get more sleep. Only now he couldn't blame the lights.

They stared at each other for a long second. Not awkward, though. More like they both were caught up in whatever was humming between them. Because he could practically hear the buzz coming off the connection.

Or was that just wishful thinking?

"You haven't moved?" his mother asked, coming back toward them.

Peter jumped at the same time Lara said, "I really should be going."

She hurried away but shot him a smile over her shoulder as she went through the door to the jingle of the bell.

His mother came up to stand beside him. "Pretty girl."

He flicked her a glance out of the corner of his eye. "Yup."

"You make her laugh."

He'd noticed. He didn't make anyone laugh these days.

His mother adjusted a book on a shelf that didn't need any adjusting. "Maybe you should offer to show her around, introduce her to a few new friends."

He grunted a noncommittal response. His family just wanted him to be happy after what the past year had wrought, but dating was pressure he didn't need.

"Only women, though," Mom tacked on. "Just to be safe."

"Hey," he protested automatically.

His mother swatted his arm and laughed not very subtly as she walked away.

"You are not forgiven for breaking our deal."

I'm lying curled up in the front passenger seat of Peter's truck, but I lift my head at that, shooting him an unrepentant look.

Because I got Peter and Lara to spend time together, and that's the secret sauce of love.

After successfully helping Emily and Lukas, and then Sophie and Daniel, find each other, I know a thing or two about matching humans. Mostly, all I need to do is force them together.

Hopefully Peter will eventually be smart enough to take advantage of the opportunities I set up. He might even move up on my list of favorite humans.

Never above Emily, Lukas, or Miss Tilly. They're my forever family. But Peter could move above Daniel. He is definitely smarter than his friend.

"I swear you just gave me a satisfied smirk, runt," Peter grumbled, shooting me a frown.

See. Smart.

I lay my head on my paws and purr, loudly, so that he knows I am pleased with myself. Now I just need to come up with another way to get them together.

Lara looked over the brightly lit store, made even more so by the darkness outside the windows, as though The Elf Shop was a sparkly Christmas ornament. Pride, happiness, and nerves churned, brewing a potent cocktail inside her, all three elements only growing more knotted inside her the closer she got to opening day.

The rest of this week leading up to her opening, she'd taken to sleeping in the office of her shop, just to save time. But not anymore. She'd already packed up the sleeping bag she'd been using and set everything to rights. Time to look professional, even if a small voice inside her whispered that maybe she was going to fail at having a shop. That she wasn't smart enough or experienced enough to do more than sell toys out of her home. All words Lance had hurled at her for months before she'd moved here.

She thought she'd gotten good at blocking him out. All it took was concentrated determination, the ability to think of other things while he droned on, and maybe a pair of industrial soundproof earmuffs probably wouldn't have hurt.

But some of the doubts and worries still lingered. Better to play Pollyanna and focus on the excitement.

Tomorrow was her opening. Tomorrow.

Saint Nicholas Day and the first day of the Christmas Market. Maybe she should have done a soft opening on Friday or Saturday before, to work out the kinks. She shoved the thought, one that she'd had a million times already, aside. Too late now. Either this worked tomorrow or it didn't.

She could hardly believe it, even with the proof in front of her eyes. For the thousandth time, she mentally ticked through everything that she'd had to get done, making sure she hadn't missed anything.

Shelves stocked, computer systems for inventory and sales and taxes all sorted, advertising about the opening had been going out all week already, a schedule posted for workshops that would start her second week open. No one had signed up yet, though, but she'd deal with that hurdle after the opening. She'd hired and trained two women as salesclerks. Sally Ann was older with kids out of the house and looking for a little extra income. Cassie was in high school and working her first ever job. Both would be here tomorrow, in case there was a rush of people.

Lara had no idea how much foot traffic to expect. Hopefully the Santa she'd arranged for the kids would help draw folks inside. The storage space in the back of the shop could be in better shape, but customers wouldn't see that part. She'd deal with that eventually, too. For now, she couldn't look past tomorrow.

It needed to go *perfect*. Everything was riding on the success of her store.

The bell over the door rang and she turned to find Emily walking through. She'd hardly had time to chat with her shop neighbor since the last time. Just quick waves as they passed each other.

"What are you still doing here?" Emily's smile edged toward tired, shoulders drooped, and no wonder. She was up early baking every day. Lara would know, because she'd smelled it in the mornings. But today was Sunday, and the shops were all closed on Sunday.

"Getting a head start for tomorrow," Lara said. "Opening day. Just finished and I'll go home in a second." And probably not sleep a wink.

Emily grinned. "I remember my opening. I thought I was going to throw up, I was so nervous."

Lara laughed. "Does it get any better?"

"Sort of. Eventually." Stepping farther in, Emily ran her gaze over the shop, shaking her head in what appeared to be awe. Awe was good, wasn't it? Or maybe it was too much? Had she gone overboard with things?

"I can't believe you did all this yourself," Emily murmured, still gazing around.

Okay. That sounded like too much. *I knew the dancing nutcrackers in the window display was over the top.*

A small nod to the handle she'd used on the forum—Nutcracker. Given Right Rudolph's sarcastically passive aggressive response of "Good luck to them," this small rebellion had made her feel better.

At least he hadn't posted anything new since. Maybe responding the way she had had worked. Convinced him to leave her to fail or succeed without his commentary.

"It looks amazing."

Oh.

Oh!

"Thank you." Deep breath in and out as Lara's fingers itched to tweak this shelf or revisit that display. After second-guessing herself on everything, she was forcing herself to leave it. She needed to see how everything worked with customers in the store and then make changes. "A lot of work, but worth it."

"I was surprised you didn't hire anyone to help you stock it."

That would have been great, but she was trying to save money for emergencies, and that didn't count as one.

She'd been denied the business loan she'd applied for. Thanks to Granny's inheritance, even after taxes, she'd still been able to pursue her dream. She really could have used the loan money to get her through the first year or two of a new business, though. Instead, now she was doing this all on her own. Christmas season for her opening would be the determining factor in her success.

Not that she would lay any of this on Emily. Lara wasn't one to spread her troubles around. "I enjoyed doing it. That way I could make sure every detail was exactly how I wanted it."

Emily chortled. "A control freak, in other words."

"Guilty." Lara laughed, then scooped up her purse, thinking through what she needed to do tonight. The machine she used to cut some of her wooden pieces was too loud to run at this hour, so probably best if she got out the materials to stain the Xs and Os she'd cut for her tic-tac-toe games yesterday. The Xs worked better in a darker stain.

"Want me to walk you to your car?" Emily asked.

Lara shook her head. It might be dark, but Weber Haus, and all of Braunfels for that matter, felt . . . safe . . . somehow. For a city girl, it hadn't taken her long to lose her wariness. Though she might not ever leave her front door unlocked like many apparently did in the area.

After she locked up the shop, they walked side by side toward the house. Lara had gathered that Emily and Lukas lived there with Lukas's aunt Tilly, who owned the property and focused on the bed-and-breakfast based in the house itself.

"Best of luck tomorrow," Emily said at the back door.

"I've been talking it up to everyone who comes in the bakery. I know it'll be great."

Lara took a deep breath, trying to calm the skitter of nerves that had taken up a permanent roost in her stomach. As though the Mouse King nutcracker in her window display had invaded. "Thank you. I really hope so."

Hope, pray, wish. She might even write a letter to Santa at this point.

Twenty minutes later, she dragged herself into her town-home. She'd only been in here to shower and change period-ically over the last ten days. She'd really cut herself short trying to open when she was. But being open for the festivi-ties kicking off the holiday season officially had seemed a smart business decision.

"I'll sleep when I'm retired," she murmured to no one in particular. Slurred more like.

Retirement suddenly seemed a long way off. Exhaustion was turning her sluggish, and she would need to be up early tomorrow and on all day. Forcing her body to move, despite feeling as though someone had sewn lead weights into her muscles and eyelids, Lara ate dinner, showered, set out her clothes for the next day, then, instead of working on the tic-tac-toe staining, settled into bed with her computer on her lap. She could at least get a little paperwork done.

When she turned it on, though, the first screen to appear was the town forum, and she didn't mean to look, but her hand just sort of clicked anyway.

But Right Rudolph was silent.

Why did that make her more nervous? Almost as though Right Rudolph's lack of comment was just as much of a con-demnation.

But really, her own doubts were making her feel that way.

The foot traffic visible to everyone would be an indicator of her success or failure. Maybe even subtly encouraging people to show up . . . or not.

In her head, Right Rudolph and her brother were there, telling her she was making another huge life mistake.

According to Lance, dropping out of college to make toys had been the first one. Trusting her college ex, Elias, the second. The kind of mistakes one might make when they were fresh out on their own, running a business and didn't really know how to handle finances and, most importantly, trusted the wrong person.

She'd met Elias at a college club event for young entrepreneurs. He'd been older, and she'd foolishly thought wiser and more mature, than the other boys. In school for his master's degree in accounting, Elias was the president of the club. That had been a year before she'd dropped out to start her own business, and Elias had been so eagerly helpful when she did. At least she'd thought so. Turned out he'd been helping himself, not her.

Still . . . she'd learned from that. She didn't make the same mistakes twice.

Tomorrow would be telling. Lara dropped her head against the headboard with a thump, visions that weren't exactly of sugar plums dancing through her head. Her sitting in an empty shop with her two helpers for hours and hours as people passed by with pitying looks cast at her door, more like.

Tomorrow could be an unmitigated disaster.

"Just a few customers," she whispered, pleading with God and Santa. "Don't leave the store completely empty all day." Lara sighed. "Put a good word in for me, Granny," she added, talking to her grandmother's spirit.

Then she rubbed at the spot under her ribs that hurt when she missed the woman who'd raised her. This was Granny's dream for her as much as it was for herself, and she wasn't here. She wasn't here to see it, to talk to or debate with, or to ask advice of.

Lara was on her own for all of this.

Too tired to deal with what she'd wanted to get done, with a click, she shut her laptop and turned off the light. Work could wait an extra day. Rest was more important, and clearly, she needed to work on her own faith in herself.

Tomorrow was important, and she was going to make it the best opening in the history of toy shops.

Chapter 4

Peter had promised himself that he wouldn't go anywhere near The Elf Shop on its opening day. He'd even skipped his almost daily run to Emily's bakery for his breakfast. So why he found himself driving toward Weber Haus on his lunch break was still a mystery. At least three times he considered turning back around and grabbing lunch from somewhere else. Anywhere else that wasn't in the Weber Haus shops.

But before he knew it, he was rounding the bend in the road, driving past rolling, snow-covered hills, to the inn on the outskirts of town. The house itself had always been a sight to see. Set back off the road down a long drive, the pristine white wood-sided building was two stories, three if you counted the large attic, with a wraparound porch and a red roof. Built by the Weber family during the Victorian era, it was a classically beautiful example of a Victorian home.

At least, that's how his mother and Emily described it every time he insisted on calling it a house.

"Good grief," he muttered at the sight of cars packing the gravel lot off to the side of the home.

Terrific.

He should have known better than to come today. Saint Nicholas Day and the kickoff of the Christmas Market all on the same day was sure to be a draw. The place would be a zoo. In fact, he followed a busload coming from the town down the drive, something that the town did during the Christmas Market because the parking wasn't enough and Miss Tilly refused to let people park on her pristine, currently snow-covered lawns.

Peter spent all of ten minutes searching for a spot. In the end, he cheated and parked in the family's private parking that was fenced in near the house, out of the way of the shops. Then he slowly, reluctantly made his way toward the sound of merriment and a ton of people.

The sounds of the shops and Market grew louder until he rounded the corner into the main strip that was set up at the back of the property. Peter really had to give it to Daniel. He and his crew had done a remarkable job retrofitting what had originally been the barn and carriage house into permanent shops while still keeping that original Victorian ambiance.

White with red roofing and ornate iron scrollwork here and there, the two buildings formed a quasi-main street of sorts, in the center of which sat a large, matching gazebo that was new, intended to match the rest of the buildings. A focal point for shoppers and also a makeshift stage when needed, it was currently being used by a barbershop quartet singing Christmas carols.

In addition, for the Christmas Market, temporary stalls had been set up all around and even into the field beyond. He hadn't been here for last year's events—having been laid up in the hospital at the time, dealing with what eventually would change everything about his life—but this was more booths than he remembered there being when the Market had been held in town. That was for sure.

He intended to not even glance at the toy shop—which should have been his family bookstore reopening on this perfect weekend—as he went into Emily's. But how could he miss it, after all? The bakery was right next door. The booths meant he didn't see the store until he was standing directly outside it. And the second he did, his feet slowed.

"Whoa."

He blinked at the sight of all the people inside. So many that he couldn't really see the layout or decorations or even the toys. Just a crush of humanity through glass that had been hand-painted to look as though he was looking into Santa's workshop at the North Pole.

Wait . . . were those nutcrackers *dancing* in the window display? How'd they do that?

You don't care, he told himself firmly. But he didn't move away, either.

This was not what he'd expected. At most he'd thought maybe two or three families with children would be interested in a toy shop at any given time, but the store was crammed. Jam-packed. Sardines had room to spare compared to that mob.

The door was propped open, probably to cool things off inside with that many bodies. The dings and whistles and bells of various toys could be heard even where he was standing outside and over the sounds of the crowds and the quartet. A hell of a lot of racket, if you asked him. All that noise.

And people were *smiling*.

On a *whoosh* of realization, there went all hope of the shop not doing well and giving him a chance to get the bookshop into this perfect location. Maybe he should have counterbid. Paid out the nose for it. Eaten into his profits.

No. He'd been right about this. Whoever outbid him would regret that move on their own. Especially a sole proprietor just struggling to get started.

For a brief second, a flash of fluffy white fur caught his eye inside the shop. On instinct, after watching Snowball for his sister, he craned his neck to be sure, but didn't see her anywhere. He had no intention of going inside the store to search. Besides, the cat was Emily's to deal with, and Snowball tended to wander the entire grounds of Weber Haus, including the shops, with no problem. In fact, she'd become a bit of a mascot for the place. Better to just leave her alone if she was in there. The new managers would find that keeping her out was impossible anyway if she wanted to be in there.

With a grumbling sigh, Peter plodded away, jerking the glass door to Emily's bakery open perhaps a little too hard.

"Steady on." Emily was standing behind the glass display of goodies, giving him an exasperated look over a bunch of super-fancy Christmas cupcakes she was busy arranging. "I know all those muscles from the navy make it hard to do things normal-human style, but try."

"What?"

She wrinkled her nose. "Don't break my door, brother dear."

He gave another grumbling sigh and stepped farther inside. "I didn't."

"What's got you in a mood?" she asked, moving behind the counter to stand in front of where he stopped.

He shrugged, with zero intention of sharing. She could put it down to lack of sleep for all he cared. And she wouldn't be entirely wrong.

"The toy store seems to be doing well," he said without meaning to.

Emily's eyebrows twitched. "Did you expect any different?"

Hoped was more like it. "Well, with the Market going on, that will help. I'll be curious to see how it does after the holidays are over and people aren't buying gifts and whatnot."

"The town is full of young families," Emily pointed out. "I'm sure it will do great. It's adorable inside. You should see it."

No thanks.

He had no intention of bumping into the manager who'd beat him out on the bid for the space. Peter pictured an older man, Geppetto-like, hoping his puppet would turn into a real boy. He'd be wobbling around the store with a smile under a big mustache and talking to all the kids. That or some slick twentysomething kid, fresh out of business school and who wanted to be CEO of a huge franchise tomorrow. Either way, Peter wasn't interested.

"What can I get you?" Emily asked, her expression more concerned than usual. Probably because he'd gone off into thoughts instead of answering her.

He saw that expression on her face way too often lately. Hers. Mom's. Dad's. Their brothers'. A concern that had never been directed his way before . . .

She was staring at him now, the concern only deepening the line formed by her scrunched-up brows. What was the question? Oh, right. Food. "I'll take your lunch special."

"I think you should have moved the bookstore into these shops to save you the trip here every day." She winked.

Yeah. Me too.

She knew he was looking for a new space for the bookstore. Everyone in his family did. But he hadn't shared much more than that, including being beaten out for the spot the toy shop got, mostly to keep his parents from getting their hopes up. At this rate, moving the bookstore could be years from now.

If the shop survived that long.

"No, I understand completely, Mr. Ayers. You shouldn't come if you're so sick." Lara paused, listening to the man apologizing on the other end of the line.

"Really. I wouldn't want the children exposed, anyway. Just take care of yourself," she assured the man who was supposed to play her Santa. For her opening day. The one she'd advertised for.

What in heaven's name had she been thinking?

The number of people pouring into the shop was a dream come true. Her first day of business was a fantastic, if astoundingly overwhelming, start to things. But with just two helpers, she was already run off her feet. And now her promised Santa was a no-show, thanks to a severe bout of stomach flu.

"We'll find someone, I'm sure," she assured the distressed, and miserable-sounding, Mr. Ayers. Then hung up on the sound of retching.

Sinking onto the chair in her office in the back of the shop, she allowed herself ten full seconds of desperate panic. *What am I supposed to do now?*

Picking up the red Santa hat with its fluffy white trim and puff ball at the tip, Lara wrinkled her nose. She didn't know any other men around here to ask and doubted finding another "regular Santa" player nearby and ready to go in thirty minutes was going to happen.

Wait! She jerked upright on a flash of revelation. *Except Daniel.*

Sucking in a sharp breath, she reached for her phone. But as she did, a streak of white caught her eye a blink before a fluffy white cat—a *familiar* fluffy white cat—sprinted across the office, snagged the Santa hat from her fingers, and took off into the store.

"Snowball!" she cried, jumping to her feet and rushing after her.

Only the tiny cat, nimble and small, easily weaved through the feet of all the patrons packed into her store. Pasting what she hoped wasn't a panicked-looking smile to her face, Lara had to force herself to move safely around people, which slowed her down.

She burst out the open door just in time to see Snowball take advantage of a customer leaving Emily's bakery. The cat—with the Santa hat hanging from her mouth and dragging on the cobble-stoned ground because it was practically bigger than she was—dashed inside, the glass door closing behind her with a soft thump.

At least there she'd be a little corralled.

Lara rushed into the shop after her. The whiff of sugary baked goods hardly penetrated as she searched the ground. Then she sighted Snowball. The little cat had run right to the feet of a man standing at the counter paying for his food, his back to her.

"Snowball," Lara called, and hurried closer.

Only the cat didn't run. She sat down, tail curled around her feet fastidiously, looked Lara directly in the eyes, then gently laid the Santa hat right on the man's booted feet.

"Snowball? What on earth?" she heard him rumble in a familiar voice. He leaned over and picked up the hat. "What do you have here?" he asked the cat just as Lara skidded to a stop beside him.

Recognition hit in an instant. Peter. A small rush of pleasure mixed with relief that she had the hat back, and embarrassment at how she lost it.

Along with . . . a terrific, wonderful, ludicrous idea.

Sometimes, when desperate, ludicrous was the only way out of a tricky situation. After all, if Santa could do it, then so could Peter Diemer.

"I'm afraid that's mine," Lara said, a smile blooming, because she had the answer to her prayers standing right in front of her, only he didn't know it yet.

Thank God for Snowball, that's all she could say.

Peter blinked. "Lara? What are you doing with a Santa hat?"

"Actually, about that . . ." She put a hand on his arm. "I'm in a bind and could really use your help."

His brows lowered in a questioning frown. "I'm happy to—"

"The man I hired to play Santa got the flu at the last minute and I'm desperate."

Horror sparked in his eyes, the lines deepening around them, making her want to laugh if she wasn't in a bit of a hurry. She'd left her helpers alone in the store and clueless as to why she'd abandoned them to the chaos.

"You need a Santa?" he asked slowly, as though he was sure he'd misheard her. "Are you running one of the booths at the Market?"

"The new toy shop, actually. I own it, and Santa starts in"—she pulled her phone from a pocket to check it—"in fifteen minutes." She tugged at his sleeve. "Please? I'm desperate."

While he hadn't been smiling, his expression had been vaguely pleasant. But at her words, all pleasantness faded away, not just from his lips, but from his eyes as well. "*You* are the new toy store owner?"

Something in his voice was off, but she didn't have time to identify what. "Yes, I just opened today."

"It's really adorable, Peter," Emily said from where she stood behind the register.

"But . . ." Peter was frowning now, looking as though the real Santa had put used coal in his stocking instead of a gift. Then he shook his head, expression blanking out. "I'm sorry, but I have to get back to work."

"Please," Lara said again. Begging would happen next. On her knees if she had to.

"For heaven's sake, Peter," Emily piped up. "I'll call Mom and Dad and let them know. They'll understand and can cover for one day."

Lara curled her hand around the hunk of shirt she still held on to, as though she could drag him over there. "I don't know anyone else."

He grimaced, an actual contortion of pain. "I'd be a terrible Santa—"

But she wasn't lying. She'd take anything that could walk and talk at this point.

"All you have to do is dress up, smile for the camera, ask

each child what they want and whisper it to Cassie, who is playing your elf. She'll write it down and include it with the picture they get."

"Lara—"

She took a deep breath and stepped closer into him, lowering her voice. "I'm not kidding when I say I'm desperate, Peter. I know it's a lot to ask. I'll pay you back somehow. I promise. But . . . I don't have any other options."

"Peter!" Emily snapped. "I'm going to cut you off from all breakfast bagel sandwiches and lunch specials if you don't help her right this second."

The man might be handsome, but the reluctance twisting his face was almost comical. Lara would have felt sorry for him if she wasn't in such a bind.

"Fine," he finally gave in.

Thank God. Prayers answered before she'd even prayed them. Someone was definitely looking out for her.

She glanced down to find Snowball still sitting at their feet, watching them with interest. Did cats smile?

"Thank you," she mouthed, semi-embarrassed to be thanking a kitty-cat-slash-Santa-hat-thief.

With a quick smile at Emily for her help, Lara proceeded to tug a visibly reluctant Peter right out of the bakery, into her shop, and to the office in the back. She pointed at the Santa suit hanging off her standing lamp. "I'll leave you to change here. Cassie is already dressed in her elf costume. I'll send her to get you when we're all ready for Santa to make his big appearance."

She bit her lip, considering his rather crabby expression. "Would a big *Ho-Ho-Ho* as you walk into the room be too much to ask?"

"I've landed in hell," she thought he muttered under his breath. But before she could take it back, he said, "I'll see what I can muster."

"Thanks." Before she scared him off with more requests, she scooted out of the office, closing the door behind her.

Talking with both her helpers, Lara started organizing all the children into a line. A line so long already that it ran out the door and through the crowded Market stalls outside. Nothing she could do about that. They needed to leave room for people to shop or leave the store and at the same time lead up to a seat fit for the real Santa, a red velvet cushioned seat wide enough to fit him and one, or even two, children at a time. Even with Peter's broad shoulders.

Oh no! She'd forgotten the belly. Peter didn't have a belly, as lean and muscled as he was. Even through his thick winter coat she could tell that. She sighed. Too late now. "Go get Santa, Elf Cassie."

Cassie, with her dark hair piled into two high buns and big green eyes, looked precious in a green elf suit with red-and-white-striped leggings. The teenager had gone a little sexier than Lara would have preferred when they'd ordered the outfit online last week, but nothing objectionable.

With visible enthusiasm, Cassie hurried away.

A few seconds later, a hush fell over the crowd as the tallest Santa Lara had seen in a long time stepped into view. She glanced at his feet and had to swallow down a loud laugh that wanted to escape at the sight of his red velour pants barely coming to the tops of his black boots. *His* personal boots, she noted, not the shiny fancy ones that came with the suit. Good thing the jacket was made large for the belly, or he'd be popping out of it. As it was, this Santa was ripped.

Peter planted his feet wide and crossed his arms, which strained the seams of the jacket enough that she thought she could hear threads popping. He looked over the tops of the wire-rimmed glasses perched on his decidedly-not-button-shaped nose.

"Ho. Ho. Ho," he boomed. Though he sounded more like

he was barking orders, his gruff, gravelly voice also decidedly not jolly.

Dismay sunk in her stomach. Her new Santa was going to scare these kids into tears in ten seconds flat. What had she been thinking, dragging Peter in here? The man was the grumpiest Santa to ever take on the role.

"Now . . ." His blue eyes were far from twinkly as he stared at the gathered children waiting in line. "Who has been naughty and who has been nice?"

Lara lifted her gaze to the ceiling, seeking a miracle, and waited for the tears as silence hung heavily over the store for a solid, excruciatingly long ten seconds.

Then a little girl giggled. "Mama, he sounds like you when you tell me to clean my room."

Which started the adults twittering with laughter. Seeing that they thought it was funny, the other children started to giggle, too, the laughter building.

Peter, seeming to play up his crotchety Santa bit, cocked his head, eyeing them narrowly. "Hmmm . . ." was all he said.

Then he stomped his heavily black-booted feet over to the throne, plopped down, and looked at his helper. "Elf Cassie, I hope you brought me only nice children today."

As though shot from a BB gun, Cassie escorted the first child—the same girl who'd giggled and started the laughing a second ago—to sit beside him on the chair.

Lara held her breath, waiting to see how he'd handle this.

"Ellie Markingham," Peter Santa boomed. "I *know* you've been a good girl." He cocked his head. "Except . . . I wonder if you've been eating all your vegetables?"

Ellie's big blue eyes went wide at the sound of her name, and wider still at the mention of the veggies. The other children in line, hearing how he'd known that, started loud whispers. "He knows about the vegetables."

Now how on God's green earth had he known that? Or

was it just a very good guess, given most kids didn't like to eat veggies? But he knew the girl's name, too. Peter glanced over Ellie's head, caught Lara's own wide-eyed stare . . . and lifted a single eyebrow, as though daring her to break his cover right there and then to ask.

Caught staring, Lara jerked her shoulders back and moved away, leaving him and Cassie to it as she manned the register. Sally Ann, her other clerk, traded out to help customers around the shop and to keep the line organized.

Lara grinned to herself as Peter's gruff words floated over the heads of her customers to where she worked. So far, no tears. Maybe her first day as a shop owner wasn't going to be a disaster, after all.

Though it had been a near thing, and they still had the rest of the day to go.

I prance across the snow-covered yard, not deep today luckily, just cold on my paws. The kick in my step has every-thing to do with a successful scheme to bring Lara and Peter together.

Watching Peter playing Santa had been worth almost get-ting my tail caught in the door when I'd run into Emily's. Even if doing that meant he and Lara aren't spending actual time together, that had been hilarious.

Seriously, I hope someone takes a picture of him in that getup.

Hopping up on the white wooden fence that separates the back of the shops from the house, I pause as a movement snags my attention from the corner of my eye. I balance on top of a post to peer closer.

In the distance another cat is walking through the yard to-ward the wooded area to the east with a prowling gate that piques my interest. I sniff the air delicately. A boy cat. From here the other kitty appears to be about my age. Handsome with a sleek black coat interrupted by a T of white fur on his chest, and maybe his paws, though that could be snow. A new cat, too, because I've never seen him around here before. He is more interesting than the old, cranky tabby to the other side of the property.

Much more interesting.

I sit and watch, hoping he might look over. Suddenly, he pauses and swings his gaze my way. Trying to act nonchalant—this is my home, after all, and I have every right to be sitting on this post—I pretend to be busy daintily preening myself. Maybe he'll notice my soft white fur, or how petite and elegant I am.

Risking a peek to see if he's watching, disappointment drops into my stomach like icicles falling off the house with a chilly crash.

Not only is he not watching . . . he's gone.

I sit very still, searching the horizon for any sign of him, but neither hide nor hair is visible. Moving with a little less prance than before, I leap down from the post and continue on toward the house, wondering all the way who the new cat in the neighborhood might be.

I stop on the small steps leading up to the back kitchen door and meow loudly. The new cook they'd hired last year to replace Emily to make food for guests staying inside the house is a softie and lets me in and out whenever I wish. Sure enough, the lock clicks and then the door swings open.

"There you are," Mrs. Bailey says, pleasantly round face pinched with worry. "Miss Tilly has been looking for you everywhere."

Is it time for our daily nap? I wince. *Whoopsie.*

Though Miss Tilly would understand if she knew what I had been doing. Not that a kitty can tell a human anything. Humans are a little silly that way. After all, I can understand animals other than cats. Why can't humans understand animals?

Hurrying through into the hallway, I scurry through the foyer to the burgundy velvet-covered wooden staircase with its beautifully carved banister—original to the house, Miss Tilly was always proudly telling guests. I am two steps up when Sophie appears at the top.

"Snowball," she scolds. "You're late for naptime. We've been looking everywhere."

I lift my chin and tail and prance with attitude up the stairs. I'm not *that* late, after all. Besides, you'd think Sophie would be a little more grateful after I helped her and Daniel figure out they were in love last year. That ring on her finger is entirely because of me.

The ring of the doorbell has me pausing, though, and I turn on the stairs as Sophie passes by on her way down and goes to answer it.

"Mr. Muir!" Sophie is grinning wide. "I didn't see your name on our books."

A new irritation swirls with the disappointment from my encounter with the cat. Mr. Muir is here? Terrific.

He'd stayed here last year around the same time—bringing a pair of turtledoves with him. I spent days and days trying to get at those taunting birds who would coo and coo at me through his bedroom door.

"I registered under my wife's name—God rest her soul. I wanted it to be a bit of a surprise."

I narrow my eyes, tempted to growl. A surprise for who, exactly?

Sophie seems to know because her smile widens. "You left too soon last year."

Mr. Muir shrugs. "The family seemed to be dealing with a lot at the time, and I didn't like to intrude. After that, I'm afraid it took me the rest of the year to work my courage back up."

Courage for what?

Sophie reaches out and squeezes his arm. "Well . . . you're in luck. The family is here this time with no plans to leave and much less going on."

The family? That could mean only three people—Miss Tilly, her great-nephew Lukas, and maybe Emily, though she married into the family. Who does he want to surprise?

"Although I should warn you," Sophie continues. "We have work going on in the basement right now. We're replacing the air-conditioning system while it's winter, but unfortunately this was the only time they could work on it."

"Snowball! There you are," a voice that is turning frailer by the year sounds from just above me.

All three of us—me, Sophie, and Mr. Muir—turn to find Miss Tilly standing at the top of the stairs. Still-thick white hair is twisted into an old-fashioned bun on top of her head, whisps of curls framing her temples and kind blue eyes dulled only slightly by time. She is dressed in black slacks and a green knit sweater with deer appearing to jump across the design.

Only she isn't looking at me, she is looking at Mr. Muir.

Her papery-thin skin goes pale, fast enough that I worry for a second that she'll faint. But then Miss Tilly flushes, pink staining her cheeks. "John Muir?" she asks in a shaken voice that has a tone I can't quite figure out. "Is that you?"

Chapter 5

———⌘———

"And a dolly who looks like me, and a new bed for my new dolly, and new colored pencils, pastel ones please, and an oil paint kit . . ." The little girl sitting on his lap, ebony curls bouncing around her eager face with every word, had an enthusiasm that was hard to resist. Especially as her list continued on and on and her mother, lips tilted in amusement, shrugged from behind her as though to say, *What am I supposed to do with this one?*

The girl's brother had named only one item he wanted, and so quietly that Peter had had to ask him to repeat himself, at which point his sister had spoken up for him. Now on her turn, it was clear she was the talker.

"Well . . . do you feel like your behavior this year deserves as much as *all* that?" he asked gently when she paused.

Her shoulders came back, expression almost offended. "Yes, I am a *very* good girl." Then her eyes narrowed. "But don't you already know that?"

He couldn't help himself, giving a low laugh. Maybe the whole Santa costume and hours playing the part, though rather reluctantly, had sunk in against his will, because he did sound slightly jolly.

"Thank Santa, Cora." Her mother jumped in, stepping forward to take the girl's hand.

"Thank you, Santa." Cora's smile was automatic. Then she leaned forward suddenly, tugging against her mother's grip, to kiss his cheek, precariously close to knocking off his glasses or his beard or both. "And thank you for playing along for my brother," she whispered.

Ah. So this one had figured a few things out. That was young.

"You're a very good big sister," he said back.

"I know." Dark brown eyes twinkled at him as she hopped down, overflowing with confidence and life and the future ahead of her.

He watched her go, hoping that future didn't knock any of that confidence or joy out of her. He hardly remembered being that age. Though, according to his parents, he'd been too serious even then. Not shy. Just solemn.

Lara followed the family to the door, wishing them a merry Christmas as they left. Then she locked the door behind them, turning the sign hanging in the window from "Open" to "Closed." A sign decorated to look like an open present on one side and a closed present on the other. Did she make that? Or buy it?

Why do I even care?

Peter pushed to his feet, ready to get out of the way-too-tight Santa suit. Lara's helpers had been sent home about fifteen minutes before. The Santa rush had taken much longer than he suspected she'd thought it would, well past closing time. But he'd been the one to insist that every child who'd come to see him would get their chance. He might be in a bad mood, but he wasn't ruining any child's day on top of everything else.

His conscience was tweaked enough without piling more on.

With a sigh, Lara turned and leaned against the door, the smile lighting up her face making her appear to glow in the soft lighting that the store had switched to as evening shadows had crept through. "Well done, you," she said in a voice so full of gratitude it took everything he had not to wince.

Because she didn't know what he'd done to her. She was thanking the wrong guy.

"I'd better change," he said, stepping carefully off the raised platform where Santa's seat sat. Not ripping the Santa suit at the seam all day long had been a challenge. Especially helping boys and girls on and off the seat beside him.

"Of course." Smiling huge, eyes sparkling with thankfulness, she crossed to where he was standing, smile turning almost shy. "This way."

He followed her through the various rooms.

He would give it to Lara, she was creative. The inside of the store was practically a playland. Daniel had worked on it, of course. He did all the Weber Haus construction. How Peter hadn't found out from his friend that the owner was not a corporation but was Lara, he had no idea.

Except that he'd been a bit of a hermit lately, at home when he wasn't at the bookshop. Mostly because he didn't want friends to see how he couldn't really control his gruffness. Even knowing it was a bad knock on the head causing it. So yeah, maybe he'd been pushing people away.

He'd hand it to both Lara and Daniel, the place was . . . impressive. She'd had Daniel make the main part of the store look like Santa's toy shop, with elves all over. An arched entryway, with massive doors covered in glitter that he suspected really did open and close, led to the next area.

Inside the second room, the space was set up to look like the North Pole, with snow, including glittering flakes, hanging from the ceiling. And the ceilings in this shop, once part of the Weber Haus barn, went up to the second story, so in one corner she'd had what looked like a real Christmas tree with its limbs hanging out, the piney branches covered in bright-colored lights, ornaments, and what appeared to be fluffy white snow that actually seemed to sparkle.

He wondered what she'd do come spring or any other season. Or would she just leave it?

Of course, having the ice cream in the snowy, winter wonderland décor was sort of weird. Meanwhile, both inside and outside the North Pole were decorated for Christmas with garlands and wreaths and lights everywhere.

See . . . creative.

But expensive, too, both in money and in time. With paying for this setup, plus the high rent, she'd run out of money at the pace she was going. After all, how much business could a person do in toys?

She led him through a decorated door that looked as though it led to an ice cave, but really took them to the back room, which he'd seen earlier in the day. Mostly storage, her office took up about a quarter of the space off to one side.

Where did she make the toys?

At the door to her office, she turned to face him. "I really can't thank you enough. This made my opening day so much more special."

"It was nothing." He'd tried to emphasize the nothing, not able to summon a fake smile for her.

Staring down into soft gray eyes that beamed her appreciation, guilt struck like the clanging of the gong in the clock tower in Town Hall. He'd stood in that tower once, on a dare, as it went off, and hadn't been able to hear properly for a solid week afterward. This felt like that.

She must not have picked up on any of his tension, though, because she reached out to put her hand on his arm. "It *was* something," she insisted.

Nothing he could say to that, so he went past her into the office and closed the door behind him.

Peter had never been so thankful to get out of a costume in his life. Not that he'd ever worn a Santa costume, but even the odd, annoying costume party had never been this bloody uncomfortable. For more reasons than one. Including the woman on the other side of the door waiting for him to dress.

The woman who owned this store.

The same woman who outbid him for this space and triggered a landside of behavior that, looking back, he'd been regretting already. Even before he knew the owner wasn't some faceless corporation lackey.

With a frustrated flick of his fingers, he tossed the Santa hat on top of the beard and glasses he'd removed, already lying on her desk.

How on earth had this happened?

He undressed and got back into his own clothes quickly, but somehow transforming back into himself only made it all worse. Peter dropped to sit in her chair, staring at the closed door, reluctant to face her.

He'd sat for hours as Elf Cassie had escorted each child— some eager, some nervous or wary—up to sit with him. And he swore every single time, Lara would glance across the store from whatever she was doing and visibly melt a little bit. As it stood, every lingering glance, every soft smile, only snagged at the tatters of his own guilt.

What a mess.

Peter ran a distracted hand over his hair.

Of course the new toy store owner would turn out to be Lara. All that spite and bitterness he'd thrown at her—in public on the forum no less . . .

"I'm such a jerk," Peter muttered.

At the same time, as much as he hated to admit it, he still needed a new location for his store. He'd already resolved to find a different spot and give up on the Weber Haus shops, but still . . . he remained certain the bookstore would have been better for this location. And the months—months no less—wasted in that bidding war . . .

He and Lara were on opposite sides of this situation, whether she knew it or not.

A soft knock at the door made him jump. "You all done in there?" Lara called out.

He pushed to his feet. He needed to get out of here.

Peter Diemer was oddly . . . wonderful.

Yes, the man never smiled. And normally that would remind her of her brother. Not exactly the best association. But something about Peter . . . she just liked. As though all that bluster hid a softer man underneath.

The laughing guy she'd met two Christmases ago was in there somewhere. Or maybe it was the way he'd been as Santa—firm and yet gentle with each child. Or maybe the magic of Christmas and her excitement over the success of her first day of business had sunk in. Never mind sunshine, Lara was walking on stars and glitter.

And Peter was part of that.

The door to her office opened, and Santa was gone, replaced by a man who made her heart flutter for reasons that had nothing to do with holidays or children. He really was harshly handsome with a jaw that said no-funny-business softened by firm but kind lips and crinkles around his eyes that told her he at least knew how to smile, even if he didn't use it.

"I really need to get going."

See. Words and expression said "loner." Even so, something inside her wanted to see if she could bring out those smiles she knew hid in there somewhere.

Still, she could tell now wasn't the best moment. Stepping out of his way, she waved for Peter to go ahead. "I'll . . . walk you to the door."

"No need," he said.

"I need to lock up after you, anyway," she pointed out cheerfully.

He said nothing to that. Following her to the door.

He did at least pause while she held it open for him, serious gaze skating over her features with an odd expression in his eyes. If she didn't know there was no reason for it, she would have said regret. But that couldn't be right. What was going on inside his head, anyway?

Probably better not to ask. "Thanks again."

"I'm glad I could help," he said.

"Let me know how I can repay the favor."

He paused, frowning as though he didn't like that, then nodded and, without another word, walked into the crowded darkness. The booths outside were also just starting to close, though customers still lingered. They'd be open again early in the morning, just as she would, and she had so much to do. Cassie had been busy as an elf, and Sally Ann had done the best she could to restock shelves on her own as the day progressed. So had Lara. But the place needed to be put back to rights and fully restocked before she could even think of going home.

Or making a cranky bookstore owner smile.

With a shake of her head, she forced her feet over to the nearest shelf and got to work. An hour later, a soft knock at the glass had her turning to find Emily's smiling face in the window. Her shop neighbor held up a bag with the bakery logo on it and grinned.

Smiling back, Lara hurried over to unlock the door and let her in.

"I saw you were still in here when I left earlier and figured you might be a while and could use food and reinforcements."

Would it make her appear foolish if she cried right now? She hadn't counted on how long this would take one person alone. "That is so nice of you," she said, taking a breath as she did.

She'd forgotten after the past two years, with Granny dead, what it felt like to be looked after. Lance certainly didn't try.

Quickly, she led Emily to her office, where she put down the bag and started unpacking it. Lara's brows rose with each new item—noodles with chicken and a cream gravy, green beans with bacon, fresh fruit, and an apple crisp for dessert.

The scrumptious scents filled the office and her stomach gave a gurgle. "I only had an energy bar for lunch." And a lot of coffee throughout the day. Hopefully she could sleep tonight.

"I figured as much. I remember my own opening day." Emily shook her head as she set about putting items on plates.

"I didn't realize you served meals in the bakery," Lara said, sitting down with a grateful sigh.

"Only one special a day, but this isn't mine." Emily nodded at the dessert. "The crisp is mine, but the rest is from the dinner that Mrs. Bailey, the cook for the inn, served the guests staying in the house."

Lara forked a bite into her mouth and groaned—hardy and comforting, the kind of meal that would stick to her ribs, as Granny would've said. "It's *wonderful.* Please thank her for me, too."

Emily sat down. "So was opening day everything you'd hoped?"

"Hoped and prayed for," Lara said around a bite. "And more. I can't believe how busy we were."

Emily nodded, eyes wide. "I know. I didn't get to be here during the Christmas Market last year, so I can't compare, but I've been like Santa's elves on Christmas Eve trying to keep up."

"That's terrific! Although your poor feet." They shared a grin. "I've been dreaming of this since I made my first toy by hand."

She'd only been ten and had made a rag doll that she'd given to a little girl in her class at school as a gift after the girl had told her she'd never owned a doll. The process of creating combined with the look on her friend's face had been everything.

"I'm so glad," Emily said, sincerity in her voice.

Peter's sister really was a sweetheart. Maybe they could be good friends as time went on. Lara liked to hope so.

"I was so scared no one would show up," Lara admitted.

Emily sat back, frowning. "Why would you worry about that? Of course people would come for a toy shop."

She lifted a single shoulder. She hadn't mentioned Right Rudolph to anyone else. After all, this was a small town and she didn't want to stir up trouble. After that single post, she'd decided to let her store—successful or otherwise—do the talking, and that was working out just fine.

So far.

"Do you read the town forums?" she asked.

Emily blinked. "Sometimes. I like the group for recipes."

Which made sense. Lara smiled. "Well, there's a room that is dedicated to all things town business—what is moving in where, or what is closing their doors, et cetera."

"Okay."

"There is a person who goes by the handle Right Rudolph, and they . . . well . . ."

Hard to explain, easier to just show her. Pulling up her phone, she logged into the forum and scrolled, then showed Emily.

Emily who read. Frowned. Scrolled. Read some more. Frowned harder.

"Good grief. What kind of Christmas Scrooge would be against a toy store?"

Which at least made Lara smile. "None of his, or her for all I know, posts are mean or wrong. They just . . ."

Emily was huffing by now. "I can't believe someone from Braunfels would write this."

At least Emily didn't secretly agree. "So you don't think I'm overreacting?" Lara asked slowly.

Emily huffed again. "About 'Right Rudolph'?" She wiggled the phone. "No. Though I don't think you should listen to them."

Hard not to when this was her first try at a brick-and-mortar business. There was so much she didn't know. Sure, she'd thought through as much as she could to create her business plan to apply for loans, but even then, that had been a learning curve and a half. No doubt she was missing stuff. She just didn't know what she didn't know. Half the time she felt as though she was barely treading water, that she might go under at any second and not come up. And her brother's voice in her head telling her she was bound to fail—well, that didn't help anything, either.

"You know what I'm going to do?" Emily said, holding her phone out to her. "I'm going to figure out who this is. I know everyone in this town. I'm sure I can figure it out."

Lara paused in reaching for the phone. "I don't want to start anything."

"This guy started it," Emily insisted, plunking the device down into her hand. "Don't worry. I won't do anything public. But I'm sure going to give him or her a piece of my mind."

"I really wish you wouldn't. It's best to ignore it and prove myself. Don't you think?"

The steam of righteous anger leaked out of Emily like a steam train coming to a stop at a station. She sighed. "If that's what you want."

"It is."

Emily nodded, then perked up. "Then today was a great start."

"Yes." Lara glanced around her shop, picturing all the happy faces. And Peter in the Santa throne that she'd already put away. "It was."

Then Emily's grin turned amused. "I still can't believe you got my brother into a Santa suit, let alone for hours."

Still picturing his face afterward, Lara winced. "I was a lit-

tle worried at first, but the children seemed to think his gruffness was funny."

"Gruff Santa." Emily hooted. "I'm going to tease him
about that for the rest of his life."

Oh dear. Peter already wasn't all that thrilled with what
she'd made him do today. "Please don't. He did me a favor
and I wouldn't want him to regret it."

Emily sat back with a thump that knocked a precariously
balanced kite off the shelf, comical disappointment etched
across her features for a beat before she bent over to pick up
the toy. "Oh, all right."

"I hope his time away from the bookstore wasn't a
problem."

Emily shook her head at that. "Not likely."

What was that supposed to mean? The question must've
reflected in her face, because Emily shrugged. "He's never
said, but I get the impression that the bookstore isn't exactly
a labor of love for my brother."

"No?"

Who ran a business they didn't love? The amount of work
involved . . . it would only succeed if passion was the impe-
tus, and even then, odds were against you.

Emily shook her head again. "My parents inherited it from
my dad's side of the family. It's been a staple in Braunfels
since shortly after World War II. Peter just retired from the
navy and offered to take it over. Mom and Dad were thrilled,
of course. Our other brothers, Max, Paul, and Oscar, all have
jobs they love, and I have the bakery. None of us have any interest in running a bookshop."

Actually, Lara thought a bookshop might be fun. Not
quite as amazing as a toy shop, but that's because she liked
the creative process. "When did Peter start there?"

"Just in the last year. He wants to move the location,
which I don't think my parents are thrilled about. The shop
has always been there, and they own the store location out-

right, rather than leasing. But Peter insists they need to be somewhere that gets more foot traffic."

"I'm surprised he didn't try for this spot, or one of the other shops here when it first opened."

She'd been up against five other bidders initially, so she knew how coveted the spot was. It had taken a hefty bid to knock the last man, or woman, standing out of the running. Stretching her poor budget even more.

Emily fiddled with the hem of her blouse. "I thought he might. It would have been nice to have him so close."

"I'm sure." Too bad there weren't a few more spots open so that he could have had one. A small twinge of guilt nagged at her for snapping up the last one, but she hadn't known. Then again, this spot was perfect for her shop, too, and she'd bid on it fair and square. She'd have to develop a thicker business skin if she wanted to thrive. Still . . . "I hope he finds something equally perfect."

Emily just hummed noncommittally, then sat forward, a twinkle in her eyes. "Now . . . tell me all about your opening day. I peeked in several times and it was packed in here."

Chapter 6

Working the cash register, Lara hadn't moved from behind the small checkout counter for a solid hour. Terrific business, but mental note to put a padded mat on the floor back here. Her feet were killing her, and she was even wearing cushy sneakers.

Surreptitiously she kept her eye on Becky, her newest helper. By her second day, she'd realized that the Christmas Market traffic meant she'd have to hire a few more seasonal employees for the shop. Something she should have thought about before then. The first hire had been Joshua, a college student home for the holidays, who she'd snapped up off the town forum for jobs the very next day. Now she'd made it to Friday and her second new worker was just starting.

Less than a week.

Open Monday through Saturday, the shop had been going almost a full business week. One still-dizzy-from-spinning workweek. So busy she fell into bed at night, asleep before she'd hardly touched her head to the pillow.

Also five days without a word or sighting of Peter Diemer.

Thank goodness all the Weber Haus shops closed on Sunday, otherwise she probably would have tried to stay open nonstop through the holiday. Not that she'd been surprised he'd disappeared. After all, he was only her neighbor and she'd made him play Santa.

Lara didn't have time for disappointment, though—which was a strong word for what this was, anyway.

Or so she told herself for the umpteenth time as she watched Becky. Cassie had taken the newest addition around the shop explaining how everything worked before moving behind the ice cream counter, leaving Becky alone to help customers. So far, the girl was proving to be a bit of a chatterer. But not about the store.

"Hello, Mrs. Epherson!" she greeted a young woman negotiating a double stroller around the twists and turns of the displays. The woman had a tiny baby asleep in the front, and in the back a toddler whose chubby arms kept shooting out of the sides to reach for toys.

Becky stepped right in front of the mother, stopping all traffic in the central part of the store thanks to the blockage. Lara winced at the way the two or three people behind the mom leaned over to see the cause of the stoppage, then backed up to go a different route.

Mental note to try to widen the aisles a bit if she could or have a place to park strollers.

"How adorable!" Becky squealed, bending over the baby. "I hadn't heard that you'd had your new baby yet."

"This is our first outing," the young mother admitted, and Lara's heart went out to her. She sounded nervous.

"Well, you're doing great."

Lara relaxed slightly. Maybe Becky, who seemed to know every living soul who lived or visited Braunfels, would be good at setting customers at ease.

"How was the birth?" Becky asked next.

Lara swallowed a groan as the mother instantly launched into a terrifying story of long labor, failed kidneys, and an emergency C-section. Not the best place to share such things, and several folks seemed suddenly in more of a hurry to leave the store than they had been a second ago.

Before Lara could try to gently direct both ladies back to shopping, her cell phone under the counter rang.

"I've got this," Sally Ann murmured in her motherly way, bustling across the shop.

Glancing at the number on her phone, Lara frowned at her sister-in-law's name. An elementary school teacher, Angela never called her during the day. Actually, she didn't call in general. Lance was almost ten years older—Lara had been a bit of a whoopsie-daisy baby—and he'd already been out of the house and off to university when their parents had died and Lara had gone to live with Granny. He and Angela had married four years later, when Lara was only twelve, so they'd never gotten particularly close.

Lara glanced at the line still backed up in front of her to check out. Oh dear.

With no choice—she'd just have to call Angela back in a few minutes—she rejected the call. But a few seconds later, her phone was ringing again. Maybe it was an emergency?

Biting her lip, Lara rejected the call again, finished up with the customer she was helping, then waved Sally Ann over to man the cash register before she'd had a chance to move the stroller-mom along.

"I'm sorry," she said.

Though Sally Ann, who, after raising five kids, didn't seem to flap at anything, just shushed her and took over. Then the phone started ringing again in her hand. She showed it to Sally Ann. "I think it's important."

"Of course." The older woman smiled, completely unruffled. "You take it in your office. We'll handle all of this."

She then proceeded to look at Becky, still chatting with the young mother. "Becky . . . I see four other customers who could use your help," she called across the store loudly enough for everyone to hear. Not sharply. How she managed to sound kindly and motherly while still basically telling the teenager to stop chatting, Lara had no idea. But Becky jumped, and with a smile at Mrs. Epherson, moved away to help another customer.

Lara, at the same time, answered the phone as she walked through the store to her office. "Angela? Is something wrong?"

"About time you answered. Were you ignoring me?"

"I was in the middle of ringing up a customer," Lara explained with as much patience as she could.

"But this is an emergency."

"I'm sorry to hear that." With Angela, less was more when it came to conversations.

"You could have had the courtesy to answer my call."

Lara said nothing.

"After all, I never call during the day."

"I answered as soon as I was able." Before Angela could continue to complain, Lara tried to redirect the conversation. "What's the emergency?"

A pause, and she pictured her teacher sister-in-law—probably wearing an over-the-top Christmas-themed sweater paired with matching leggings and, if she knew Angela, elf shoes on her feet with curly, bell-tipped toes. How Angela could be every child's dream of a teacher and still also be the rather sharp-tongued relative she was, Lara still hadn't figured out.

"My mother fell down the stairs on her Caribbean cruise," Angela finally said, her voice turning as sharp as broken glass. Lara tried to chalk it up to worry. It's not like this was her fault, though Angela's tone seemed to indicate it could be. "She broke her hip, among other things."

"Oh, I am so sorry."

"Are you?"

Lara ignored the quip. Angela was probably in shock. Benefit of the doubt and leeway for worry and all that, right?

"Anyway, Lance and I have to fly out immediately to go help her. She's in some hospital in Bermuda. We'll have to get her through this and home somehow. I imagine it will take most of the month."

Most of the month? What a mess.

Sympathy had Lara sinking into the chair behind her desk, actually feeling sorry for her brother and his wife for once. No matter how they treated Lara—especially since Granny died and left everything to her, rather than splitting the inheritance between Lara and Lance—they were still family. The only family she had left. Besides which, Angela's mother was a sweetheart.

"How can I help?" The offer was somewhat empty given that her brother and sister-in-law lived a five-hour drive away.

"We need you to take Ben until we return."

Her nephew? They wanted her to take in a six-year-old boy? "Isn't he in school?"

"They've agreed to allow him to finish his work from your house virtually."

While Lara was what? At the store leaving him alone? She looked around her office as though he was going to pop up there like a jack-in-the-box. Or as though she could find answers to solve this new one somewhere on the shelves around her.

Which actually . . . She supposed he could sit back here in the office and do his work. Except this was a toy store. What six-year-old would be able to do that?

"School is only another week before he's on holiday break anyway," Angela said.

That was something, at least. A week of home schooling her nephew while she ran the shop. Could she handle that? Maybe she needed to hire another helper for the store? Except she was already at the edge of the budget she'd given herself for expenses.

Think. Think. Think.

"Of course I'll take him," Lara said.

"Good—"

"But I'll need you to pay for a tutor to help him through his schoolwork during the day." She tried her best to state that firmly but kindly.

An ominous silence descended over the other end. "We are already having to pay to fly to Bermuda. We can't afford that."

"And I can't afford to be away from the shop. It just opened."

"Use all that money from your grandmother to hire another helper."

"I'm afraid I can't do that."

"Don't tell me you already ran through your inheritance." Angela's voice rose a decibel or two. "Lance just knew you were going to do that."

"My finances are none of your business, or my brother's," Lara stated, more firmly.

"She should have put that money in trust and we could have made sure you didn't—"

"I imagine you have so much to do to get to your mother." Lara cut her sister-in-law off before she could get on a full-steam rant, or before Lara ignored the fact that Angela was dealing with a difficult situation and said something she'd regret later. "I'll find a tutor and give them your information to handle payments. Otherwise, I'm sorry, but you'll need to make other plans."

Another pause, and then Angela burst into tears. "In our hour of need, you do this?"

Lara blew out a long breath and lifted her gaze to the ceiling, remaining quiet while Angela worked herself through her emotional outburst.

"*Mrrrow.*" A small meow sounded a heartbeat before Snowball jumped up on her desk, her big blue eyes brilliant against her pure-white furry face, open wide in what appeared to be a question.

Lara shook her head at herself for such fanciful thoughts, though Peter claimed the little cat spoke human. Reaching out, she ran her hand over Snowball's soft-as-feather-down fur and instantly a tiny bit of the tension of dealing with her family drained from her. How could she stay upset when petting such a sweet cat?

Angela chose that moment to wind down.

"And Ben will already be so upset to have his Christmas ruined," she was saying.

That Lara could help with. "This is a Christmas town and I run a toy shop," Lara pointed out. "I will do everything I can to make his holiday lovely. But I can't both help him with schoolwork and run the shop. I'm sorry. I wish I could."

"You just don't want to—"

"Because you are upset about your mother, I will stop you now before you say something you regret." Lara loved her nephew, and despite Angela's sharp tongue, she was a very good mother. And most of the time she wasn't quite this bad with Lara, either.

A huff reached her down the line. Then silence. Then a slowly released breath that spoke volumes about Angela holding on to her patience. Lara ignored all of it.

"Fine," Angela finally said. "Send me the tutor bill. Now, about getting Ben to you . . . Our friends, the Dochersons, just happen to be coming your way. They are leaving for their own holiday and are happy to drop Ben off with you."

Already arranged before she'd said she could? So like Angela and Lance to assume. Though this was an emergency. "What time should I expect them?"

"They're driving, coming up from Bremen, and said they'd get there around two in the afternoon today."

Today?

Good grief. Friday . . . at least that gave her two days to

sort out the tutor situation before Ben would need help with his schoolwork on Monday. "They'll need to drop him at the shop then," she said to Angela. "I'll text you the address as soon as we hang up."

The pause following that was one filled with silent ire. How Lara knew that for sure was more about experience than actual sounds being made. If Angela had been a witch, Lara would probably be a smoldering ash stain on the floor by now. "That's a terrible inconvenience," her sister-in-law finally said.

"For everyone, I imagine," Lara murmured sweetly. "But the shop is open until eight tonight—holiday hours thanks to the Christmas Market—so I will be here, not at home. Besides, it's right on their way into town from the direction they'll be coming, so easier for them to reach as they go than my townhome."

Silence as Angela couldn't really say anything to that.

"Well . . . I hope you'll do all sorts of things with Ben that are seasonally appropriate. A visit to Santa, and shopping, and maybe even skiing."

Lara wrinkled her nose at the last bit. She was not a coordinated skier, let alone finding the time. Not that she had any intention of saying that out loud. "Has he ever been?"

"No, but it can't be that hard."

Keeping her thoughts to herself, Lara considered how expensive ski lessons might be. She could hardly get herself safely down a mountain. No way was she risking Ben's life trying to do that on her own. Still, trying to hold on to her holiday cheer and Christmas spirit, she thought of poor Angela's sweet mother laid up in a strange hospital somewhere across the ocean, and in pain, and how worried Angela had to be. As an only child, she was very close with her mother. Plus, Lara loved her little nephew, though she didn't get to see much of him. He was a good kid, a bit quiet, but then, so had she been at that age. Always in her head.

"I will do everything I can to make Ben's holiday magical," she promised. And sincerely meant it.

She owned a toy store, after all. That sort of made her a Santa with training wheels. Right?

"Call me when he arrives so I can stop worrying," Angela said. Then followed up with a quick goodbye and hung up abruptly. No thank you, though.

Lara put down her phone on the desk, then closed her eyes, trying some breathing exercises she'd seen online just last night.

They didn't help.

"Mrrrow," Snowball meowed again, and Lara swore it sounded like the cat was asking what was wrong.

She sighed and, opening her eyes, reached out to pet her again, instantly feeling a little better. How on earth was she going to get a tutor hired by Monday and be ready to take care of a little boy? Also, where on earth was she going to put him? Her one and only guest room was her workshop space, for heaven's sake, with all sorts of dangerous tools and things.

"Snowball," she said. "Life just got more complicated."

"Oh, that's too bad," a woman murmured, disappointment rife in her voice as she stopped walking directly in front of Peter. He was crossing through the Christmas Market after leaving Emily's bakery. Mom had sent him with a new cookbook that Emily had ordered through their store, and he was trying to avoid Lara, so he'd hurried and deliberately not looked over at The Elf Shop as he'd passed by.

The fact that the woman making the comment was now blocking his way was the only reason he stopped long enough to see that she was staring at the toy store. An *empty*, dark toy store with a sign in the window that read, "Santa is giving his elves an early break for the day, but they'll be back at it tomorrow, right on time."

Peter ignored a slight sinking sensation in his stomach, because this was none of his business. Lara was probably fine. There could be any number of reasons why she'd have to close early. On a Friday evening. The first weekend of the Christmas Market to boot. Although . . . had she been closing early a lot? He didn't think so. No matter how early or late he made it home, her car was never parked out front.

She'd work herself into an early grave if she kept up that pace.

Maybe that was why she'd needed to take off early today. Or maybe the shop wasn't doing well. All those customers might have just been there to see Santa, but not bought something.

"I was hoping to see the nutcrackers do their dance," the disappointed woman said to him as though they were both there for the toy shop. "I heard that each hour a new song comes on and they do a new dance."

They did?

He thought about when he'd been sitting in the store as Santa. He hadn't had a view of the window display from where he'd sat, but he'd vaguely noticed the music changing and hadn't thought much of it.

Given the extravagant Santa's Workshop decorations, nutcrackers doing different dances seemed right up Lara's alley. Yet another example of great creativity but perhaps not the best business sense. How long had it taken her to set those things up, after all? Hours she could have been getting other things done, he was sure.

Which only soured his mood, obscuring his original bout of guilt at being the one trying to overturn her store on the forums. Because if she wasn't a good steward of the space, and ultimately went under, that would look bad for all the shops here at Weber Haus.

The bookshop definitely would have been better for this location, allowing them to expand their inventory slightly, but not outgrow themselves. Plus simpler in design. Cozier. He'd pictured people grabbing Emily's baked goods and bringing them over to snuggle into comfy chairs and read.

Not that the toy store wasn't cozy. A bench built around the base of the tree inside had got a lot of use when he'd been there. Plus, the tables inside the "North Pole" area designed to match the aesthetic provided more seating. But still . . .

Turning on his heel, he left the disappointed woman and made his way back to his car and home.

Lara's car wasn't parked in her drive. Again.

Another gut sinker of worry combined with relief. Because the thing was . . . he *wanted* to see her. Only he knew pursuing her beyond being casual neighbors was a bad idea. Heck, being around people in general was a bad idea lately. Not being sure the bookstore was the life for him was one thing. He'd loved his previous career. He'd been good at it. But, thanks to that whack on the head, he also didn't feel like himself or know who he really was. The anger and frustration weren't him, but he couldn't make it stop. So relationships were out . . . why be with someone if he couldn't even like himself?

Plus, there was the guilt over those previous posts. He'd been so caught up in that bidding war, so sure that space was meant to be for the bookstore, that he'd taken out all that disappointment and frustration online. He couldn't take that back now. They were out there.

Maybe he could turn the ship around, so to speak.

After popping a meal in the microwave to cook, he grabbed his laptop and hopped on the town forum, bringing up his Right Rudolph account.

"The Elf Shop closed early today," he wrote. "I hope everything is okay."

The next morning, he made it to Emily's bakery for his regular breakfast bagel, a habit he had no intention of changing. Or maybe he was checking on Lara to see if she'd taken his questioning to heart. He hadn't heard her come home last night, and her car hadn't been in the drive this morning. But his steps slowed as he neared the shops and could plainly see she wasn't there, either. The store was dark.

"I'm surprised the toy store isn't open yet. They closed early last night, too," he said to Emily as she handed him his food in a bag along with a cup of coffee, black the way he liked it. The savory scents of ham, eggs, and cheese—his daily breakfast sandwich—wafted to him and his stomach rumbled.

"Lara—"

A sound of a cat challenge blasted in a *meow* of epic proportions before a white streak shot directly at him. Snowball jumped up, sinking her claws into his jeans, and the skin underneath. Before he could even yelp, she snagged his keys, dangling from his fingertips, in her mouth. Then she jumped down and sprinted out the door, open as another customer entered.

"Snowball!" he and Emily both yelped, and he ran after the cat. That was his only set of keys.

He emerged outside just in time to see her trot into the toy store, the door now propped open.

Peter growled his irritation, reluctance to follow now dragging at his feet. But he needed his truck keys, so he made himself go. He entered to find a young boy, not more than six or seven, kneeling down in front of the white cat who had dropped Peter's keys on the floor in favor of being petted and cooed over by a new admirer.

"Aren't you cute," the boy was saying as he gently stroked her fur.

Even from the door, Peter could hear the motor of Snowball's purr start up like a toy car engine. Then the boy looked up, eyes going wide at the sight of a strange man standing there, no doubt. Wide and wary. "Um . . . can I help you?"

Which meant the boy wasn't shopping here? If not, then

who was he? Peter frowned as possibility struck with all the subtleness of dropping a thick, hardback book on his head. Was Lara a mother?

He studied the kid's face, noting some similarities in the shape, and even the eyes, though the little boy's were brown. The fact that the kid started to back up had Peter shoving the jumble of thoughts aside and holding up both hands. He even tried to smile.

Except the boy's eyes widened even more in visible alarm. So he wiped his expression free of any rusty, apparently scary-looking smile.

"That's okay," Peter said. "I'm here for my keys. I'm afraid Snowball there likes to steal shiny things."

Though usually not right out of the owner's hand. She was generally sneakier than that. The boy dropped his gaze to the keys on the floor and Peter could practically see his thin shoulders drop from around his ears to a more natural position.

"Oh," the boy chuckled. "Her name is Snowball?"

"Mm-hmm." Peter moved slowly so he didn't startle the kid and crouched beside them both. "She brought a wedding ring to my sister once."

The boy giggled, though he didn't look up from petting the cat. Peter grabbed his keys off the floor and Snowball didn't stop him. She was such an odd cat sometimes. "Well . . ." Where was Lara, anyway? "I'd better get going."

The boy nodded.

But Peter couldn't just leave him by himself. "Are you here with someone?"

"My auntie Lara is in the back."

Auntie Lara. The whoosh of satisfaction wasn't something Peter should be feeling. Not that he would have had anything against her being a single mom. Besides which, they weren't dating or anything. Just neighbors.

"Are your parents visiting for Christmas?" he asked.

The boy shook his head.

"Ben—" Lara's voice preceded her out of the North Pole entrance, but she paused as Peter rose to his feet.

He tried his hardest not to frown, because she looked . . . exhausted. As though a puff of wind would knock her over—dark shadows under her eyes and a droop to her shoulders. She was wearing jeans and a sweatshirt, her hair pulled up into a messy ponytail. Having seen her in her toy store attire of slim-fitting black slacks and a long-sleeved red button-down shirt with the store logo on the breast, he was pretty sure this was Lara at her most disheveled.

What in the name of St. Nick had happened to her?

"Peter?" she asked, a confused smile gracing her lips. Confused and distant. His fault after ghosting her like he had been.

"Snowball stole my keys," he said, waving at the cat on the floor, who was ignoring him while continuing to bask in the boy's—named Ben apparently—attention.

A small twitch to Lara's lips came and went. After the Santa hat–stealing incident, he figured she wouldn't question that reason. The real question was . . . what did he do now? Tell her he needed to get to work and walk away, that's what. Only he couldn't make his feet or mouth do either of those things.

She just looked so . . . tired.

"This is your nephew?" he found himself asking instead.

Was that a flash of worry in her eyes as she smiled at the kid? "Yes, Ben is coming to stay with me for the rest of the month."

Ben glanced up, big brown eyes earnest. "My grandmother fell and broke her hip and she's in Bermuda and my mommy and daddy have to go help her. And Auntie Lara is going to take me ice skating."

And Lara was stepping in as mother while trying to open a brand-new store in the middle of the holiday season? What was she thinking? He glanced up to find her smiling at Ben, but as soon as her nephew dropped his gaze, the smile faded, replaced by a look that could only be categorized as pure panic.

"Is this why you closed the store early last night?" he asked, the question just popping out. This was really none of his business. He shouldn't get involved. She was a big girl and could fix her own problems. Except he didn't like that look in her eyes the same way he didn't like the shadows or the droop.

Though her eyebrows winged up in gentle surprise, probably that he'd noticed at all, she nodded. "The family that was supposed to bring him to me had car trouble and got stuck. I had to go help them. It took most of the night and we ended up staying at a hotel halfway back to here."

Which explained the dark circles. *Not to mention the closing early*, a small voice in his head pointed out. "I'm sorry." What else could he say?

"Auntie Lara and I had to share a small bed because she didn't have enough money for two beds."

Peter glanced down to find Ben looking at him as he offered this insight. Out of the corner of his eye, he caught the way Lara lifted her gaze upward as though asking for heaven to intervene. She couldn't even afford two beds at a hotel?

"The only room with two beds was the large suite, and way overpriced," she clarified in a tight voice.

Right. Still . . . maybe he'd been right about the poor business sense. Only, shouldn't any loans she'd got for the store cover the business side? Did she have no personal savings? Something told him not to dig into that topic. Maybe the way her lips were pressed together. Very un-Lara-like.

"I'm surprised you can leave school," Peter said slowly to Ben instead. "Or are they out for winter break already?"

Lara was the one to answer. "Due to the emergency circumstances, the school is letting Ben do all his work virtually."

And he had a feeling her panic went up another notch just voicing that out loud.

Was she really thinking of trying to get her nephew through schoolwork while running the shop, in the middle of Christmas Market madness? Surely, she must have other family who could have stepped in to help with the kid?

A second later, before he could say anything, she grimaced, then raised her gaze to look him directly in the eyes. "I don't suppose you know a good tutor who might be available for a week and can start Monday?"

Here he'd been posting, bringing her business into question on the town forum last night, and she'd been in the middle of a family and personal crisis. Could he be any more of a holiday humbugger?

He doubted it. If his mother knew, she'd be so disappointed in him. Emily, too, for that matter.

"Or maybe a good babysitter?" she asked next. "I need to open the shop . . ." She trailed off, biting her lip.

"Do you like books, Ben?" Peter found himself asking without even realizing he intended to.

Ben glanced up. "I *love* to read."

Remembering the kid's reaction to his previous effort at a smile, Peter just nodded. "Then I bet you would love my bookstore."

"A bookstore? Really?" Ben's brown-eyed gaze actually abandoned Snowball to stand up, little face turning eager. "Is there a children's section?"

"A huge one with comfy bean bags so you can lay around and read as long as you like. Would you like to spend some time there today?"

"Yes—" The childish eagerness fell away as he remembered himself and glanced at his aunt. "Can I go, Auntie Lara?"

"I . . ." She glanced at her nephew's face and then at Peter, clearly undecided. "I wouldn't want to impose. I already owe you for the—" She winced. "For the Santa thing."

"Don't worry about it. My mother adores children, and the kids' section is pretty terrific. How about he comes to hang out with us for the morning while you get situated. Then I'll take him to Em's for lunch and bring him back here for the afternoon?"

Given the North Pole setting already in play, when hope lit up her gray eyes as she looked at him, suddenly Peter felt like he'd topped the nice list in one fell swoop. Granted, he no doubt fell several positions after his post last night.

"If you're sure—"

"I'm sure." Maybe helping her out a bit would make up for his actions last night. At least a little bit. No more posting things about the shop, though. That was for sure. Time to let her succeed or fail without his commentary.

Lara blew out a long breath. "That would be very helpful. Thank you."

Another successful moment in kitty matchmaking!

One of these humans really should acknowledge how good I am at this stuff. After not seeing Lara or Peter in the same place at the same time, or even near to each other, for almost a week, I just had to intervene when I spotted him in Emily's just as Lara was opening her shop.

And now he's helping with Ben. That will mean lots of time together for Lara and Peter.

I love Ben, by the way. Unlike many children his age, he knows how to properly treat a cat. No poking, tugging, flicking, or squeezing. Just a nice, gentle petting and a lovely tickle under the chin. He can come snuggle with me anytime.

Good deed done for the day. As the cobblestone "street" of shops and now Christmas Market booths start to fill up with more people, I make my way through a maze of feet toward the house. Then in through the back door—Mrs. Bailey doesn't mind letting me in as usual—and up the dark and narrow set of back stairs to Miss Tilly's room.

Only Miss Tilly isn't there.

With a little frown, I make my way back down to the main level and start poking my head in random rooms, until I hear her voice down the hall.

"You were here last Christmas?" Miss Tilly was saying. Something in her voice is off, but I can't tell if she's shocked or irritated.

Knowing Mr. Muir, whose distinct rumble I can hear, probably irritated.

Although, all week, they've been spending a lot of time together. "Getting reacquainted," she tells me at night when we curl up to sleep.

I turn the corner to find him sitting way too close beside her on the settee in the parlor, both partially hidden by the Christmas tree in the room. Their knees are touching and he is clasping both her hands between his . . . and he's staring deeply into her eyes in a way I recognize all too well.

Look away, Miss Tilly! Look away!

I give a little snarl deep in my throat, and they both turn their heads slowly. Miss Tilly frowns at me. "Hush, Snowball."

I blink in surprise, because she never uses that tone with me. In fact, I plop my butt on the floor and tilt my head, waiting for her to apologize. But she doesn't. Instead, she turns back to face Mr. Muir. "But why didn't you say hello? And why did you leave Christmas Eve last year?"

"Because the timing wasn't right," he says, brusque voice almost imploring. "You'd been away, dealing with a family emergency, and were just home. You had a houseful of guests. And I didn't want to interrupt . . . all that."

He tips his chin down, though his gaze remains on hers. "Our timing always seems to be off."

Miss Tilly just shakes her head, seeming confused.

"Why didn't you tell me all this the first day you arrived this week?" she says next.

"Because I . . ." He glances away. "Aw heck, Tilly. I needed to gather my courage, and maybe see how you reacted to my being here at all first."

Courage for what? Better not be to do with those darn birds he had here before. At least he had the sense to leave them at home this time.

"Courage?" Tilly murmurs, echoing my thoughts.

"I came here last Christmas chasing the memory of a sweetheart."

Miss Tilly's eyes widen and Mr. Muir takes a deep breath. "When we were young, and my family visited this place that one summer, I fell so deeply in love with you I didn't know which way was up. But we were young, and I had my first big job waiting. You said you would only stay here, run this inn that's been in your family forever, and I couldn't see a way for us to stay together. I was stupid enough to leave you behind."

"We were so very young," Tilly whispers.

But she's sort of smiling, so I try not to worry that he's upsetting her.

"We were," he says. "And I blamed the distance, and how expensive long-distance calls were at the time, as an excuse for why we lost touch. But really, it was too hard to hear your voice, wishing I was here."

"Me too." Tilly looks on the verge of tears.

"As I've already told you, I eventually married, quite happily, though I often thought of you. My wife was a good person, and I loved her. I'll always miss her. But . . . my heart belonged to someone else then, even through a long and wonderful marriage, and it still does today."

"Oh my," Tilly murmured, color turning her weathered cheeks pink.

"I've come back to see if this old fool might still have . . . any chance with you."

I feel light-headed all of a sudden. Miss Tilly has a beau? One with birds? One I didn't approve of first? This can't be happening.

Chapter 7

The bell over the door jingled and luckily Lara wasn't engaged with a customer, just putting stuffed animals back into the tall bin they lived in. She looked up just in time to see Peter walk in right behind Ben.

"Auntie Lara, I got a book!" Her nephew practically floated across the room, his little face breaking out in a smile. "It's the next book in the Astronauts series. I didn't even know it was out yet, but Peter had some in the back."

Over the boy's head, Peter gave her a wink. An actual wink. "Technically, it doesn't release until next week, but for my favorite customer . . ." He shrugged.

Ben's chest puffed up at the words as he waved the book, which he'd been clutching to his small frame, beaming like she hadn't seen since she'd picked him up from her brother and sister-in-law's friends. Only . . .

"That is a very big book," she said slowly, trying to sound impressed more than worried. "Can you read that all by yourself?"

Her nephew was six. In first grade. Though her sister-in-law had had him working on the alphabet and easy words long before grade school, he'd been in school only a year and a half. That looked like a book for a ten-year-old at least.

Sure enough, Ben shook his head. "Mom helps me read these before bed each night."

Before bed? That was Lara's only time to work on the business side of things, or prep for workshops, or work on toys, or make ice cream. But . . . Ben was her nephew and she loved him.

Right. Okay. I can squeeze this in.

How long could reading a chapter a night take, anyway? "I—"

"Peter said he'd come over and read with me each night, but that I had to ask you first. Can he, Auntie Lara? Can he? Can he?"

A small twinge of disappointment tweaked at her, because after that moment of panic, she'd been looking forward to the simple pleasure. Still, Peter's offer was a good solution, especially since he conveniently lived next door, so she nodded. "Of course."

Ben took off, bouncing like a rubber ball all over the store in excitement. She shared a smile with Peter over his head, wondering why he'd even offered. His sudden bout of helpfulness was . . . well . . . sudden. "Are you sure?" she mouthed.

"It's fine," he mouthed back.

Another emotion tangled with the others. A twinge of . . . what? It couldn't be excitement at the thought of Peter in her house each night. That would be silly.

I'll just have to stay downstairs and work while he's there.

Giving herself a mental nod for being sensible about this, she summoned a more grateful smile. "Thank you so much for watching him this morning. I really appreciate it."

"My mother was thrilled to have a kiddo around to entertain. No grandchildren yet, so I'm afraid she spoiled him a bit."

"Nothing wrong with that. It's Christmas and his parents are away." Lara glanced over at Ben, who was now sitting on the comfy bench around the base of her North Pole tree, his book open on his lap.

"I don't think I told you the other day," Peter said, moving to stand beside her, his arm almost brushing hers. If she reached out ever so slightly, she could hook her pinkie finger around his.

Now where did that idea come from?

"The decorations in here are . . . elaborate," he said, breaking the sweet picture in her head.

Elaborate?

She tried not to frown, looking everything over and trying to see it from his point of view. "I wanted something that the kids would want to come back and see or spend time in or tell their friends so their friends would want to see."

Now she was explaining herself. She'd promised herself she wouldn't do that for anybody.

Part of the reason for moving here, instead of setting up shop where she'd grown up with Granny, was to get away from having to explain herself to an opinionated brother and his wife. They couldn't just drive by the store anytime they wanted and make comments.

"Well, I hope it works." Peter's words were encouraging, but his tone was . . . Actually, it wasn't anything bad.

She flicked him a glance. "Me too."

"Will the tree stay snowy year-round?"

That had her grinning. "Of course. The North Pole is always winter," she said. "But I will change out the decorations seasonally."

"Really?" He eyed it doubtfully.

"Mm-hmm. I found a post online with the idea with different Christmas tree decorations for each month. You know . . . hearts at Valentines, shamrocks for St. Patrick's Day, that kind of thing."

"Sounds time consuming . . . and expensive."

She checked his expression again, but he was smiling. Or

smiling for Peter, the tips of his mouth tilted up slightly. Still, she couldn't shake the impression that he was warning her or disapproving or something.

Maybe she was just being too sensitive after dealing with Lance.

"It *will* take me a full Sunday to remove one set of decorations and put up a new set, but I figure once a month won't be that bad."

Peter grunted what could have been an agreement or doubt. Hard to tell with him.

"Ben . . ." She waited a long beat for her nephew to blink and then raise his head to gaze at her a little owlishly. Definitely a reader like she'd been. "I have a workshop starting in about twenty minutes. We're going to build a toy airplane from wooden pieces that fit together like a 3D puzzle."

He blinked again.

"Would you want to do that? Or do you want to sit there and read your book? I won't be able to help you much, I'm afraid." She bit her lip.

She'd be lucky to run the workshop at all. Sally Ann and Becky had both called in sick. Cassie had been able to come in on her off day and help Joshua, but as busy as the shop had been this week, they'd needed at least three people manning the shop and ice cream bar at all times. Which meant they were a man down with her doing the workshop.

Hopefully Cassie and Joshua could handle it.

All good problems, she reminded herself for the seventeenth time that day. Better to be feet-soreness-inducing busy than sitting alone and bored in an empty store that was losing money instead of making it.

"Everything okay?" Peter asked.

Tipping her head back to look up at him, she forced what she hoped was an easy smile and nodded. "Right as rain."

He'd helped her out with Ben for hours today. No way was she leaning on his help more than that. That would be taking advantage. As it was, she owed him two favors now. She'd have to think of a way to repay him after the holidays were over and things slowed down a bit.

Only Peter narrowed his eyes, suddenly turning slightly intimidating, the military man in him making an appearance as he searched her expression. "You don't sound sure."

Not one to be intimidated, she plunked her hands on her hips and grinned, because she knew exactly how to get rid of him. "Unless you want to make another appearance as Santa. That would be great—"

"No, no." His hands shot up in the air like she was holding up a bank teller with a gun and he backed away. "I have . . . things to do."

She would have laughed if she wasn't actually trying to get rid of him. Poor guy. Apparently, that had been a traumatizing experience.

Peter had the door open before he paused. "What time does Ben go to bed?" he asked.

Trying to remember what had been written on the four pages of neatly typed instructions—ones Angela had sent along with Ben and his three suitcases of stuff, and two bins of Christmas presents that Lara had been told to keep hidden from him—Lara scrunched up her nose, drawing a blank. It had been a *lot* of information.

"My bedtime is at seven," Ben piped up from behind her.
Seven? How did I miss that?

She closed at eight for the next few weeks the Christmas Market was open. Even after that, when her hours dropped to a more reasonable six o'clock closing, she doubted she'd be home by seven, let alone feeding them both dinner and doing bath time before bed.

How did single parents without family nearby do this? They skyrocketed to the top of Lara's hero list, right along with nurses and teachers.

She'd deal with bedtime later. First, she needed to get

through the day. Thank heavens tomorrow was Sunday and the store was closed. She'd have more time to figure everything out then.

"Seven it is," Peter said. "I'll be there to read then."

"Actually, eight thirty tonight. The store closes at eight." She could come in and do all the stocking and cleaning in the morning.

"Sound good?" Peter asked Ben.

Ben nodded and buried his nose back in the book.

"What do you say, Ben?" she prompted.

He slowly raised his head. "Thanks, Pete," he said.

Pete? When did that happen?

"Anytime, bud. Don't get too far ahead without me." He pointed at the book.

Ben grinned, expression clearly a six-year-old version of, *Challenge accepted.*

She didn't need to ask about the planes activity again. She had a feeling Ben would be reading the rest of the day. At least he'd be occupied and able to sit still where she could see him.

With a nod, Peter left, long-legged stride eating up the ground and taking him swiftly out of sight between booths and people outside. And a small part of her acknowledged that the store felt a little empty without him in it.

But the independent woman in her said that was only because he was so tall. That she had everything under control and didn't need more help than he'd already given. Deliberately, she turned away from the view.

"How about some ice cream?" she asked her nephew. The workshop was all set up and ready to go.

That brought Ben's head up sharply with a grin from ear to ear. "With hot fudge?"

Maybe she should have asked what the Diemers had fed him for lunch. Too late now, though. "Why not? Go pick your flavor."

*   *   *

Peter's feet crunched on the frozen, icy grass that filled the small patch of land between the strip of townhomes and the sidewalk, his breath misting on the cold night air. At Lara's door, though, he hesitated.

What had he been thinking, offering to read with Ben? It meant seeing Lara. Every single night. There was nothing between them, and there wouldn't be.

Not that he was doing a bang-up job with that. After leaving Ben with her, Peter had spent most of the day wondering about that pinched, worried look that had come over her face when she'd mentioned the workshop. But she'd seemed adamant that nothing was wrong, and he wasn't the pushy kind. *And* he was supposed to be keeping his distance. So he'd left and then felt guilty the rest of the day for not staying.

Which was ridiculous. If she needed help, she'd ask.

He made himself knock on her door. Then stood there blowing on his hands and stomping his feet. Since she was right next door, he hadn't bothered with a coat or gloves to come over.

When no one answered right away, he knocked again. Then, a minute later, tried the doorbell.

The door swung open, only he had to drop his gaze way down to find Ben gazing up at him, blond hair a darker shade than Lara's sticking up every which way. The kid was wearing only pajama bottoms—ones patterned with Santa hats at all angles on a field of snow—and the kid's skin glistened damply and his hair was still damp.

And something smelled . . . off.

"Who is it, Ben?" Lara's voice shouted from somewhere inside.

"It's Pete," Ben shouted back, over his shoulder. Then to Peter, "Come in. It's cold."

"Of course it is." He stepped inside quickly, closing the

door behind him. "It's winter in the mountains and you're all wet."

Ben grinned. "Auntie Lara thought—"

"Oh no!" Her distraught wail had him and Ben raising their eyebrows at each other and then hurrying toward the sound that came from the direction of the kitchen. Or at least he thought that direction. It took Peter a second to orient, because her unit was built as a mirror image to his, everything on the opposite side. Then he sighted Lara standing over a pot on the stovetop stirring at something or other with a frustrated frown on her face.

Dinner?

He glanced at the clock. He'd been spot on time. Eight thirty. Past Ben's bedtime, but when she'd told him to be here. Seemed like she was still sorting out timing with dinner and the shop and now her nephew.

"What happened?" he asked.

"I burned the noodles."

That accounted for the smell. Her frustrated tone combined with the way her nose wrinkled put him in mind of Snowball when she got into a snit.

He moved closer to try to help. "I'm sure you can salvage—" He got a look inside the pot at a lump of noodles practically cemented together and to the bottom. "Never mind."

She sighed and, with a shake of her head, put the pot in the sink and filled it with water to soak. "No worries. The chicken is fine and so are the green beans."

Behind her back, Ben made a retching face, and Peter held on to a chuckle with difficulty. He must've not cleared his expression quick enough, though, because she looked up, then closed her eyes, sucking air in through her nose as though trying to find some sort of zen.

Which was when he noticed the exhaustion etched into her face with lines and shadows that were deeper than they should have been. Maybe even worse than earlier today. Of course, traveling to get Ben had already exhausted her last night.

A well of something . . . protective . . . surged up. Something he put down to his previous occupation. Protectiveness was part of his makeup, and that wasn't something he intended to ever lose. But letting it loose in regard to Lara was probably a bad idea.

"Tell you what," he found himself saying despite that. "The chicken and . . . errr . . . beans will keep for five minutes. I have some microwavable instant rice at my place. How about I get that and get your dinner dished up while you finish drying Ben off and getting him dressed for bed."

Lara's eyes slowly opened, a combination of hope and reluctance at war in gray eyes that had gone dull with her tiredness. "I can't—"

He cut off any arguments before she could make them. "I won't take no for an answer."

A puff of defiant air left her in a rush, her shoulders dropping. "Thank you."

"No problem." Peter waved her upstairs and he made his way back to his house.

By the time he had everything on the table, he could hear the pad of Ben's tiny bare feet down the wood stairs, followed by a more hushed tread. He glanced up. Socks. Lara was wearing socks. Nothing special. Just a pair of straightforward plain white cotton socks. Why did that make him want to kiss her all of a sudden? Press his lips to hers gently and tell her to eat and then go to bed and he'd take care of the rest.

Because of socks.

What the heck?

He cleared his throat. "All set?" he asked, maybe more abruptly than he intended.

Beyond a small pause of her foot on the last step, Lara didn't acknowledge that, though. "Yup."

They sat down, all three of them, him at an empty spot since he'd already had his dinner. Lara practically fell on her food, shoveling it in, enough that even Ben noticed and was staring.

"Did you eat today?" Peter wondered aloud.

She shrugged, which he took as no.

Irritation spiked, because she really should take care of herself. But he had nowhere to put that irritation. Partly because the logical side of him knew it was part of his healing brain, and not really him feeling that way. But also, it wasn't as if they were close enough for him to henpeck. Plus, he wasn't the henpecker or worrier type. Not usually. Reluctant to ask her anything to do with the shop, he cast about for another topic, a safer topic. "Did you hear from your brother?"

"Just a text that they arrived in Bermuda."

He nodded and fell silent, letting them both eat. The trouble was, he wanted to ask a lot more questions. About her. About the store. About her family. And he shouldn't want to know. He'd already decided. Lara was just his neighbor, and—unwittingly—the person who badly outbid him for the best storefront in town. He'd tried to make amends on the forum of a sort, and he'd helped her with Ben, and that was doing more than his neighborly best.

They sat in quiet, the other two eating. Ben finished well before Lara did and hopped up. "Ready, Pete?"

Peter stood up too, trying not to chuckle at the name. The kid had heard his father in the bookstore call him Pete and glommed right onto the name. He didn't mind. "Sure."

He raised a brow in question at Lara, who, still chewing, waved them to go ahead, and he followed Ben up the stairs, asking, "How far did you get?"

Only he didn't hear the entire answer as Ben led him into what would be the second bedroom in the townhome. Only, this wasn't a bedroom. This was clearly Lara's workshop.

Laminate wood floors were probably a good idea, because

she clearly worked a lot with wood. She had all sorts of tables with tools—some of them big tools—set up throughout. Another station looked like where she painted things. An entire wall dedicated to smaller hand tools and pieces like dowls and nails and whatnot. And it smelled of woodchips, reminding Peter a lot of Daniel's construction sites.

"You're sleeping in here?" he asked Ben.

"No, I left my book in here, though."

"Oh." There were only two bedrooms in these units.

Sure enough, after grabbing the book, Ben took him across the hall to the master bedroom. "You're sleeping in here with your aunt?" Peter asked.

"Yup." Ben had to sort of jump and crawl to get up on the tall queen-size, four-poster bed. An antique that matched the chest of drawers and a dressing table and mirror. The buttery-yellow bedspread was entirely Lara—though he'd semi-expected a Christmas-themed color scheme. Still, bright and cheerful fit her to a T.

Only he didn't feel entirely right being in here without her permission.

"Come on." Ben patted the bed beside him.

Apparently, he had no other choice. Climbing up with the kid, Peter immediately smelled the peppermint that seemed to linger around Lara, and almost smiled. Then frowned, because he shouldn't be noticing what the woman smelled like. Or imagining what her lips might taste like if he kissed her.

Forcefully putting all that out of his mind, he focused on Ben and the book. Thirty minutes later, lost as far as the plot went because the kid had managed to read the first two chapters on his own—smart boy—Peter closed the door of the bedroom, then paused, curiosity drawing his gaze into her toy-making room again, looking around longer.

Boxes.

Boxes everywhere. He'd noticed the same thing in her bedroom, and the family room, though no boxes were in sight, was bare. Just the basic furniture. As though Lara had only bothered to unpack things she absolutely needed—the kitchen, her clothes and toiletries, linens for the bed—but everything else was on hold.

Because The Elf Shop was taking all her time?

The answer to that seemed a little too obvious, and that twang of guilt ping-ponged around his insides like a pinball machine.

Forcing his feet to move, he went back downstairs to find Lara still at the kitchenette table, head resting on her bent arms on the tabletop, her plate of half-eaten food pushed to the side.

"Lara?" He tried not to startle her by lowering his voice. Maybe too much, because she didn't even twitch.

He cleared his throat and said her name again. Louder.

Nothing.

Peter moved closer and squatted down to the side she had her head turned to. Surprisingly, dark lashes fanned out over pale cheeks that had picked up a pink tint.

He frowned. Was she feverish?

Brushing aside her hair, silky against his fingertips, he pressed his palm to her forehead. She did feel a little warm. At his touch, she stirred, and he pulled his hand away as she slowly blinked awake. Dazed gray eyes gazed at him, confusion swirling for a long blink, then realization struck and, on a sucked-in breath, she bolted upright in her seat.

"It's just me," he tried to assure her. "You fell asleep."

After another blink, she nodded and then yawned big, reminding him suddenly of Snowball when she would yawn and stretch after an extra-long nap in a sunspot.

Shaking her head, Lara huffed a laugh. "Sorry about that."

"After the last few days you've had, I'm surprised you made it this far," he said.

Ben had filled him in on a lot. For only six, the kid was observant, and talkative once you drew him out of his shell. Books and candy had been all the bribery Peter needed.

She sighed. "It's been a lot. I don't know how . . ." She paused, seeming to reconsider sharing her burdens with him. Sure enough, her next words changed the subject. "Is Ben asleep?"

"I left him with the bathroom light on and the door cracked," Peter said, trying not to be foolishly disappointed that she didn't want to tell him all her woes. "But you may want to check in a bit. He didn't want to stop reading."

She nodded. "Thanks again for that. You've been a huge help today."

"No problem." The manners drilled into him by his mother, combined with that protective thing inside him, especially and oddly for *this* particular woman, tugged at him to offer more help. He clamped his lips shut on the words.

When she didn't say anything, he cleared his throat, then, needing something to do, he grabbed her plate.

"You don't have to do that," she said, getting to her feet as well.

Peter waved her off. "I already put the other stuff in the dishwasher. I just need to do your plates and then I'll run it and get out of your hair so you can go pass out and catch up on all that sleep you missed."

"Not possible," he thought he heard her murmur, but pretended not to hear. Because he was supposed to be not caring beyond that of a casual acquaintance. Keeping that firmly in mind, he finished the chore. To the sound of the dishwasher humming quietly, he shot her a friendly but deliberately distant wave. "Let me know tomorrow if Ben still wants me to read to him."

And then he hotfooted it out of there before he could do something like offer to take the kid again in the morning. After all, tomorrow was his day off.

Lara could handle it.

* * *

Something wakes me up—I'm not sure what and I'm not going to rush to see. Instead, I yawn and reach my paws out in front of me in a stretch so good I unsheathe my claws and knead the air. Once I'm done with that, I, of course, have to give the pads of my paws a tongue bath.

Finally, I look around to see what woke me . . . and frown.

Where did Miss Tilly go?

I spend every other night with her and the other nights with Emily and Lukas. Tilly never leaves the room in the morning without me because she has to take me down to the kitchen to feed me.

Hopping down from our bed, I trot into the bathroom that is attached to her room, but it's dark and cold. Empty.

No Miss Tilly.

The bedroom door is cracked just slightly, so I head over there and then bat at the thing with my paw until I get it to open just wide enough to squeeze through and pad into the hallway beyond, only to pull up short.

Because I found Miss Tilly.

She's there. And she's in her nightgown—white and frilly, down to her feet, with a high-necked collar and long sleeves gathered at the wrist. No dressing gown, which is unusual. She always insists it must be worn if she ever leaves her room in this "state of undress," as she calls it. After all, guests are here all the time.

And she's kissing Mr. Muir.

Kissing him.

She's kissing Mr. Muir wearing nothing but her nightgown in the hallway of Weber Haus, where any guest—or cat—could walk right out and see them.

He's been courting her. Tilly's words again. I knew that already, because she's been spending so much time with him, and because I heard that declaration of . . . I guess it wasn't love, but close enough, that he made to her the other day. I wasn't sure she was convinced, though. After all, she hasn't talked with me about it, and Miss Tilly talks things over with me all the time.

A little bit hurt that she'd keep this from me and sneak around behind my back, I slink the opposite direction down the hall to the back stairs that will take me down to the kitchen. As I pass by the air vent, the banging from the man working in the basement—and seems like all over the house—on the air conditioner can be heard easily.

Just one more thing making the house somewhere I don't want to be.

"You're early, Snowball," Mrs. Bailey says, glancing over her shoulder from where she's fiddling with something on the stovetop.

Huh. Only because Miss Tilly has some man's tongue stuck down her throat. I run to the back door and meow, pawing at the door.

"Okay, okay." Mrs. Bailey hurries over and opens it for me.

The sun isn't up yet, so I have a good idea of the time. It's Sunday, so the shops are closed, but I bet Lara will be in hers. She never seems to leave. I can definitely go visit her.

As I pass from the snow-covered grass onto the cobblestones that mark where the shops start, I catch sight of Peter clumping through the snow drifts that piled up near the family parking area, heading in my direction. He's muttering to himself and his face looks like someone took away every single one of his Christmas presents. He doesn't go to the house, but toward the shops. Curious, I wait, despite how my paws grow colder by the second, and then follow him straight to The Elf Shop.

Only it's locked when he tries the door, so he knocks.

Chapter 8

———⊗———

A beam of light shone in the dark of the toy shop. Coming from the back, he thought. Probably from Lara opening her office door at the sound of his knock. Peter stomped his feet as he waited for her to come let him in.

What am I doing here?

Sunday was supposed to be his day off. He was supposed to be doing other things. Anything other than this. But not even an hour ago, he'd vaguely heard the sound of Lara's car starting up, then driving away—far too early in the morning given how beat she'd been last night, asleep practically in her dinner. She was going to wear herself into nothing at this rate, and she was already pretty dang slender.

Knowing Lara wouldn't have left Ben on his own, Peter figured that meant she'd gotten up in time to get her nephew and herself both fed and dressed and intended on looking after him and whatever she had to do at the shop on her own.

Which is up to her, he tried to tell himself. She was an adult. She should be aware of her limits.

But none of those self-assurances had helped Peter get back to sleep. Instead, he'd stared at the ceiling, thinking about how he'd seen Emily go through opening a new business. But Emily had had Lukas, and their parents, and him and their brothers, and Miss Tilly, and Daniel, and lots of other help. Lara was on her own, as far as he could tell. He'd pictured her harried and tugged in a thousand directions, and Ben bored, and both of them dragging back to the house at a terrible hour only to do it all again tomorrow but with customers and Ben's schooling.

Which was why Peter had gotten up, gotten dressed, and driven his backside here at a ridiculous time in the morning.

On. His. Day. Off.

Lara appeared in the part he could see through the glass, walking through the dark space, the brightness of her pale hair giving her an ethereal, almost Ghost of Christmas Past appearance. Her face when she recognized who was standing outside knocking was a frowning combination of perplexed and questioning. But, even in the dim, with dancing nutcrackers paused at odd angles blocking his view, he still caught what he thought was a flicker of relief across her features.

She moved to the door, unlocked it, and pushed it open for him. "Peter?"

"Mind if I come in?" he asked. "It's cold."

She blinked, then stepped back. "Sorry. Of course."

Inside, he stomped and blew on his hands some more to shake off the lingering bite of winter clinging to his skin, despite the thick coat, hat, and gloves.

Lara crossed her arms and waited, eyebrows raised and lips only slightly smiling, but not exactly in a welcoming way. More like a "what are you doing here?" kind of way.

And darned if he didn't suddenly want to kiss her all over again.

This time it had nothing to do with socks and everything to do with the stubborn written all over her face. Maybe coming here to help her had been a bad idea. If anyone found out the guy she'd outbid, and who had retaliated by posting on the town forum, was now helping the new toy shop owner he'd be laughed out of town. If Lara found out . . . Well, he'd stopped now, and he'd helped with Ben. That was all he could do.

Lara was still waiting.

"It's my day off," he said, as though that explained everything.

She tilted her head, then glanced over his shoulder at the still-darkened sky. "And you decided, on your day off, to get up before dawn and come to a toy store? Or are you an early riser?"

Not really. Not even when he'd had to be. "I thought you might need someone to watch Ben," he said instead. "I should have offered last night."

Only she waved a hand as though shooing that offer away. "You've done too much already."

He shrugged. "He's no trouble, really."

"Mrrrow."

They both glanced down to find Snowball underfoot.

"Now how did you get in here?" Lara asked, bending over to pet the ball of fluff.

"The runt is a Houdini cat." Peter shook his head at her, only to be blinked at from guileless blue eyes as Snowball leaned into Lara's touch.

He wouldn't mind leaning into her touch, either. *Jeez, Diemer. Get yourself together, man.*

He and Lara looked at each other at the same time.

"Actually—"

"Auntie Larrrraaaaa?" Ben's voice sounded from inside the North Pole.

"Uh-oh," Lara muttered under her breath. Then raised her voice, "Coming, sweetie."

She hurried away, leaving Peter and Snowball to follow or not. He followed. So did the cat.

To find Ben's small form bent over a box on the floor practically twice his size. He was half in/half out of the ice cave–

style door leading to the storeroom area and Lara's office, obviously trying to drag the box into the North Pole room, but now wedged neatly in the doorjamb.

"Sorry. Sorry." Lara hurried over and bent at the waist to help her nephew tug.

Peter lifted his gaze to the ceiling, because . . . well, he was a man after all, and that view was temptation even for him. Was this a last-minute test of his resolve on Santa's part? Seemed as though he'd be earning his name on the Nice List again this week.

But the sound of a feminine grunt had him sighing and lowering his gaze so he could cross the room to the struggling pair. "Here. Let me," he said, shooing them both out of his way.

After an initial tug on the box, he could see it was stuck and not going to be forced. So instead he got on his knees and put a shoulder into it, pushing hard to back it the way it had come. With the sound of ripping cardboard, it gave with a jolt, and the box went sliding, and he went sprawling on his belly on a cement floor painted to look like a snow-covered winter wonderland.

Great job. Big, strong man to the rescue.

Ignoring a choked set of sniggers from behind him—one feminine and one childish—he got to his feet and repositioned the box to pull it through with only a slight tug, then picked it up, careful to hold the torn corner together, and turned to face two laughing sets of eyes.

"Muscles really do come in handy sometimes," Lara managed around the hand she'd lifted to unsuccessfully cover her grin.

Peter grunted. "Where do you want this?"

She pointed to the nearest table and he set it down. "What's in this, anyway?" he asked. "Bricks?"

"Supplies," she said.

Then proceeded to open the box and start to pull out stuff that reminded him of the horror of art class in grade school when he'd been forced to color and glue and glitter and cut his way through an hour of arts and crafts once a week for years.

Some kids had loved it. Art had not been, and never would be, his thing.

"What's this for?" He was almost afraid to ask.

Ben answered. "Kids are going to make Christmas ornaments."

"Another workshop?" he directed the question to Lara.

"No. These will be out for anyone who wants to use them." She pulled the last item out of the box and put her hands on her hips, staring at the pile. "Hmmm . . . What do you think, Ben? Should we do the same kinds of ornaments on one table? Or do stations?"

"Definitely stations," Peter said.

She turned laughing eyes his way. "Is your name Ben?"

Another shudder as this felt again just like grade school art class.

"Stations," Ben said, shooting Peter a look that said men had to stick together.

"Stations it is," Lara said. "Why don't you put the boxes of ornaments on that table?" she told Ben, pointing at the one closest to the entrance between the Santa's Toy Shop room and the North Pole room.

Then she started picking up all the paints and taking them to another table. Seeing what she was about, Peter grabbed the different-colored felt boxes and glue and took them to the next one. She glanced over as he set things down and nodded. Which he took to mean he'd got the gist of the idea. By the time they were finished, kids could decorate their ornaments with glitter, paint, lace, felt, construction paper, glitter glue, and more.

Halfway through organizing, Peter decided that they needed plastic tablecloths—the disposable kind—on the tables to protect the wood. Which Lara had in stock, of course. Even Christmas themed. Then he decided they needed signs for the stations and borrowed her computer to print some out and tape them to the ends.

"Not bad," he said, hands on his hips, feet set wide as he observed the results of their work.

She grinned. "I wish I'd thought of this sooner so I could have advertised."

Peter paused, then frowned. "Wait. You weren't planning on this?"

She shook her head. "I just thought of it last night before bed."

He kept a niggle of doubt to himself. He would have done things differently in her shoes. Planned it for months making sure he had all the materials, advertised, agonized over it, all for optimal participation. "What if no one bothers to do it?"

She shrugged. "I figured this would be a trial run."

A trial run. When she was exhausted. And had Ben. Those dark circles hadn't gone anywhere, even after a night's sleep. Not that she'd slept all that long apparently, with her early wake-up call.

And it's her business. Acknowledging that truth didn't make the growing pit of worry in his gut shrink any, though.

"I might have planned more," he said slowly. And actually had to pause as it hit him that he hadn't gone straight into "I'm right and you're doing it wrong" mode that would have been his reaction even a few weeks ago.

Despite how came the words came out as a grumble that sounded decidedly "clichéd grouchy old man," this was . . . an improvement. Maybe his brain was finally healing?

He was so busy being focused on this minor breakthrough, that it took a second to notice her reaction. After a long pause where, for a brief second, he thought he saw self-doubt darken her eyes, she laughed, the sound too carefree not to believe. "I would, too, usually. But it started out as an activity Ben could do in my office, and then I thought, why not put it out for any kids to join in."

That made sense. Except . . . "But you'll lose money on the supplies."

She waved that off as if it were no big deal. "Just for a few weeks won't matter. If it's popular enough, I'll think about charging for similar things in the future."

Think about it? Frustration welled again, but Peter managed to grit his teeth around more words about poor budgeting decisions. Except the way she was bouncing on her toes . . . she really did love this. So he kept his mouth shut and tried not to ruin it for her. For now.

Lara pulled out her phone and took a picture, then glanced at the screen and blinked. "Heavens, is that the time? I still need to restock from the last two days."

Peter sat with Ben as Lara swooped around the store doing the same things he and his parents and other workers did at the bookstore after closing or before unlocking the door at opening time.

He was just about to get up and offer to help when Snowball suddenly jumped up on the table beside him with a little blip of a meow. Except this was the glitter table, which had disaster written all over it. Even with the easy-to-clean tablecloths. Definitely no place for a cat.

"Oh no, you don't." He lurched for her. Only he managed to knock the table with his knee and a tub of glitter knocked over and basically dropped into his lap, upside down, dumping the entire sparkly contents all over him.

"Oh—" He cut off the expletive, barely managing to keep his cool around Ben, and instead changed it to "nuts."

Somehow, he also managed to hold on to the cat.

"Don't move," Lara said, her voice wavering with laughter that she was trying to hold back.

At the same time, Ben's eyes grew wide before he laughed, the sound bouncing off the high ceilings. Of course *Peter* would be the one to get doused with glitter. She disappeared into her office and a second later returned with a dust brush and pan that she used exclusively for all things glitter.

"Here," she said. "Let me."

Except the glitter had fallen all over his lap. As he shifted slightly—arranging Snowball so that he could cradle her in his arms without her fur touching the glitter—a tiny water-fall of shimmering pieces dropped to the ground with a soft shooshing sound, and Lara bit back a giggle at his put-upon expression. Also at the sight of this man, who was intimidating on his good days, cuddling a tiny, fluffy white cat, all while covered in sparkly stuff.

Soooo tempting to whip her phone out and take a quick picture. For posterity, of course. She managed to rein in the urge.

"Actually . . ." She handed him the items and took the cat so that he could brush himself off. As much as he could. The problem was, even without glue, glitter had a tendency to stick to stuff. Especially skin and jeans apparently.

"I look like I've been to war with Santa's elves," he grumbled, mostly to himself.

"It should wash out," she tried to assure him. "Only . . . make sure you don't put anything else in the washer with it."

Now she was picturing this burly, tough guy wearing clothes that had a little extra sparkle in the sun. It really shouldn't be funny, because he'd come here to help, but . . .

"Who has an open bin of glitter around children?" he asked no one in particular, still trying his best to force the glitter off him with the brush and not making a dent.

"It's so they can roll the ornament in it and cover it all at once," she explained, still holding on to her giggles, because now he'd managed to get one big, star-shaped sparkle on his face right where Marilyn Monroe's beauty spot had been . . .

and he had no clue. Should she show him to a mirror? There was a small bathroom in the back just for employees.

Maybe after he'd finished trying to clean himself up out here.

Because even after sweeping himself aggressively, the man was still covered in glitter. Basically a stripe of it across his lap.

"I'd better go home and change, I guess," he said, standing up.

Another whooshing waterfall, which had apparently been trapped on the bench under his backside, rained down onto the floor, and Lara couldn't help it. She burst out laughing. Then immediately apologized. "I'm sorry. It's not funny. But . . ."

"Uh-huh." He was definitely unamused. "See you later, kid," he called to Ben as he stepped away from the table.

Ben looked up from gluing a red pompom to a brown felt cutout that looked like a reindeer head, and Lara couldn't miss the disappointment that had her nephew drooping a little as he realized Peter was going.

"You're leaving?" he asked Peter.

"Yeah."

Then her nephew lit up, and before she could wonder why, he piped up with, "Auntie Lara and I are trying a new ice cream recipe tonight. Want to come over and help?"

That's right. She *had* promised that. She winced, because she didn't want to impose, again, and yet at the same time found herself holding her breath for Peter's answer while also steeling herself for a rejection. Because if playing Santa had driven him away, the glitter bomb would probably mean she'd never lay eyes on the man again.

Except the expression Peter turned to her was frowning. Almost disapproval, which couldn't be right. Who disapproved of ice cream?

"You make the ice cream yourself?" he asked, glancing at the glassed-in case at the other side of the room.

She shrugged. "I have an industrial-sized maker. It's fun."

"Fun," he repeated. As though he'd never heard the word before or had serious doubts that ice cream making could fall in that category.

Lara found herself wondering what Peter Diemer did for fun, anyway. Maybe he needed more of it.

The lines around Peter's mouth deepened with his frown. "That seems . . . expensive."

Actually, she'd inherited it, along with recipes and fifteen of the inserts that then converted to ice cream tubs that fit into the glass-covered, refrigerated cooling case. All from her grandmother who'd run a tearoom out of her home.

Before she could explain all that to him, Peter seemed to shrug himself out of whatever thought he was having and shot a wave at Ben. "I may be busy," he said. "But I'll pop by tonight if I have time. I'll at least come to read."

Busy? Like a date? Or . . . *None of my business.*

Peter scooped Snowball right out of her arms and walked away.

"Thanks," she called after his retreating back.

He paused, turned, and nodded, then, with Snowball tucked under one arm, left the shop. Why did the day suddenly seem . . . less . . . without him here?

Lara shook her head. She was just being silly. He'd been helpful, but except for one small moment when he'd first come in the shop and she'd thought maybe he wanted to kiss her, she got the impression that he didn't approve of her somehow. She really didn't need another Lance in her life.

Not that Peter was that exactly. After all, he'd been the one to drop by so early to help. He wouldn't do that if he didn't approve of her.

Would he?

No one would, really. He was just an adorably grumpy kind of guy was all.

Shrugging off the odd feeling, she focused on the shop and

Ben, who seemed right in his element with the ornaments. Maybe she could have him show other kids after he finished his schoolwork tomorrow. She grinned. The ornaments had definitely been a stroke of genius.

Hours later, with it dark outside again already, she locked up the store, satisfied she was as ready as she could possibly be for the workweek to start again tomorrow. "You know what we need?" she asked Ben.

"What?"

"A fabulous home-cooked dinner."

"I know where you can get one of those," Emily's voice sounded from behind her.

Lara glanced around, eyebrows raised. "Oh?"

In answer Emily tipped her head toward the house, but Lara frowned. "Aren't those meals just for guests of the house?"

"Where I happen to live and can invite my own guests from time to time." Emily waggled her eyebrows in open invitation.

Not to have to cook something when they got home did sound tempting. "You don't have to—"

A brush against her ankles cut her off and she looked down to find Snowball winding around her snow-booted feet. "*Mrrrow,*" the little cat greeted.

"Snowball!" Ben dropped to his knees, ignoring the way the newly fallen snow was soaking into his jeans, his little face an eager study of enjoyment as he petted the cat gently.

"See," Emily insisted. "Snowball wants you to come, too."

To which Snowball meowed again, as though in agreement. Maybe Peter was right and the cat spoke human.

Lara thought about the mostly empty cupboards in her kitchen and her dread at the thought of trying to cobble together an edible and filling concoction that a six-year-old might eat from that hodgepodge. Either that or she'd have to go to the grocer. Her growing exhaustion combined with

Emily's smile and Ben petting the cat, and she gave in gracefully. "That would be more lovely than you probably realize."

Emily chuckled and gestured at her face as they started to move toward the house. "I recognize that glassy, up-for-days, starting-a-new-business look in the eyes."

"Is it that bad?"

"Bad? No. Just . . . normal."

"But it gets easier, right?"

Emily laughed at that. "You get into a routine that works for you. But easier?" She shrugged. "It's my passion. My dream. So easy is relative. I could work every waking hour of the day and not notice the time going by. Lukas, who is just as devoted to his photography, worries about what's going to happen when babies come along."

The way Emily's hand seemed to unconsciously move to cover her still-flat belly, Lara had to wonder if the first of those babies was already on the way. But she didn't want to push.

"Are you in a place where you can hire more help at the bakery?"

Emily nodded slowly. "The question is, do I want to? I love what I do."

A tough question, one extremely personal to the individual. Every person had their own way to handle their situations. Given that Lara was only an auntie, and not managing that all that well as a temporary parent, no way was she going to give any advice. "I'm sure you'll figure out what works for you and your family."

"I hope so."

"I lived with my grandmother after I turned eight and she ran a tea house out of her home for income. I loved helping her. I'm not sure what she would have done during the baby or toddler years, but . . ." Lara shrugged.

Emily grinned as they stepped up to the back door of the house. "You're right. We'll figure it out."

The next few minutes were a rush of being introduced to Mrs. Bailey, taking off all the layers of winter clothing to hang them up, and leaving their boots melting on plastic pallets by the back door. Then they moved into the dining room, where they met the guests staying at the house. Everyone was already lining up to move through a buffet line and waiting for Mrs. Bailey to put the food out, so Lara took Ben to the back of the line with Emily.

The scrumptious scents of a pot roast with thick brown gravy, potatoes, carrots, and warm, fresh-baked rolls had Lara's stomach growling in appreciation. Especially as she pictured the ruined noodles from last night—out of a box no less. Pathetic.

The line backed into the foyer and they were at the end of it. Would it be rude to bowl these paying guests over so that she could fall on her food sooner?

"Hello, my love." Lukas came down the stairs, wrapping his arms around Emily to give her a lingering kiss, as though they hadn't seen each other all day and didn't have an audience. He let her go with a grin. "Aunt Tilly is canoodling with Mr. Muir in the hallway upstairs," he whispered loudly, blue eyes alight with laughter.

Emily's dark eyes, not like her brother's at all, went wide, sparkling right back at her husband. "Really?" She glanced over his shoulder as if she'd be able to spot the couple.

"Who is Mr. Muir?" Lara asked, careful to keep her voice low.

"According to Sophie," Lukas said, "he's an older gentleman who stayed here last year while we happened to be away. Apparently, he has been carrying a torch for my great-aunt for years, but we were all out of town when Peter was in the hospital, so it didn't work out for them to reconnect last year."

Peter had been in the hospital? Her heart gave a worried

thump. Had it been serious? Was that why the uber-serious man she knew now differed from her memory of a man who knew how to flirt and smile from the first time she'd visited Weber Haus?

The front door opened at that moment and Daniel came stomping in with his wife, Sophie, who Lara had met shortly after renting the space in the Weber Haus shops. Still dressed in what seemed to be her uniform of smart slacks and elegant blouse, her honey-blond hair pinned up, Sophie smiled, gray eyes full of laughter. "Someone"—Sophie elbowed her husband—"burnt our dinner."

Daniel offered a sheepish grin. "I fell asleep on the couch."

As hard as the man worked—and physical work, too—Lara wasn't surprised.

Unwinding a long scarf from around her neck, Sophie started down the hallway past the stairs to the back entrance to the kitchen. "I'm going to ask Mrs. Bailey if there's enough for us, too."

"Oh . . ." Lara winced. "She said there was, but that's when she thought it only needed to stretch for me and Ben. We can go somewhere else, though."

After all, they weren't family. Pizza would be fine. She'd order it and pick it up on the way home.

"No, no," Sophie laughed. "If there's not enough, *we* will go somewhere else."

"But you're family. I can't—"

"You can, and you will," Sophie insisted, and Daniel nodded.

"Of course you'll stay," a deceptively frail voice sounded from the top of the stairs.

They all glanced up to find Tilly at the top with an older gentleman standing slightly behind her. Perhaps Lara was looking for signs after what Lukas said they were getting up to just now, but it seemed to her that Miss Tilly's white-haired bun was a little lopsided. And was that a fresh coat of lipstick? The man, who had to be Mr. Muir, did appear to be a little stunned, unable to take his eyes off Tilly.

In front of Lara, but where Tilly couldn't see, Lukas poked at Emily as if to say, *See. I told you so.*

Emily ignored her husband.

"I'll still go ask." Sophie scooted away into the kitchen before anyone could tell her not to.

By the time the older couple made it down the stairs—moving carefully, but that didn't fool Lara any, because she'd seen with her own eyes a few years ago just how feisty Miss Tilly could be—Sophie was back. "Mrs. Bailey says not to worry. She made enough for a Christmas truckers' convention."

They all chuckled at that.

In short order they'd served themselves. Since the dining room, even with its extra-long table, couldn't seat them all as well as the guests, Tilly had led all the "family" members into a separate sitting room, where she pulled bamboo lap trays out of a built-in cupboard at the bottom of the bookshelves. Ben sat beside Lara on the carpeted floor, tray balanced over his crisscrossed knees and Snowball curled up beside him.

Please don't let him spill anything, she silently begged, watching him closely. The rug had to be expensive . . . and old. An heirloom like everything else in the house no doubt.

"You've found a friend for life," Miss Tilly said, directing the words at Ben with a nod at the little cat.

He perked up, as though he'd sighted Santa's sleigh in the night sky. "Really?"

Faded blue eyes crinkling around the corners, Miss Tilly nodded solemnly. "Oh yes. She doesn't pick just anyone to love on."

"Trust me," Daniel said. "She took a while to warm up to me."

Lara chuckled as Sophie patted his knee. She'd seen the

cat—only a tiny kitten at the time—attack him like a banshee the first time she'd stayed here. Snowball lifted her head from her paws to look at Daniel as though to say, *You're still on thin ice, sir.*

Which made Ben laugh.

"So, Mr. Muir . . ." Lukas said. "What exactly are your intentions with my aunt?"

The entire room went still and quiet, and Snowball again lifted her head, this time with a disconcerted little expression, as though truly concerned with the answer.

"I told you he saw us," Mr. Muir murmured at Tilly, who assumed a prim expression and whispered back, "It's none of his business."

"As your nephew, who cares about you very much," Lukas said, "I beg to disagree."

"Don't act pompous, babe," Emily quietly teased. "Tilly is an adult."

"I'm an adult four times over," Miss Tilly said in such a dry voice that Lara grinned.

Lukas, meanwhile, settled into a pout only to get pinched by Emily for his trouble.

Mr. Muir, expression reminding Lara a bit of Peter when he was at his most stoically cantankerous, harrumphed. Then he eyed Lukas closely. "I appreciate that my Matilda has people who care about her," he said. "But she's right, youngster. None of your business."

Tilly actually beamed at her suitor for that, and Lara had to cover her smile by shoving food in her mouth and chewing. This was family business.

Lukas grunted, still clearly in protective nephew mode. Not that she blamed him. His relationship with his great-aunt reminded her of her own relationship with Granny, setting up an ache of memories just behind her left ribs.

"Just don't play with her heart," Lukas warned.

Lara winced at the same time Emily did, but it was Daniel

who spoke up. "He wouldn't do that, Lukas. Mr. Muir is good people, and I know he cares for her a great deal."

Lukas slowly turned to Daniel, eyebrows rising to his hairline. "And how would you know that?"

Daniel glanced from Lukas to Mr. Muir. "Because he told me last year."

But that only made Lukas frown harder. "Why?"

Daniel leaned forward, clearly trying to impress the truth on his friend. "To make me realize that I'd be a fool to lose Sophie."

"You did that?" Sophie murmured quietly, aiming the words at the older man, who shifted in his seat uncomfortably, face turning slightly red.

Daniel's expression softened as he looked down at his wife. "The day I came to get Snowball from you at the hotel . . ."

Sophie softened right back, the two living in the memory of that moment, so sweet to witness. What would it feel like to be looked at that way?

Lara had once thought she had that with an ex from college a while back, but she hadn't. Hindsight was funny that way. It took off the rose-colored glasses and the haze of wishful thinking to show you that while things had been fun together at first, he would never, ever have looked at her as though she were the center of his world. The piece that kept it turning for him. Because she wasn't.

She'd been . . . a gullible fool for him to take advantage of, and he'd left her in a hole of debt. Deep enough that she'd had to ask Lance for help digging her out. She'd paid him back, eventually, but . . .

All thanks to her poor choice in men.

But she still believed in love. Now . . . nothing less than what these couples had would do for her. And she doubted it would come. Her business was her focus, and she was happy with that. With herself.

Except maybe for Peter . . .

Mr. Muir cleared his throat, shaking her out of that thought. "While our relationship is none of your business," he said to Lukas, "I appreciate that you care for Matilda. I assure you, I do, too."

Lukas studied the older man. Lara thought of Mr. Muir as the epitome of a salty sea captain, thanks to the neatly trimmed beard of white and the deeply entrenched lines around his eyes, but with the clothing of Dr. Doolittle. After a second Lukas nodded his appreciation and Mr. Muir nodded back as though the two men had silently come to some sort of agreement.

The room eased, like a leaking balloon, all the tension just blowing away slowly. Lara shoveled another bite into her mouth and had to contain a groan at the way the tender meat just sort of melted on her taste buds. Real food.

When was the last time she'd had it this good?

She paused, realization floating down like snowflakes. Actually, she hadn't eaten like this since Granny passed away. Gosh, two years was an awfully long time to go. Lara twisted her lips around a sudden rush of sadness and loneliness. Yes, technically, she still had her brother, but that was different. Wouldn't Granny love to see what she'd done with the shop? Or feed her when she was too tired to cook? Granny loved feeding people. That was her love language.

Although, if Granny had been waiting at home with food last night, Peter would never have needed to come over and rescue her with microwavable rice.

Lara bit her lip.

What a disloyal thing to think. And meaningless. Because Peter had clearly changed his mind about any interest he might have in her. Besides, she'd rather have Granny in her life more than just about anything.

"Hey?" Emily murmured softly from where she sat in a wing-backed chair beside Lara.

"What?"

"I have an idea about how to find the Right Rudolph."

Lara lifted her eyebrows, glancing around, because she really didn't want others to know about that, despite how public it already was. No one was paying them any attention, though. "How?"

"I had this idea that the person might be posting due to sour grapes. What if they were one of the people you outbid trying to rent the space you got?"

Lara frowned as she thought through that. Multiple people had been in the running, which was why she'd bid as high as she had, but the posts hadn't started until she'd knocked the last contender out. Could it be them? "I guess that could be true."

Emily nodded. "So I thought I might check with Tilly. A management company runs all things shops for her, but she has access to them. I could see if I can find out the names of everyone who bid for it."

Lara's frown deepened, as did her exhaustion all of a sudden. The thing was . . . knowing wasn't going to fix anything. It would only make her bitterly uncomfortable around that person. "Maybe we should just let it go."

Emily wrinkled her nose, visibly reluctant. "Really? Are you sure?"

Lara nodded.

"Why don't you think about it a bit?"

She wouldn't change her mind, but she nodded anyway. "Thanks." A yawn suddenly sideswiped her.

Lukas picked up on it and grinned around his wife. "No one ever warns you how opening a new business is the hardest thing you'll ever do in your entire life."

"Maybe not the hardest thing," Emily said.

The way he glanced at her belly just added to Lara's suspicion. The lovely couple were expecting. Hiding a secret smile, happy for them, Lara redirected the conversation in general. "So . . . what are the traditions here leading up to Christmas?"

I drop my chin to my paws and listen vaguely to the humans chatting. Every once in a while, Ben runs a hand over my fur and I give a little purr for his efforts. But mostly my mind is on Miss Tilly and Mr. Muir.

If Miss Tilly is going to fall in love with him, I need to rethink things a bit. Still . . . I want Miss Tilly to be happy.

Chapter 9

⁂

The flash of headlights across his ceiling had Peter up and at the window. It was after eight, and Lara was just getting home? He checked the time on the microwave. An hour after Ben's bedtime? What happened?

He stepped back from the window as they got out of the car, then rolled his eyes at himself, because the voice in his head whispering about bedtimes had sounded just like his mother. When had that happened? Ben and Lara were none of his business, except . . .

Without thinking about it further, he stepped outside. "Hey!" he called, and she paused with her hand on the door.

"Hey, Pete!" Ben grinned, bouncing on his toes. "We got to eat dinner at Weber Haus. Mr. Muir is going to be my tutor for school. He offered and Auntie Lara said no, but then she said yes. And I'm one of Snowball's favorite people. We didn't get to go ice skating—Auntie Lara says maybe another day. But I got to eat black forest cake that Emily made. And Mr. Muir and Miss Tilly's gonna get married."

Peter paused on the last step down from his front door. "Whoa," he said, glancing between Ben and Lara. "Sounds like a lot happened."

Ben nodded.

Lara chuckled. "I'm not sure if they'll marry, but they are . . ."

"Courting?" Peter asked. Because "dating" didn't seem like the right word somehow.

"Exactly."

At least that all explained why she and Ben were running late. The tightness banding his ribs eased. Nothing bad. Just getting fed and getting home.

"Emily's black forest cake is my favorite," he said. "Did you save me any?"

Ben's face fell, and Peter elbowed him playfully before the kid could get upset. "Don't worry. She usually puts a secret slice with my name on it in the fridge for next time she sees me."

"Sounds like a nice little sister to have around," Lara murmured. Why did her smile dim as she said it, though?

"She has her good points." Peter shrugged. "Now . . . bedtime for you?"

The question had Lara grimacing. "We'll skip bath tonight." She ruffled Ben's hair. "Go brush your teeth."

"I'll be up to read in a few minutes," Peter told him.

With a whoop, Ben skittered up to the front door and let himself in with the keys Peter assumed Lara had given him.

After he was out of earshot, Peter looked at Lara, falling into step beside her. "You should probably go get ready for bed, too."

Which had her lips twitching as she put her bags down just inside the door. He should probably reword that. Make it sound less like a nagging husband. He wasn't going to, though. Besides, she was already giving excuses.

"I have a few train sets that need my attention. Time to paint them." She kicked a box on the floor with her foot.

Peter shook his head. "Uh-uh, young lady. You look dead on your feet."

"Gee thanks."

"Gorgeous, but dead on your feet," he corrected, and got a smilingly wrinkled nose.

She sighed. "You're probably right."

He crossed his arms, giving her an unwavering stare. "I usually am."

"And so humble."

He shrugged. "Humble and right don't usually go together."

"I'll remember that." Lara started up the stairs and Peter followed, close behind because she looked like a puff of wind could blow her off her feet.

Then she suddenly stopped and turned. "I forgot. I need to start a batch of ice cream—"

The action brought her down onto his step facing him, crowded into him thanks to the rather narrow stairway. The side of him here only to help with Ben and otherwise determined to keep his distance told Peter to move back and let her pass.

But wide gray eyes drew him like a child to a candy store window and he found himself staring, unable to look away. The scents of peppermint and candy, as though she'd absorbed Christmas, wended around him.

Step away, his brain said.

But he didn't want to. What he really wanted . . . "I want to kiss you, Lara Wolfe."

Those beautiful gray eyes widened, and a tinge of pink bloomed in her cheeks, chasing away the exhaustion. "I'd . . . like that."

Oh. "But I can't."

Hell. This impulse control thing was going to get him into trouble. At least, he thought this was a brain injury thing. Wasn't it? Regardless, the sudden disappointment shadowing her eyes now was like a solid kick to the gut.

"Why, exactly, can't you?" She tipped her head, eyeing him oddly.

A question he was already debating. Peter put one hand up on the wall behind her head, to brace himself, to stop himself from giving in, but unfortunately bringing him closer to her. Close enough to discover silver ribbons of lighter color within the gray. "We're neighbors."

She slow-blinked. "That's it?"

Exactly what the irrational part of him was saying. But that wasn't everything, and he knew it. How could he kiss her knowing he'd let himself do the things he had? Plus, she didn't deserve someone in his current state of mind.

Except her lips looked so soft. Would she taste of peppermint? He'd been wondering for weeks. Peter swallowed.

"Eventually things will end, and we'll still be neighbors, and you'll be next door to my sister in the shops. I think staying friends is . . . a better idea."

A safer idea. But what he was doing right now was far from safe.

"This feels like friends to you?" she whispered, her voice turning slightly husky, and he almost groaned at the impact.

"Not really," he grumbled. This felt like an avalanche.

The corners of her mouth tipped up at that and he dropped his gaze to her lips, still trying to talk himself out of what he shouldn't want. He curled his hand on the wall into a fist, willing himself to step back, but not doing it. She never looked away, as though waiting for him to decide what move to make.

"Not at all," he muttered, and leaned forward slowly, giving her time to change her mind, because he was going to kiss her despite all the reasons he shouldn't.

"Hey, Pete!"

Ben's voice at the top of the stairs had them both jerking apart guiltily, just in time for Ben to peer over the banister at the top.

"I'm ready," the little boy said, then frowned at the two of them. "What are you doing down there?"

Lara cleared her throat. "I remembered I need to make that batch of ice cream."

The way Ben's face lit up and then Lara mumbled "whoops" under her breath, Peter guessed that was probably the wrong thing to say.

"You said I could help you with that." The boy clearly was not in the going-to-bed frame of mind. "Right?"

Lara grimaced. "We'll have to do tomorrow's batch together, because you should have been in bed a while ago."

Ben's little face fell, chin jutting out in silent mutiny, and he opened his mouth on what Peter was pretty sure was going to turn into a half hour of whining and wheedling.

"Let's go hit the books, Ben," he got in before the kid could say anything. "I need to get to bed, too."

Ben closed his mouth slowly, glancing between the two of them, clearly pulled in two directions. Then nodded.

"Don't do the Scrooge Face–flavored one without me," the boy pleaded with Lara.

Peter was pretty sure Ben didn't catch her sigh. "I'll do the peppermint one tonight, okay?"

"Okay," came a slightly sullen agreement.

"Let's go, buddy." Peter started up the stairs.

He turned at the top to find Lara still there watching and darned if he didn't want to go right back down the stairs, pull her into his arms, and kiss away the tired. Too late now. The rational side of his brain was in charge again. Santa had better be watching, because being a good boy really sucked sometimes.

"Thank you," she mouthed.

He frowned. For what? Almost kissing her? Almost making this even more complicated?

She tipped her head at Ben, who was retreating down the hall without him.

Peter flashed her a thumbs-up, then hid a grimace because he wasn't a thumbs-up kind of person. Or a helper. Or a children's book reader for that matter.

He was a fixer, and that's all this was. *All* he would let it be.

Lara grinned, as though she'd caught all those thoughts, and turned away, heading to the kitchen for ice cream making. He glared at the offending appendage even as he lowered his hand to his side.

"Come on, Pete," Ben called from his room.

Right. Read to the kid, then get the heck out of here before Santa cemented his name under "naughty."

Lara blew a stray strand of hair out of her eyes as she stood over the stove stirring her latest ice cream concoction over low heat—the simple syrup, milk, and egg yolk mixture that would become the custard. Unfortunately, the peppermint recipe was one of the longer and more involved of the ones she had. But she'd bought ingredients for only two recipes, and she had to save the Scrooge Face one for Ben. She'd promised. Meanwhile, standing here stirring, her mind had plenty of time to wander.

Especially to that almost kiss that didn't happen.

Heavens, Peter Diemer smelled amazing. Whatever subtle manly, woodsy cologne he used, she'd been tempted to bury her face in the crook of his neck and just . . . breathe. Let all the tension leach from her muscles.

That was probably a bad thing, right?

The fact that around him, she felt as though she even could take a moment and breathe, as if the pressure she was putting herself under was all going to turn out fine. She frowned at the slowly thickening mixture, going over his words again. Peter was already worried about their breakup when he hadn't even asked her out?

Definitely the kind of commitment-phobic guy she should

be avoiding. If Peter was that kind, then he was right and it was better they just stay friends. She didn't have time to date, anyway. Even if she really, really . . . really . . . really, really wanted to kiss him.

"Still going?"

The sound of his deep, rumbly voice had her jumping and turning at the same time, knocking her hand against the side of the metal pot she was using. Lara hissed at the sudden flare of pain, dropping the wooden spoon in the pot to jerk her hand back. Peter was across the room, in total "guy getting things done" mode, tugging her over to the sink and shoving her hand under running cold water. Which she was about to do, anyway. In a second.

"The stove . . ." She tried to pull away. She needed two more minutes of stirring or she'd scorch the mixture and have to start over.

Peter blocked her path, stepping over to the pot. "I've got the stove. You take care of that."

Okkaaaay. She put her hand back under the water. "You have to stir it constantly, scraping the sides and bottom until the timer dings."

He nodded and went to work with all the focus of a man with a mission. One not unfamiliar with the kitchen, either; it hadn't seemed like Peter would be, but one never knew about people.

When the timer went off, Lara turned off the water and moved to take over, but he waved her away. "Now what?"

She pointed. "I've set up cream in an ice bath. You'll pour the custard mix through the strainer over that and then stir it all together until it's all cooled off."

"Right."

He turned off the burner and grabbed the pot holders she'd already gotten out, lifting the large container off the stove. Lara leaned a hip against the counter and gave herself full permission to just enjoy the view. The muscles of his forearms, on display thanks to rolled-up sleeves, flexed. So did the muscles in his biceps, stretching the material of his shirt. All thanks to his previous job, of course, but she idly wondered if he still kept up the strict physical regimen from that time in his life. The muscles certainly indicated he did.

He finished carefully straining the mix, then set the pot and strainer aside and proceeded to stir. Which pulled Lara right out of her reverie. "I can take over now."

He glanced over but didn't stop stirring. "How's the hand?"

"Just a little pink is all. I barely touched it."

He nodded and still didn't move.

"Really, I can—"

"How is this supposed to be peppermint ice cream?"

She raised her eyebrows at the question. For a man who had basically told her that they were just going to be neighbors, he certainly paid attention. "I'll add extract when it's cooled, and then halfway through the freezing process I'll stir in crushed candy canes."

He tipped his head, focused entirely and intently on the ice cream ingredients. "You know what would be terrific with that?"

He wanted to mess with her ice cream recipe? *Granny's* ice cream recipe, actually, but he wasn't to know that. "What?"

"Chocolate chips. Or even better, a fudge swirl."

Lara paused. Because he was right, but even more so because there was just something incongruous about this tall, tough man discussing chocolate chips and fudge swirls in ice cream that just sort of struck her as . . . endearing.

Not that she'd tell him that. "I'll have to try that."

She considered his casual shrug, which basically said "whatever." Was he trying not to care? Or maybe he really didn't. Either way, she'd taken up enough of his time today.

"Thanks for all the help." She tried to scoot him away from the bowl, holding her hand out for the spoon.

"Let me just get this part done and I'll pour it into the freezer thingy for you," he said.

Actually, that part was always tricky since she made such a big batch and it was always heavy. "Thanks," she said again. Then . . . "Is there any way I can repay all the help you've given me lately? Maybe something for the bookstore? A favor for a favor, so to speak?"

Another shrug—lots of shrugs tonight—and a glance that looked almost uncomfortable. "I can't think of anything."

"Maybe I could do a workshop in the bookstore one day. Something book related might be fun."

"Maybe." Now he sounded reluctant.

Why? Her workshops brought in a fairly good-size group of people and usually made other shoppers curious. Maybe it was the cost?

"I'd waive my fee," she offered. "And other than paying for materials out of the registration fees, you can keep the profits."

The reluctance thickened, hanging over him like a tattered blanket in wet snow. "I'll talk to my parents and see what they think."

"Okay."

If he didn't want her, she wasn't going to push. She just . . . She was having a hard time figuring Peter Diemer out. He blew hot and cold faster than Jack Frost in summer.

After Elias, and even Lance, she should be more guarded. Lara shouldn't be so eager to get involved with someone so difficult to read. Still . . . she'd definitely find a way to repay all these favors.

Maybe she'd go over his head to his mother and see what she thought. Or Emily might have some ideas.

I revel in the refreshing cold air, or at least try to convince myself I'm reveling as I prowl the outer edges of the Weber Haus property. I haven't done my due diligence on bird patrol in some time. Too busy with the humans and their love lives. If, while I've been distracted, things have gone the way they did last year—not just Mr. Muir's turtledoves, but the geese, and swans, and partridges—I'm in trouble. Good grief, what a mess that was.

I can't do anything about the hens in the coop. Those are part of the house and grounds and petting zoo. But I can scare off a crow or ten. Maybe even bring one to Mrs. Bailey to add to dinner.

Mostly, though, I needed to get away to think about Miss Tilly.

If she really does love Mr. Muir, that means things are going to change. Would Tilly go away with him? Daniel and Sophie had moved into the small cottage on the grounds, so they'd stayed close. But maybe Tilly would be like Peter, though, living too far away for me to check in on her regularly like she needs me to.

What about our naps!?

Or maybe Mr. Muir will move here. If he does, he'll bring his birds. He loves them too much to leave them behind. That was clear last year. And those darn birds and I cannot live in the same house peaceably. No way. No how. It would be like that human story of Cinderella and the two terrible stepsisters.

I'll end up eating them, and then Mr. Muir will cry, and Miss Tilly will hate me.

A rustle up ahead, coming from the thick underbrush at the edge of the woods that lines the property, has me slowing and then crouching low to peek over the top of a drift of snow, using my white fur as camouflage. Whatever bird is out there is about to learn who's boss around here.

Only a bird doesn't appear out of the woods . . . that boy cat does.

I stop wiggling my backside in readiness to pounce and straighten. So I hadn't been mistaken the other day. I *had* seen him. I'd also been right . . . he is very handsome with green eyes that make me think of the fields in the spring, striking against his sleek black coat even in the dark of night.

A good kitty neighbor would go to greet him—say hello, find out where he is from. Maybe offer a mouse or two as a welcome gift.

At least, that's what Tilly would say. Maybe that was only humans, though.

Either way, a sudden bout of shyness stays my paws. I really don't see many other cats around here, and none my own age. I am more human than cat according to both Daniel and Peter. What if he doesn't like me? Or he thinks I'm a snob, living in such a nice home? Or what if he is one of those cats who is mean to anything else with whiskers?

He hasn't seen me yet. I could sneak away and he'd never know.

I risk poking my head up to peek again and freeze as still as a deer in a meadow. Because he is looking right at me. Green eyes glint with interest and . . . amusement maybe. Is he laughing at me?

Yes . . . well . . . I am not in the mood to be laughed at by some strange cat who doesn't know anything about me. I have bigger problems than him.

Forget being shy.

Straightening fully, I lift my head and tail up in a regal pose and walk away with attitude . . . and maybe just a little bit of a sassy sway in my walk.

Take a good look, I want to say. *Because I'm something special.*

Chapter 10

Peter walked into the bookstore through the alleyway door they accessed from where they parked behind the store and where deliveries came through. Which meant he walked right into his mother's slightly plump figure bent over a series of boxes. She seemed to be transferring books around, filling several empty boxes, and muttering to herself as she worked.

Nothing new. They were always moving inventory around back here depending on how things were moving on the shelves, the change of seasons, and the weekly deliveries of new releases. And the muttering was just part of who she was.

"Morning, Mom," he said.

He made to pass by, headed to the office with every intention of burying himself in the computer, running reports on last month's figures. His favorite thing to do for the bookstore. He would focus on that and not on how soft Lara's lips had looked or the ridiculous urge to search up ice cream recipes for her. Easier ones, or faster at least, than what she had been doing last night, for sure.

Though . . . with his mother working back here, he should probably be up front with his father helping with customers.

Peter grimaced, keeping his back to his mom to hide it. A people person he really was not. He had to talk himself into working up there every time. He'd been hoping that he'd get used to it sooner or later. Later seemed to be the way things were going.

"Oh, Peter." His mother stopped him. "I just got off the phone with Lara, who is so nice by the way. . . ."

Peter frowned at the shelf of boxes in front of him. Lara had called? Wait. Called his mother? Or the bookstore? Either way, why?

He turned. "Was she looking for me?"

Maybe she needed help with Ben again. Mr. Muir was tutoring him for schoolwork, but no doubt that didn't take all day.

Not your problem, he told the guilt that wanted to make him rush over and try to help. Fixer was part of who he was. A doer. That was all, and he should ignore it. The trouble was, the guilt could just as well be eagerness. The tightening in his belly could go either way. Hell, he shouldn't have almost kissed her like that. It had muddled his thinking.

"You?" his mother asked, slightly perplexed. "No, she called to thank me for helping watch Ben and to offer a favor in return."

A favor? Darn it. She went over my head.

The familiar burn of irritation crawled up his neck. He'd *told* her to back off. Maybe not in those words, but he thought he'd been clear enough with her last night. She didn't need to return any favors. "I told her she didn't need to—"

"Actually, her suggestion was lovely, and I think we should take her up on it."

His mother liked Lara's suggestion? Which one? The workshop thing? More than that, there was a light in her eyes that looked more than generally pleased. It was downright satisfied with a hint at motherly machinations. What was going on here? "What was it?"

"She offered us some shelf space at her store where she could sell a selection of our children's books on consignment."

Peter's brain decided to go on strike at that moment and significantly slow down on processing time, his mother's words seeming to come at him in slow motion. "What now?"

The question earned him a patient frown, and his mother repeated what she'd just said, ending with, "Don't you think that's fantastic?"

Not the word he would use.

His brain caught up all in a rush along with a healthy extra whack of irritation. Their bookstore was doing fine. Yes, they needed a better location, but their sales were just . . . fine. Including the children's section. They didn't need any handouts. Especially not from the person who overbid on her space. What? Now she wanted to make money off them?

The last thought stuttered and, unlike any other time in the last year, the anger fizzled like a can of soda left out in the sun. Lara wasn't like that. That had been a stupid thing to think. Knee-jerk reaction.

"I'm sure she means well, Mom—"

"It's an extra place to sell children's books. She's even going to put up a sign that reads, 'Find a bigger selection at Braunfels Books.' I think it's generous."

Too generous.

His irritation picked up new steam and swung the other direction. Lara would be losing money on the shelf space that she probably couldn't afford, and they might lose money on the books if they were on consignment.

"What portion of the sales is she getting?"

"She offered ten percent, we agreed on twenty-five."

Peter clenched his teeth and tried not to growl like a bear. Definitely too generous. Twenty-five percent of the cover price of a book wouldn't cover the amount she'd net from most of the toys in that shop, especially the ones displayed on shelves. She was practically giving the bookstore that space for free.

"We should wait until after Christmas," he tried. "I'm

sure she needs all the shelf space she can get for the holiday shoppers."

"That's what I said." Mom nodded, as though he was spewing wise words instead of trying to get out of this.

"And?"

"She suggested all holiday-related books for the season, but children's only."

He frowned. They always stocked for the season and did displays that went with whatever holidays or events were coming up, but . . . "Do we have enough holiday children's books to fill a shelf for her as well as our own?"

"I've been pulling them and I think we do. Especially since she said she could fill in any gaps with toys that match the books. How adorable is that idea?"

Peter scooted over to the boxes his mother had been reorganizing, and sure enough the titles facing him were ones she'd selected for this new development—the usual selection like *The Velveteen Rabbit* and *'Twas the Night Before Christmas*, plus newer ones releasing this year, and a selection highlighting other seasonal holidays, including Yuletide, Hanukkah, and Kwanza.

Great.

If his mother had already done this much this morning, she was definitely excited by the idea. That meant he couldn't talk her out of it.

"Can you think of any other titles we should include?" she asked now, following his line of sight.

Peter sighed. "I would add copies of Dickens's *A Christmas Carol* in there as well. We have those illustrated ones left over—"

"From last year," she said, brightening. "Wonderful idea." And started bustling around to find them. Peter moved toward the office, needing solitude more now than he had when he'd walked in. From somewhere in the back, his mother's muffled voice called his name.

He paused again. "Yeah?"

"Later this afternoon, I'd like you to take these boxes over to Lara's shop and help her set up the display."

Peter tipped his head back to glare at the ceiling and reached for some sort of calm, because he'd just identified that eager light in his dear mama's eyes from earlier. The light of a matchmaking mother. She was trying to set him up with Lara.

Which . . . of course she was. After all, he'd played Santa for the woman, and been doused in glitter, and watched her nephew a good chunk of a day. Of course his mother was hearing the pitter patter of little grandchildren feet.

"I'm doing the books today," he said in a voice that brooked no compromise or argument.

Except this was his mother, who ignored the voice and patted his shoulder as though he were a little boy arguing about brushing his teeth before going to bed. "Your father and I are too old to be hefting these big boxes around, and the display needs to go up quickly since it's holiday themed. Only a few more weeks to Christmas, you know."

And just like that, he was spending more time with Lara Wolfe. The last thing he wanted.

Liar.

He ignored the small inner voice and the spark of excitement that curled tighter in his belly despite his sensible thoughts. Mocking him if anything.

"And bring her and Ben over to our house for dinner when you're done shelving," his mother dropped on him next.

Peter blew out a harsh breath. "I can see what you're thinking, Mother."

Her eyes went wide and overly innocent. "I don't know what you're talking about, child of mine."

"Uh-huh," he scoffed. "She's my neighbor, and Emily's storefront neighbor, and that's it."

Mom picked up a book from one box and moved it to another. "You can say that, but I saw the way you looked at her two years ago when she was a guest at Weber Haus."

Right. Lara had arrived at the inn Christmas Eve and that was when Emily had hosted the whole family. He'd flirted. In fact, with Daniel and Max, and Paul, and Oscar all there, even with dates, it had practically been a flirting competition for Lara's attention.

But that had been *before*.

Back when he knew who he was and what his place was in the world and didn't struggle with anger and frustration.

Peter shook his head, pushing doubts down deep where they couldn't disturb him. He'd settle into running the bookstore eventually. After all, it hadn't even been a full year.

"What time?" he asked.

"Seven should be fine."

Seven. "She closes at eight while the market is happening, and that's after Ben's bedtime."

His mother pursed her lips, thinking. "How about we have a later dinner, then? Eight thirty? That might be pushing it for his bedtime, but she can put him to bed in one of our spare rooms after he eats, which will let her stay a little longer."

His mother really didn't give up. Sure enough, she brightened even more all of a sudden. "And then you can help her get him home and into bed later."

He recognized defeat when he looked it in the eyes. "Great."

She gave him a look that brooked no arguments.

Peter just nodded and turned away, heading into his office. The only way to put a stop to his parent's little fantasy was to ignore it and go on with things the way he'd already planned.

For the first time all day, Lara had a chance to sneak back into the storage room and look through her inventory. Marta Diemer had given her an idea of which children's books she'd be sending, so Lara figured she'd see what toys she could display with those titles.

"Where do you want these?" Peter's voice sounded from directly behind her.

Lara yelped as she spun to face him, hand to her chest to find him standing inside the doorway hefting a large box.

His eyebrows shot up. "You okay there, jumpy?"

"Sorry," she chuckled. "You scared me."

He glanced around. "You work in a toy shop, in a group of shops at a Victorian bed-and-breakfast, and in a town where people don't bother with keys because they leave their homes unlocked twenty-four/seven."

"The scariest place I've ever been," she quipped with a wink. Then pointed to a table in the center of the room. "There, please."

Only one box? She'd planned on clearing one entire section of shelving for this. *I'll just have to fill it with more themed toys if I can.*

He put the box down with a thump, then turned and crowded closer to her, leaning a fist on the table beside her. This close, his blue eyes were hard. Beautiful, but definitely hard. "You went over my head."

True. She tried an apologetic smile on for size. "Sorry?"

"I believe I said you didn't owe me, or my family, any favors," he said in a quiet voice that was no less forceful.

Only, she was pretty sure his tough-guy display was having the opposite effect of what he intended. A delicious shiver slid down her spine—a situation he probably wouldn't appreciate right now. She certainly didn't because she had no intention of backing down on this topic.

"I don't like to owe people," she said, also softly and just as uncompromising.

A frown flickered across his features. "Why?"

"What?" She wasn't expecting the question.

"Why don't you like to owe people?"

Through all that irritation, he'd picked up on that? "Don't most people not like to be in debt?"

He gave his head a decisive shake, and she swore his blue eyes softened. "Most people would say they want to return the favor, not that they don't want to be in debt."

Mental note that Peter paid attention to details. He wasn't going to let this go, either, she could tell. Lara dropped her chin because for some odd reason she *wanted* to tell him all about why. About her relationship with her brother, something she didn't tell anyone. Weird.

"So . . ." He put a gentle finger beneath her chin, tipping her head up so she'd look at him. "Why?"

Lara cleared her throat. "My ex for one. Elias insisted that we always go dutch so that neither of us was constantly paying for things."

It had seemed a fair point at the time, since they were both working to establish their careers and needed every penny. What it should have been was a red flag, especially since he was helping himself to her pennies behind her back.

"Not very gentlemanly, but I get it."

She shrugged. "So did I. Until we broke up, he left town, and I learned he'd set up multiple credit cards in my business's name without my knowledge and then maxed them out."

"Wow." Peter whistled low. "Real prince you found yourself."

"Yeah, but there's more. My brother is a whole different . . . thing." She bit her lip, because Lance was still family. Talking about him like this felt disloyal.

Only, Granny had been gone when this happened, and Lara had had no one to share the burden with, even just to complain to at the end of the day. And Peter's shoulders were broad, and he was looking at her like he was still irritated but he cared. Like he really wanted to know.

"Where's Ben?" he asked, flicking a glance over her head though he didn't change positions.

"He's in the house with Mr. Muir, getting his schoolwork done."

Right. Peter nodded at her to continue.

And she found the words tumbling out. "My ex left me in a decent amount of debt. He'd been sweet, and I thought a decent man, the unassuming type, you know. I thought he supported my dream. In fact, one of the ways he did that was helping me with my books. I accepted the help because he was an accountant, and he was supposed to love me. But after he was gone, I discovered what he'd done as soon as the debt collectors started knocking. Lance loaned me the money to pay them all off. Then, my grandmother died, just before I met you, actually. In fact, that was why I was alone for Christmas."

His eyes flickered with something akin to sorrow.

But that wasn't the part that had made her the way she was. "Anyway, she left me everything."

"I'm sorry to hear that." He cocked his head. "Nothing for your brother?"

"No. Granny raised me, but not him. When our parents died, Lance was already out of the house and in college. He has a terrific job that he loves and is pretty well set, if you get my meaning."

He nodded.

"But when the will was read, he was furious. I was still paying him back at the time—and used part of the money to finish that. But he said I owed him half of Granny's estate, which wasn't a ton, but she'd been very clear it was for me."

"Did he contest the will?"

"I get the feeling that he tried, but the lawyer assured me there was nothing he could do. So . . ."

"So he badgered you."

"Badgers," she corrected. "Present tense. It got worse when he learned about the toy store plan because of the previous . . . thing."

"I see." His lips flattened to a grim line. "But he expects you to jump in and watch his kid for a month after all that."

Lara shrugged. "I love Ben."

"And he knows that." He let out a long breath. "I have to say I'm not too impressed with your brother so far, Lara."

She shrugged. "He's worried about me in his own way. And he's still family."

Peter shook his head, though she got the impression he was shaking it at himself more than her. Then shook it again. He let out a long breath. "What am I going to do with you, Lara Wolfe?"

Something needed to be done?

"You could let me do this favor for your store," she said. "That would be nice."

He hummed a noncommittal sound. "That's one idea."

What other ideas could there be?

Except his gaze dropped to her lips. *Oh.*

"Kissing you is such a wonderful, awful idea," he murmured in a low, gruff voice. Although she got the impression he was telling himself as much as her.

"Why?"

His gaze rose slowly to hers again, and suddenly he was letting her see the interest there. Even more than the day he'd asked her on that date that never happened. Sparking at her from blue eyes that suddenly seemed even bluer. Had there always been a hazel-ish ring around the pupils? Lara's breath snagged in her throat at that look, ribs suddenly feeling too tight around her lungs.

"Are you going to kiss me, Peter Diemer?" she whispered.

"I'm thinking about it."

Just thinking? Good heavens, what would it be like if he made up his mind?

"Do you want me to kiss you?" he asked.

"Yes." The word came out a husky whisper.

He lowered the lids over his eyes slowly, blocking her from

seeing his reaction to that. Then gave a soft groan and leaned forward, placing his lips to hers tenderly, almost reverently.

She'd imagined Peter's kisses more than she cared to admit, even to herself, but this . . . this was a surprise. As big and strong and grumbly as he was, she'd pictured hard kisses, abrupt even. But this was gentle, sweet.

Hard would have been enticing, but gentle . . . his touch pierced through every protective barrier she'd put up around her heart and wrapped around it like a warm blanket.

She sank into him on a soft sigh, and Peter groaned again, a sound that told her even this gentle touch was more than he wanted to give. And yet he framed her face with his hands, burrowing his fingers into her hair, and deepened the kiss.

Gentle turned into something more, something that drew sparks through her blood and made her want to smile against his lips. Only she didn't want to stop kissing him.

Peter groaned again, only this time his muscles bunched a heartbeat before he forced himself to lift his head. He didn't let her go, though. "I knew you were going to be a temptation."

Lara's lips twitched. "Is there a reason you don't want to be tempted?" she asked, half teasing, but also half serious.

He stared at her, turning more somber by the moment. "I think I won't be good for you, Lara."

Really? This man who'd helped her in one way or another, granted reluctantly sometimes, thought he wouldn't be good for her?

"Why would you say that?" Maybe it had to do with his recent change in career? Or the time in the hospital that Lukas mentioned? Was something wrong?

But Peter just slowly shook his head, lips going flat again, and she knew he wasn't going to tell her the real reasons. Reasons she suspected had little to do with being neighbors and how that would be awkward if they broke up.

Peter swallowed, and she expected him to let go, but instead he brushed his thumb over her cheekbone in the softest sweep. Barely a brush. A shiver chased its tail up her spine and she wanted to melt into him all over again.

"I'm willing to take the risk," she said. The words were out before she even formed them in her mind completely. "But you need to make a choice, Peter. We're friends and neighbors. Or we're . . . exploring more than that."

He searched her gaze and the indecision in his eyes made her heart ache. What about her or them was holding him back?

"I—"

"Hey, Santa Pete." Cassie's chirp had them both springing apart, only to face Cassie, who was grinning from ear to ear.

Peter cleared his throat. "Hey, Elf Cassie," he said.

Cassie's grin only grew bigger because he sounded as flustered as Lara felt, which on him was almost as adorable as how focused he'd been on making ice cream for her.

Then Cassie's gaze moved to Lara. "There's a customer who has a question about a custom order."

"Okay." She moved to follow Cassie out into the shop.

"I'll bring in the rest of the books," Peter said, also following. And the words were almost like a bucket of ice water. A reminder of what she should be focused on.

Maybe he was right to hesitate about starting something up.

Right. Shop first. Love life later. If she had a love life to do anything about. She still wasn't sure.

A very distinctive coo sounds from somewhere above me, and I scowl. *No. It couldn't be.*

Running as fast as my kitty paws can go, I sprint upstairs, screeching to a halt just outside Mr. Muir's room. I press my ear to the door, listening.

At first, all I get is silence. Deciding to move things along, I try a trick that guaranteed squawking last year. I slip my paw under the door and scratch at the other side with my un-sheathed claws.

Sure enough, a squawk sounds followed by another round of cooing. Louder cooing. Taunting cooing.

Mr. Muir's birds have arrived. When did that happen?

Happy is not what I am right now. Not at all.

Miss Tilly and Mr. Muir spend all their time together and completely ignore me, and now his birds are here.

Emily and Lukas seem concerned over having me around. Something about taxidermy, or taxo-something. Either way, Lukas keeps taking me to Miss Tilly's room, even on the nights I'm supposed to be with them.

I haven't seen that boy cat anywhere.

But at least Peter and Lara seem to be on track to their happy ending. I saw them kissing. Kissing! And they were both really into it. So at least I can relax about them. My work is done there.

Good thing, too, because right now I need to focus on my forever family, who seem to be changing. Like snow that feels solid when you walk on it, then *ploof*, it gives out from under your feet.

Chapter 11

⊷⊷⊷

Peter somehow ended up beside Lara at his parents' dinner table . . . and it was killing him slowly.

His mom had gone all out for what was supposed to be a casual get-together. Emily and Lukas had come. So had their brother Max and his girlfriend of a little over a year now, Nicole. Which meant Lara and Ben were the only newcomers and therefore the center of attention.

Given the fact that all Peter could think about was pulling her into the darkened hall and trying that kiss all over again, just to see if the first one wasn't a fluke, he was in deep trouble. Especially hiding that from his family, who knew him best and were watching his interactions with Lara as though they had to know what happened next. He could even picture them in theater stadium seating with buckets of popcorn discussing whether or not he was going to do something about this attraction that everyone could see.

Could everyone see?

Kisses weren't supposed to *feel* like that . . . make him want things.

Things like dates and more kisses. Things like flirting and more kisses. Things like letting her shower him in all things Christmas and more kisses.

"So, Lara," his mother asked, in full information-digging mode all night long. "Tell us about the shop."

Peter froze and did his best not to flinch or frown. *Not* his favorite topic.

"So far it has been amazing," Lara said. "Exhausting, but amazing. Much better than I projected, so a very good start."

Peter waited for that pinch of frustration at the words. Because only a few weeks ago, when he was still hoping the shop would fail, that news would have been a big disappointment. But instead he was . . . happy for Lara.

He did frown at that. There was a difference between not working against her and being happy for her to succeed. When had he made the switch?

"I hear you hold workshops?" his mother asked next. "What kind?"

Lara put down her fork.

"Mom . . . let her get a chance to chew her food," Peter said.

"It's fine," Lara assured them both. "I'm done. And the workshops are generally crafts related. I try to make them seasonal and a mix for all ages."

"Like what?"

"Oh . . . ornament decorating, greeting card making, assembling toy puzzles, wreath making, candle making, those word signs that are so popular right now."

"Word signs?" His mother perked up at that. "What are those?"

"You stencil sayings—funny or inspirational or whatever—onto something you hang up. These days I usually go with rustic wood or chalkboard as the background."

"Wait . . ." Emily grinned. "Like the one in your yard?"

Lara slid him a conspiratorial grin and Peter actually, for a blip of a second, wanted to grin back. "Yes," she said. "I had an . . . extra strand of lights. I thought that would be a cute way to use them."

"Other than Christmas stuff, what kinds of sayings?" his mother asked.

"Anything you want." Lara sort of bounced in her seat, obviously enjoying the topic. "There's the cliché 'Live. Laugh. Love.' But I like the funny ones best. Like, 'The dishes are looking at me dirty again.' "

"Dishes are the worst," Peter found himself saying.

Lara turned wide, laughing eyes his way. "I know, right? I don't like to cook because I don't want to have to clean up afterward."

"Exactly."

She grinned and he found his lips drawing up at the corners. Over a mutual dislike of dishes. What was happening to him?

"Can you do literary quotes?" his mother asked.

Lara blinked, as though reluctant to turn away from their shared moment, but she did. "Of course. Anything you can fit into the space is fine."

His mother straightened, eyes alight, and looked directly at him. "That might be a good idea for the bookstore."

The small glow of whatever was going on with him and Lara disappeared as though someone had tossed him out into the cold and dark with no clothes on. Because she was already doing the bookshelf space thing to pay back favors. She didn't need to add workshops to the list. Had she mentioned this to his mother as well this morning when they'd talked behind his back?

He shot the woman at his side an annoyed look. "Did you put my mom up to this?"

"Peter Diemer," his mother chided. "What a thing to say to her. Of course she didn't."

Lara, though, didn't take offense. If anything, her lips

twitched. "No, Mr. Suspicious," she teased. "It's just a really good idea."

He scoffed. "That remains to be seen."

"What idea?" his mom asked, gaze bouncing between them like a tennis spectator.

Lara raised a single eyebrow at him, because now he was the one who'd brought it up. "You want to tell her?"

On a frustrated growl, he waved at her. "Go ahead."

She chuckled. She actually chuckled at his bad mood about this. Most people avoided him when he got like this. Not Lara. In fact, she reached over and patted his hand.

Ignoring his scowling face, she turned to everyone else listening with avid interest. "When I was trying to think of a way to repay all the help you've given me, I offered to run a workshop from the bookstore and, after materials are covered, you'd keep the profits."

"But that's a wonderful idea," his mother trilled.

Exactly what he hadn't wanted.

"We're doing the consignment thing, Mom," he reminded her. "That's enough of a fair exchange."

More than enough, actually. Because Lara would likely be losing money on the setup. Maybe she'd give up the workshop idea if he continued to pop into the store to help her with things.

Now you're just making excuses to see her.

He was really starting to dislike the little voice in his head. Mostly because it was right.

"We could split the profits to make it fair," his mom insisted. "But the workshop sounds like a great way to bring in customers." She looked at Lara. "Do you have time?"

"No," Peter answered before Lara could.

Which made his parent bite her lip and study the woman beside him, who was now glaring at him in a fair imitation of his own scowl. "I'm fine," she insisted.

He put an arm across the back of her chair, leaning in so that he could lower his voice and keep this semi-between them. "You're taking on too much," he insisted right back.

"Things will slow down after New Year's," she pointed out, stubborn chin jutting. "Just a few weeks. Until then, I need to do everything I can to get my business off the ground."

"It *is* off the ground," he pointed out. "But it's going to fall out of the sky, crash, and burn if you make yourself sick trying to do everything."

She fixed him with that determined look that reminded him of Snowball in a snit, brows scrunched up and expression immovable. What would she do if he planted a kiss on the tip of her nose? Probably swat at him, like Snowball would.

Swallowing the uncharacteristic urge to grin in the middle of an attack of frustration, Peter stared right back. Because he meant it. She was riding the razor edge of exhaustion as it was, and he was worried about her.

"How about this . . ." he said when she didn't budge, either. Compromise was not usually his thing. "Christmas is right around the corner, then things will slow down. Start with the shelf space in your shop. Then, after the Market is over, relook at options."

She opened her mouth, paused, then closed it, thinking. "Okay."

"Okay?" He leaned closer to catch the word. She was actually going to listen to him?

The starch went out of her posture, and he suspected a small amount of relief replaced the stubborn. She offered a lopsided grin. "I do have a tendency to want to do *all* the things," she admitted.

"I get it."

"You do?"

He shrugged, hiding his own surprise at how, around her at least, he could be more like his old, reasonable self. "You're starting a business. If I were you, I would also be trying anything I thought that would make that succeed."

Her gray eyes warmed. Melted.

And all over again, he wanted to kiss her. Really kiss her. This was becoming a problem.

"Auntie Lara, are you going to kiss Pete?" Ben piped up, his small voice shooting between them like an arrow, and both of them straightened.

"No, sweetheart," she murmured.

Right. His family had all been watching that.

Unaccustomed heat surged, making his skin feel tighter and hotter. *Oh dang, I'm blushing.*

He couldn't remember blushing a single day in his life. What his family was going to make of this entire moment, he had a fair idea. Expectations and speculation and probably a whole lot of teasing.

Exactly what he didn't want. Not about him and Lara.

"We ready for dessert?" his father asked.

And thank God for him, because Peter had nothing.

Lara unlocked the door to the toy shop and flicked on the lights so that she and Peter could see where they were going. Earlier, when he'd dropped off the boxes of children's books, they hadn't had time to do more than remove the items on the shelf she was clearing before they had to head to dinner.

She had planned to come in super early tomorrow and set the new display up before the doors opened, but as soon as she said so out loud, Peter wasn't having that. Neither were his family. She'd never had so many people vocally invested in her state of sleep in her life.

On a rising tide of people surrounding her with determination to help, she'd had the decision taken out of her hands.

Emily and Lukas took their car and hers and went back to her place with Ben to put him to bed.

For practice? she wondered, but didn't ask. That was their secret to spill.

That left her and Peter free to come back to the shop in his truck and finish the shelf setup before he took them both back to their homes.

"Hopefully this won't take too long," she said. Probably for the third time.

She felt bad about hijacking the rest of his evening. Especially because it had been glaringly obvious that part of sending them both here together was his family's not-so-subtle attempt to push them together.

Not that she blamed them after that moment at the table.

A wellspring of heat lit her cheeks up all over again as she pictured that. All she'd been able to see was Peter, blue eyes both soft and something else that lit her up even more than this blush. Because, for a moment there, she felt like he'd let her, and only her, see the real person he was underneath.

She took a silent, calming breath and tried to will the heat to calm down. Hopefully the dimmer glow in here, with only a few of the overhead lights turned on, would hide it from Peter. "Your family is so nice to offer to help—"

"Hey." He spun her around, putting a hand on her arm. Then leaned over so that he was right in her face. "Stop worrying about owing people favors, or not taking advantage," he said. "We wouldn't have offered if we didn't want to. And favor-wise, I'd say we're even."

Was he going to kiss her again? Or was she wishful thinking it because that moment in front of his family was already on her mind?

After a long pause, where she searched his expression for who knew what and found nothing but general, generic, not-heated-at-all friendliness, Lara stuffed the disappointment down the same hole with the blush and nodded.

*   *   *

Being alone with her was turning out to be a heck of a lot more difficult than he'd thought. Already Peter was fighting to keep his hands, and his lips, to himself.

Determined, he turned them both toward the back.

"I'm not sure about us being even, though," she grumbled at him, sounding funnily familiar. Now who was the grumpy one?

I'm rubbing off on her. He almost grinned at the idea. He didn't bother to say anything, though. Too intimate.

In short order, they dragged all the boxes of books to the shelf they'd cleared. Only Lara didn't start unloading right away. Instead, she stood there, hands on her hips, staring at the empty shelves as though her will alone could make them fill up.

Peter waited for her to move. Then waited some more. Finally, he cleared his throat and she startled.

"Sorry," she said. "I was visualizing."

Visualizing? "I'm probably going to regret asking, but . . . what?"

"Arranging the shelves in my head so I have a plan before I start putting things out."

"At the bookstore, we usually just go alphabetically, and turn some of the covers facing out—newer books or the more popular ones," he said.

Simple. Easy. Quick.

Except Lara shook her head. "Since we'll be pairing some of the books with toys, I'm thinking we need a theme for each shelf."

A theme. This was getting more involved than he'd been picturing. "A theme," he repeated aloud.

She nodded. "I'll show you."

Working quickly, she started pulling out books, only particular ones, though, and arranging them on a single shelf in small groups. Then she disappeared into the store and came back with an armload of toys, which she then arranged and rearranged with the books until she stepped back and gave a happy nod.

"See?" She waved a hand at her work.

"You have a concerning obsession with nutcrackers," was all Peter said, eyeing the display.

She flicked him a mildly amused glance. "Do you see the theme?"

"Hard to miss it."

Actually, the shelf looked pretty brilliant. She'd grouped together only books about nutcrackers. Not just an illustrated version of *The Nutcracker*, but also books like *The Nutcracker in Harlem* and *Nutcracked*. In and among those, she'd put like-themed toys. A few actual nutcrackers, of course—including one that happened to match the illustration on one of the covers. But also a stuffed nutcracker mouse, a nutcracker-themed puzzle, and a ballerina doll that looked like the little girl from the story.

"Okay," he said. Grudgingly. "I see what you're doing."

She beamed as though he'd praised her to the high heavens. This woman was . . . adorable.

He mentally winced at even the unspoken use of that word. One kiss and he was losing it. "So what are you thinking for the other shelves?" he asked.

Eyes sparkling, she turned to stare at the shelves, and he had a feeling she could picture the exact setup in her head. Pointing, she said, "All things Father Christmas or Santa here. Nativity-related stories here. A Hanukkah shelf and maybe the other seasonal celebrations. Snowmen and snow days here. Then miscellaneous on the bottom shelf that we can arrange the way you usually do." She turned to him. "What do you think?"

Having gone through the books his mother was sending, Peter had to admit to being reluctantly impressed. "You got all that from looking through the boxes for, what, ten minutes?" he asked.

She shrugged. "I think decorating and arranging the shelves and windows speaks to my very right-side, creative brain."

He could see that about her, not only in the way she lit up doing it, but in the ideas she'd come up with. This store, as frivolous as he'd first thought it, was entirely and utterly Lara . . . and a bit of a wonderland. "I don't think I have any right side to my brain. When I was born, the brain fairy gave me two left sides."

She buttoned her lips, eyes laughing at him.

"What?" he asked.

"The brain fairies?" she teased.

Peter huffed a laugh, more at himself than anything. "Mom talks about the fairy blessings at birth. Speak of them with respect. They could affect your future children."

She was jiggling now with suppressed laughter. "There's more than just the brain fairy?"

"Of course. There's the common-sense fairy, the coordination fairy, the math fairy, the creative fairy, the outgoing fairy, and . . . probably a hundred others."

"I see. Those fairies must be very busy."

He nodded, totally deadpan. "Very important jobs."

And it struck him suddenly that he was enjoying teasing with her. Joking around. He used to do that more. Not as much since his life took an about-face. Maybe he needed to do something about that.

"Oh yes." Lara nodded, playing along and oblivious to his minor epiphany. "I guess they gave me two right sides of a brain on accident."

He chuckled. "If they did, I got two left sides."

She tipped her head, gaze turning speculative. "That must mean you're good with the books and taxes and stuff for the business."

"It's the part I like best," he agreed. Maybe now would be

a good time to point out a few of the overspending items he'd noted with her store.

Peter opened his mouth, but something about taking away the laughter reflecting at him and replacing that with serious discussion just didn't sound . . . fun. Maybe another time.

Lara bent over the boxes, pulling out the next grouping of books, working on the Father Christmas shelf. Knowing what she wanted for the other shelves, Peter did the same, pulling out all the snow- and snowman-related books.

"What about running your bookstore do you like best?" Her voice was muffled as she was practically half in/half out of the largest box.

Peter paused in arranging the shelf he was working on and frowned. *My bookstore.* Even after taking over, it still didn't feel like his. Maybe because his parents were still working there.

"Are you ranking the options in your head or something?" she asked, beside him now.

That would be a better problem to have. "No, I'm trying to come up with what I like."

Her eyebrows slowly lifted, head canting to the side at the same rate. "Is there *nothing* you like about running the store?"

"I like analyzing the business we're doing and trying to determine what books will or won't sell based on our previous records. It's like a competition with myself to do the analysis right and get just the right books for the people who shop with us."

Lara nodded along. "Anything else?"

"Keeping the stock organized. You should have seen it when I took over. My system is *much* better."

"You were right that one time," she said.

"Huh?"

"Humble and right don't go together." She winked, and he nudged her with his elbow as a silent protest.

After laughing, she returned to the subject. "Those are good things to like. Important for the business." However, her tone of voice sounded like that encouraging thing his second-grade teacher used to do when it was his turn to read out loud.

"But?" he asked.

She blinked, maybe not expecting him to hear that she was leaving something unsaid. "Well . . . that's all behind-the-scenes stuff. Do you like anything to do with it being a bookstore?"

He knew where she was going with that. Maybe because he'd been avoiding asking himself the same question for a while now. Since he offered to take over the store, actually. He opened his mouth, closed it, then opened it again. "Not really."

They both stared at each other, surprise definitely in Lara's eyes, and he was sure his, too, because he hadn't intended to say that. He hadn't really admitted it in his own head yet, let alone out loud.

Peter let go a long breath and ran a hand over his short hair. "Sorry. It's something I'm still . . . working through."

Rather than continue on with the shelves, though, Lara sat down on the floor beside him, crossing her legs and giving him her undivided attention. "Need to talk about it?"

Normally he'd say no. He wasn't a talk-about-your-feelings kind of guy. But the understanding in her expression, no pressure, just a sincere wish to help, had the words coming anyway.

"I'm not much of a reader. Just how-to books on things like poker or business books, really. So I don't know how helpful I am to people looking for recommendations. And I'm definitely not into gushing over books like many of our patrons. I don't fan-guy over authors. I could care less about the fun events we run."

Lara nodded. No judgment or disappointment—the two

reactions he feared he'd see on his parents' faces if he brought this up with them.

"I'm not a people person," he said.

For the second time she buttoned her lips around amusement.

"What?" he asked, also again.

"Well . . . your Santa performance—"

Right. Good point. He held up a hand. "Say no more."

"Only by the end, I think you were really into it. Maybe if you forced yourself to regularly interact with people at the bookstore, you'd eventually relax and that magic could happen again."

"Maybe," he acknowledged. "But if I have to make myself do that every single day . . ." He let the thought trail off on a shudder.

"You'll end up hating it," she filled in.

He said nothing. What was there to say?

"Why did you decide to take over the shop if it's not your thing?" she asked quietly.

Another shrug. "Mom and Dad are reaching retirement age and have been talking about selling and how wrenching that would be. My military career ended abruptly, and this seemed like the best answer to both situations."

A frown flickered over her features. "From whatever had you in the hospital last year?" she asked. Then . . . "Emily mentioned it."

Of course she did. "What happened is classified, but basically, I was in the hospital, unconscious, for a few weeks. Brain swelling."

And personality altering. Hopefully not permanent. At least, the doctor seemed to think not.

"I'm so sorry."

Normally he would just shrug it off, but with Lara, something in him didn't want to do that. "Leaving my career—I thought I'd be a lifer—and now . . . I guess I don't know who I am anymore."

He didn't know what he was expecting. Pity, like he got from everyone else maybe. Or impatience because at least he had options. He had his life. He wasn't lacking for food or a roof over his head or struggling with his health beyond the anger management thing. Other people had it a thousand times rougher than he did.

But instead of any of that, Lara reached across and twined her fingers with his. "I can see that."

"Yeah?"

She squeezed. "Of course. This"—she waved around the shop—"is a big part of who I am. What you spend the majority of your time doing is very much who you are, I've always thought. Don't they say if you find a job you love, you'll never work a day in your life?"

He didn't say anything to that, because if that was true, he was spending a lot of time on something that wasn't really him. Would it eventually become him?

"When your parents retire, what will you do about handling the front of the store, if you still don't enjoy being up there?" she asked.

"I don't know. Hire someone who loves it maybe. A partner."

"That's an idea." But enough doubt lingered in her voice that reflected what was in his own heart that he grimaced.

"Hey."

He glanced up, colliding with eyes turned the softest gray . . . like fluffy bunny gray.

"You'll figure it out," she assured him.

"You think so?"

"If I've learned anything about you, Peter Diemer, it's that you're a born fixer."

"A fixer, huh? Is that a good thing?"

"Of course. You're a guy who gets things done. You see a

problem, you fix it." She grinned suddenly. "Even if you step on a few toes."

That was how she saw him? A guy who got things done? That was how he'd thought of himself before, when solving problems was the difference between life and death, but now . . .

Lara leaned forward suddenly and pressed her lips to his. Too fast. Way too fast, because she was pulling back before he could savor the touch.

"Trust yourself," she whispered.

He stared at her, taking in each line and curve of her face, the darker rim of gray around her irises, the way her hair curled at her temples, but only there, the rest straight. But mostly the faith in her eyes.

This was the person he'd tried to run out of town. What an ass he turned out to be.

"I think you have too much faith in me," he said.

"I don't think so." Her eyes darkened with an emotion he couldn't pin down. "Sometimes we need someone else to have faith in us in order to bolster our own faith in ourselves."

Was that what she needed? Did she doubt herself as much as he'd been lately?

He gave in to temptation and closed the distance between them, kissing her the way he'd wanted to a second ago, lingering over it. Taking his time, with soft, slow, deepening kisses. No other part of them touching, and yet his heart was ready to leap out of his chest and fly.

Lara sighed into him and he reached out to draw her closer, all the way into his arms.

Except something hard and heavy smacked him in the head with a painful *thunk*.

He jerked away from Lara and looked up just in time to see another five or six books tumble off the top shelf. On pure instinct, he yanked her closer and covered her with his body, taking the brunt of the falling books to his back.

"Ow," he grunted when it was all over.

"Um . . . What just happened?" she asked from under him, warm breath whispering against his neck.

Peter risked looking up to find two blue eyes in a fuzzy white face peeking over the edge of the shelf, whiskers twitching.

"Snowball," he said.

Lara came up from underneath his arms at that and looked up only to laugh.

"Bad kitty," he scolded.

Lara got to her feet and gently lifted the cat down, snuggling her into her arms and rubbing her face against Snowball's soft fur. "She's not bad," she corrected him. "She's just precocious."

Yeah . . . well . . . the darn cat had interrupted a very nice kiss before he'd hardly gotten started. Nothing Lara said was going to make him agree right this second.

Though, oddly, Snowball's expression as she stared at him from the safely of Lara's arms was almost as disgusted as he knew his must be.

Not my best move.

Peter and Lara had been kissing. Again. I'd come over to the shop because I'd seen the light on inside when I was patrolling our property perimeter one more time before going to bed. Or that's what I told myself. But really Tilly kicked me out of her room because Mr. Muir had brought his darn cooing turtledoves in there and I might have slipped a little and hissed at the things.

She told me I need to make friends. That is *not* going to happen.

Still, seeing that light in the shop, I decided to check on

Lara. When I found Peter here, I was thrilled. I'd stuck around to see if he needed any help in the matchmaking department, but then they started kissing all on their own. So I was trying to get down from the shelf to sneak out and leave them to it in privacy.

Unfortunately, I knocked that first book off, and trying to stop it from falling, my tail knocked the rest of them off.

"Bad kitty" is right. I can't seem to do anything right these days.

Chapter 12

Lara could hardly keep her eyes open. The sandman might as well have filled bags with cement and attached them to her lids. And she blamed Peter Diemer entirely.

That kiss.

That darn kiss that was the sweetest thing and left her craving more of the same. After Snowball interrupted, though, Lara had got a good look at the clock on her phone. Way too late. She'd let Peter distract her from getting things done. And then, after she'd got home and in bed, she'd let the memory of that kiss distract her from sleeping. She'd tossed and turned, reliving it, like a teenager with a first crush.

Not even with her ex had she been like this—all fluttery and discombobulated.

She'd been flattered by Elias's initial interest and quickly they'd been comfortable together. Too comfortable even, or she would have discovered what he was up to much sooner. Thank goodness they'd never moved in together at least. He'd pushed for that, but she'd wanted to stay with Granny.

But even with Elias at the beginning and with stars in her eyes, she'd never been like this. Not like she was with Peter. Only now she was exhausted and the store wasn't the only thing on her mind. Peter was. Which was distracting her.

Sally Ann, Joshua, and Becky, who were working with her

today, had all at some point looked askance at her. Which meant she wasn't focused when she should be.

The logical part of her brain was telling her she needed to take a step back. If Peter was still available six months to a year from now, then maybe. But she was determined to do this without the same mistakes, and that meant needing to focus on the shop. Despite her logical brain, though, she wanted to see him again.

At least the books were selling well. So were the toys she'd paired with them. That had been a good idea.

If she could just make it another ten minutes without falling asleep on her feet, then she could close up the shop. She would need to clean up from the ornament stations that had been set out today. Then she could go home and fall into bed.

Well, fall into a heap in bed *after* feeding Ben, getting him bathed and read to, getting herself ready. How did parents do this?

Thank heavens for Mr. Muir and Miss Tilly, who, after Ben had finished his schoolwork for the day, had taken him sledding, promising to feed him and have him home in time for bed. Lara glanced out at the softly falling flakes, which had been coming down sporadically all day, probably making for terrific sledding. A part of her wished she could have joined them.

Maybe she'd let him stay up a tiny bit later and they could try to make a snowman in the tiny front yard of her townhome.

A glance at the clock, and she breathed a sigh of relief. Ushering out the last lingering customers, she was just flipping the sign to "Closed" when Peter showed up.

Again, logical brain said, *Send him away.* But apparently, she was correct about those right-brain fairies not giving her a truly logical side. Because was sending him away what she did?

Of course not. Unable to stop herself from smiling like

Christmas had come early, she let him in. "This is a surprise," she said. "Did you bring me more books?"

He cocked his head. "You can't already be out."

"No, but I'll probably need more stock on a few titles by the end of the week."

She could practically see the gears cranking over in his head—after all, Peter was a numbers man. "That's more than we've sold of those books in a week," he exclaimed. "It's only been one day."

Then he frowned as though both flummoxed and offended.

"I probably get more kids in the store than you do." Toy store, after all.

It still took him a second before he shook his head at whatever he was thinking, semi-erased the frown, and looked directly at her. "I am here to make sure you get home at a decent hour," he said.

Now it was Lara's turn to frown. Older brother wasn't what she wanted from him, though at the same time, part of her found the gesture sort of sweet, in a bossy kind of way. Lance would have accused her of not paying attention to the time, even though she'd closed right on time. Peter wasn't accusing, he was trying to be helpful.

"I was planning to get home a little after eight. Miss Tilly and her beau have Ben and are meeting me there."

"Yeah. I've been sledding with them."

Lara's mouth fell open. "You . . ."

She just couldn't picture Peter leaving work early to go sledding with two octogenarians and a six-year-old boy.

He raised his eyebrows.

"Today's not your day off," she stated baldly.

"I cut out at two, since it gets dark not long after four these days, so not too bad. I worked a relatively full day."

"Oh."

"Apparently Ben needed someone who liked to go fast."

Now she could picture it. Not that she'd had a chance to see him in action on the snowy hills, but something about Peter struck her as fearless. The image of man and boy flying down the side of the mountain on a red plastic disk, Ben hooting the entire way and Peter laughing. She almost giggled at the thought. Did Peter laugh? She'd heard a few chuckles, but all of a sudden, she really, really wanted to hear a full-bodied, hearty laugh from him. Had she missed that today while she'd been working?

"I wish I could have seen that," was all she said.

"Next time."

If there was one. But of course, she expected to have Ben until after Christmas. She would make time.

"So . . ." Peter glanced around. "All set?"

"I just need to clean up from the ornament stations."

"Okay. I'll help."

He followed her back into the North Pole and looked over the tables. "This doesn't look too bad."

"It's not. I want to leave most of it ready for tomorrow, so it's just putting everything back where it goes, checking to make sure caps are on tight, filling up a few things, and sweeping up a bit."

"Got it." Together they tackled the tables, setting them to rights.

"*Mrrrow.*" He hopped back as Snowball appeared under his feet, wrapping around his ankles.

"Oh no," he said. "You've already got me doused in glitter and dumped books on my head. Out you go."

Peter scooped the cat up, frowning a bit at a wet spot on one side of her fur. She must've been lying in the snow or something before she came in here. He took her to the front door, ignoring her very offended kitty face. Opening the door, he went to plop her outside. "Go home, Snowball."

Only when he went to let go and stand up, Snowball's fur . . . stuck, tugging her along with his hand.

"What on earth?"

He tugged, then tugged again.

Horrible realization struck like Santa's reindeer hitting a rooftop at full speed. That wet spot hadn't been snow.

"Lara," he called, trying not to sound panicked. He'd dealt with much worse than this. Like things blowing up around him and bullets whizzing by his head types of worse.

"What?"

She appeared in the arched doorway of the North Pole.

"I'm pretty sure Snowball had superglue all over her coat, and now my hand is stuck to her."

Lara stared at him for a single, unblinking beat. Then a giggle escaped only to be quickly smothered with a hand over her mouth.

This was *not* funny. He tried not to glare too hard, though, because he needed her help.

It took Lara another several seconds to control her humor. "Okay," she said. "I have things to deal with superglue. Come on back to the washroom."

He followed her back, pausing as she grabbed something from the storage area. In the washroom, under the buzzing fluorescent light that made them both appear purplish in the mirrored reflection over the sink, Snowball was starting to squirm.

"Poor baby," Lara cooed at the darn cat. "You must've laid down in it."

"Poor Snowball?" Peter demanded. "What about me?"

"Do you want me to pet you, too?" she asked, too innocently.

Peter growled in his throat. "I think of myself as a capable person," he said. "I have skills."

"I'm sure you do." Her shoulders shook suspiciously.

"*This* is why I don't do arts and crafts," he insisted.

"Technically, you haven't done any arts and crafts yet," she pointed out. "You've put them out and cleaned them up and put books on shelves. Maybe you should just avoid being so helpful."

Peter stared at her and tried not to laugh. Laughing just wouldn't do. He had a point to prove.

Lara couldn't help herself. Another chuckle escaped. "Maybe not," she corrected when he just stared at her. Then she snapped a pair of latex gloves she'd grabbed into place.

He didn't reply.

"Okay. Let's try to get you figured out. Set her on the counter."

Only the second he did, Snowball tried to scramble away, her claws clacking against the slick surface of the counter, then finding purchase at the edge. Peter lifted her up to un-hook her and then set her back down. When he didn't—couldn't—let go, the little cat started twisting around, frenzied, trying to bite or scratch her way out of his grip.

"Stop that, you little hellion. We're stuck," Peter hissed as she got a particularly good swipe of her claws in.

"Settle," Lara crooned, running a hand over the fur on the other side that didn't glisten with glue.

Thankfully, Snowball seemed to like that and stilled, her tiny body trembling, blue eyes wide.

"Keep that up," Lara told the man who was dead still and dead silent beside her. As though if he didn't move or breathe, maybe the cat wouldn't go berserk again.

"Peter," she had to prompt. "Keep up the petting while I work on your other hand."

"Skills," she thought she heard him mutter.

Lara grinned to herself as she soaked a cotton ball with nail polish remover. Then, slowly and carefully, started working it between his skin and the parts of Snowball's fur that she could get to.

Except every time she tried, Peter had to loosen his grip and Snowball wigged out again.

After the third time and a particularly pained grunt from Peter, she had to call it. "Right. This isn't going fast enough. Cuddle her close for a minute to minimize the damage. I'll be right back."

She hurried away to the sound of, "Hey! Never leave a man behind."

"I thought you were in the navy," she called back as she snagged a pair of scissors from her office.

In a few seconds, she was back, and as quickly and carefully as she could, she cut the fur of Snowball's beautiful coat, separating man and cat.

"Don't let her go," she warned as she got to the last piece. "We need to get all of it out of her fur."

"Great," he muttered, but didn't argue.

Finally, after a lot of hissing, a lot of scratching and wiggling, and a lot of grousing by Peter, they had the glue out of Snowball's fur.

Placing her on the ground, instead of bolting like Lara expected, the little cat squatted there and trembled, the shake of her muscles making the rest of her fur vibrate like she was in her own personal earthquake.

"Poor baby," Lara crooned. "Here." She shoved the nail polish remover at Peter. "Work on your hands while I take her to the house. She shouldn't be left alone for a little bit."

"But I'm okay to be left alone?" he demanded in a quasi-offended voice.

Lara raised her gaze and her heart did a somersault at the expression on his face. Total guy trying to be tough and yet somehow, she could see exactly what he would have looked like as a boy when he went to his mother with a scraped knee.

There was no way she could leave him with that look. On total impulse she leaned forward and placed her lips to his.

Peter breathed in sharply at the sudden contact, and she smiled against his lips before lifting her head to look at him.

"There," she whispered. "All better."

My fur.

My beautiful fur! They *mangled* it. They cut out big hunks from one side and now I'm all lopsided and I look terrible. A shambles. Unfit for eyes—human or otherwise.

Why would they do that to me?

All I'd been doing was taking a nap under the table. Sure, some wet stuff got on me, but it would dry and then I could give myself a tongue bath later if I needed to. I keep myself fastidiously clean, after all. Instead, Peter first tried to throw me out and then he wouldn't let me go. No matter how much I bit or scratched.

And then they . . . Cut. My. Purrfect. Fur. Off.

I huddle reluctantly against Lara as she walks through the quiet, closed shops toward the house. At least she seems to understand that I've been through a lot tonight. I'm traumatized.

Besides, with the giant hole in my coat where fur used to be, I can feel the winter chill so much more now. The feel of it against my skin is biting. No wonder humans protect their bare skin with so many clothes.

As her boots crunch in the layer of iced-over snow, movement catches my eye nearby. I glance around Lara, and my gaze collides with two bright green eyes and a very male kitty smirk.

The boy cat is here.

Just my luck. He's sitting on the fence post where I had balanced the first time I'd seen him, and there's no way he can miss exactly what sort of state I'm in.

I want to bury my face in Lara's jacket in shame. Of course he would be here to witness this.

This is *not* how Christmas is supposed to go.

Holy smokes, that kiss.

It had been barely a brush of their lips, but Peter was fairly certain Lara Wolfe had just knocked his socks off. He stopped scrubbing at his hands, which now reeked of acetone, and glanced down at his feet, almost expecting to see no socks. Then shook his head at himself.

It had been a tiny kiss, so why did he suddenly feel as though he was . . . spinning?

"Snowball's all settled." Her voice preceded her into the room, so he had enough time to try to set his features in some semblance of normal, going back to his scrubbing.

"How's it going?" she asked.

"I smell like a nail salon," he grumped.

"Yup," she agreed, so cheerfully he glanced up at her face in the mirror and caught her grin.

After a second, an answering grin made it past his defenses and onto his face, tipping one side of his lips up.

"Is that a smile, Peter Diemer?" Lara teased.

It was, though he had no idea why after tonight.

He finished up, his skin basically scrubbed raw, then dried his hands. "Home," he said.

Lara, still grinning, didn't argue. He followed her into her office, where she grabbed her purse, her laptop, and a box that rattled, no doubt with toy parts for her to do something or other with, and he shook his head. "Nope, no more work tonight for you."

She stilled, but not in a good way. "I can take care of myself," she pointed out.

Peter played back what he'd just said and winced. "Sorry. That did come off like an order."

"You think?"

"Some habits are harder to break than others." Because that had had nothing to do with his frustration control issue and everything to do with his previous career. He was used to telling people what to do.

After a second, she nodded.

He knew he shouldn't, but he pushed anyway. "I still think you should just get some sleep tonight."

At least her scowl didn't return. "But I'm almost out of my fighter jet kits, and I need to order some more inventory—"

"Tomorrow."

"I—"

"You're so tired, you won't know if you're ordering a hat from an elbow." He was trying his hardest not to give orders, but dang that was hard.

She chuckled, the sound burrowing right into his heart. "We don't sell elbows here."

"Well, you should. Elbows are fun."

Lara snorted inelegantly, then threw her hand up over her mouth, eyes wide. "Heavens, what a noise."

Peter couldn't help it. Between the night, the noise, and her look, he tossed his head back and laughed. Laughed like he hadn't in a long, long time—not since before the hospital—feeling more like himself all of a sudden. Recognizing the man in this room.

Lara watched him over her hand, then, dropping it, grinned, chuckling with him. After he calmed, that grin turned into a softer smile. "I like the sound of your laugh," she said quietly. "You should use it more often."

Just like that, kissing was right back to the top of his mind. He cleared his throat. "Feel free to snort anytime."

Lara rolled her eyes. "Come on, Chuckles McGee." She tugged at his sleeve to follow.

Only, as they walked through the North Pole room, her feet slowed. "Oh nuts."

"Nuts?" He looked around her at what she was looking at. The ice cream counter. "Nuts as in . . . you need to stop by the grocer to pick up more nuts?"

"Nuts as in I need to make a batch of ice cream tonight."

"I thought I made myself clear—"

She was shaking her head. "No choice. I'm out of my extra batches and I'll be missing a whole container tomorrow if I don't. I'll just do an easy one like vanilla." Though the way she wrinkled her nose, he figured she wasn't too happy with that. Probably too, well . . . vanilla for her. Too plain. Knowing Lara, she'd change her mind once she got home and make some fancy, time-consuming concoction.

"I'll make it." The words were out before he thought them. A situation that was becoming a habit around this woman.

"What?" She frowned and shook her head. "I can't let you do that."

"Why not? I had fun the last time."

"You poured stuff last time. Heavy lifting. I did all the real work."

Oh really? "That sounds like a challenge."

Lara snickered. "An ice cream challenge? Really? Who are you, Peter Diemer, and what did you do with my grumpy Santa?"

He straightened to his full height. "I was not grumpy. I was gruff."

She stared back, eyebrows slowly raising until he shrugged. "Fine," he acknowledged. "I was grumpy."

Only he had no intention of telling her the real reason.

"So how is the ice cream challenge going to work?" she asked.

"What do you say to a holiday flavor ice-cream-off?" A competition was something he could sink his teeth into. Literally, in this case.

"A what?"

"For the next eight days the store is open before Christmas, every other day we each come up with a holiday-themed ice cream flavor. I'll start tonight, and you can do tomorrow night. We trade off."

She tipped her head. "And the customers can vote on their favorite?"

He'd give it to her . . . she was savvy when it came to involving her customers in unique ways. He was just going for best flavor as far as the two of them were concerned. "Fine," he said. Then held out a hand. "May the best flavor win."

Her eyes narrowed, but after a second, she slowly reached out to shake. "I have a feeling I'm about to see your competitive side."

She wasn't wrong. "I don't know what you're talking about."

"Uh-huh. I should warn you I can get pretty competitive myself." She twinkled at him, smile full of mischief and a bit of a dare. "And I've been doing this a lot longer than you."

Using his grip on her hand, he pulled her closer. "No using previous recipes. Only new stuff."

"We already shook," she pointed out.

"I'm adding that as a rule."

She nodded her head in concession. "Then I'm adding the rule of no outside help." No doubt she was thinking of Emily. Or even Mrs. Bailey. She paused, thinking. "Except Ben."

"Only if we can both have Ben help," Peter insisted.

"Deal."

"Deal."

They shook again. Peter would rather have kissed on it, but no such luck.

Chapter 13

Dawn had yet to break as Lara urged a still sleepily yawning Ben out into the crisp morning air. A small dusting of snow had fallen overnight, leaving the moonlit landscape pristine. Fairy-like. She'd love to make the snow on her shop tree sparkle like that.

Or maybe for it to snow inside.

Hmmm . . .

"Our snowman!" Ben said.

Glancing over, she grimaced. The admittedly pathetic attempt at a snowman, one who only had a butt that looked more like pyramid and a very small head with no middle section, had been covered in snow as well. Now their poor Frosty looked as though he had a cone on top of his head. And the scarf around his scrawny neck was crusted in ice.

"We'll have to clean him up tonight, huh?" That was the best she could offer.

Luckily, Ben seemed okay with that, nodding slowly. Then he frowned. "It's cold, Auntie Lara. Do you think we could go ice skating?"

"Maybe," she offered. Actually, she had specific plans for that, given how often he'd been asking.

Good thing she'd already been out to turn the car on to

warm up and defrost the layer of ice on her windshield. She popped her nephew in his booster seat in the back.

"I'll be right back. I have to get the ice cream from Peter."

Ice cream Ben had talked Peter into letting him help with after making the snowman, despite it already being well past his bedtime. It was still a school day, too.

I'll make a terrible mother, she thought, not for the first time since last night.

But he'd been so happy, and she hadn't wanted to ruin that. Apparently, Ben and Peter hadn't nearly finished the ice cream an hour later when Peter had brought Ben back home, though. Neither of them had told her what flavor they were working on, either.

Ben grinned up at her now. "It's gonna be sooooo good, Auntie Lara."

"I bet it is."

Hers was going to be better. While she hadn't worked on her plane kits, or done anything books related, she had sat up in bed scrolling through flavor ideas online until Peter had brought Ben home. She'd listened to the rumble of his voice and the higher pitch of her nephew as they'd read their book together beside her in the bed. Then Peter had glanced up at her and lowered his eyebrows in mock intimidation. "Go to bed, young lady."

She grinned. "Go make your ice cream."

He'd winked and left.

And, surprisingly, she had gone to bed, and slept like a yule log, waking this morning feeling a thousand times better and more like herself.

Knocking on his door now, she stomped her feet, trying to hold on to the lingering warmth of her home while the winter chill tried to steal it away. On the second knock, the light on the porch turned on and the door swung open.

"Patience," he teased. Though that totally serious face

should make it hard to tell, she could still tell. "Perfection takes time."

"Perfection? Really?" She eyed the large container he was lugging to her car.

"Yup, bliss for the taste buds." He dropped it in the trunk, and she swore the back tires looked stressed from the weight. "I will win this competition."

As much as she had a serious thing for the surly, impatient version of Peter, Lara had to admit this playful man talking about ice cream flavors and taking this competition so seriously was nothing short of her kind of catnip.

"So . . . what should I label this blissful concoction?" she asked.

"Deep-dish apple pie."

Lara blinked. Holy smokes. He'd started out with a difficult one, that was for sure. "Seems a little aggressive," she murmured.

"Go big or go home, Wolfe."

She chuckled. "Have you tasted it?"

He pulled a face. "Of course. Every chef tastes his or her work before serving. Like I said . . . bliss."

Uh-oh. She might have to up her game. She'd been planning on the Scrooge Face–themed recipe tonight, because she'd promised Ben and they hadn't done it yet. But she'd definitely be thinking of other more unique options for the next one.

Peter glanced at the back seat, which couldn't be seen with the trunk top raised up, then reached out and tugged Lara closer, bending his head down to whisper in her ear. "You know what else is bliss in my book?"

Her stomach tightened as his warm breath caressed her ear, or maybe it was the way his voice lowered and yet was playful at the same time. "What?"

"Kissing you."

Then he dropped a lingering kiss on her lips. Not nearly long enough before he was raising his head to look into her eyes.

"What happened to worrying about being awkward neighbors when this ends?"

A flicker of something in his eyes—there then gone—gave her a small pause, but then he smiled. Just like last night when he'd laughed, her breath left her in a concerting whoosh. Unsmiling Peter was handsome, but all lit up, the man was darn near irresistible.

"I changed my mind," he said. "You're worth the risk."

She couldn't stop the slow smile that spread across her lips if she wanted to, and she didn't want to. Shaking her head, she went up on tiptoe to kiss him again. "Peter Diemer. Closet romantic."

He grimaced at that, which made her laugh.

"Auntie Lara?" Ben's muffled voice sounded from inside her car.

"Better go," she said.

"Hey." Peter tugged her back. "How about I swing by and pick you and Ben up after the shop closes? There's a Santa greeting kids at Wild Fire tonight and I thought Ben might want to go tell him his wish list."

He'd thought about a treat for Ben? After sledding with him yesterday and building a snowman with them last night, and making ice cream and reading to him, too. A small snag of worry caught at her. This had to be too good to be true. He had to be. Guys this good just didn't come along. Not for her at least.

Not that she'd had bad experiences, as long as she didn't count Elias in the bunch. She hadn't dated anyone else long enough to really get past the initial "best face forward" part of the relationship. But she couldn't see a single one doing what Peter had. See . . . too good to be true.

Stop worrying and have fun, a small voice whispered inside her.

Right. Because his expression was starting to turn concerned.

"I'll need my car," Lara said. "We could meet you there."

He shook his head. "I have tomorrow off, so I can bring you back to the shop in the morning."

"That's too early," she protested.

He shrugged. "I'm always up early. Habit."

She narrowed her eyes. "Wait. I know what this is. You want to distract me from ice cream making. It's my turn tonight."

Peter rolled his eyes. "I'll have you home in plenty of time, but only if you leave one hour early and let Sally Ann close up for you. Seven o'clock. Deal?"

Something about the way he said that made her consider his face more closely. Was this about her getting more rest again? She knew she was working hard, but it was only for the holiday season. Things would slow down after that. Did she look like such a wreck on the outside, though, that he really felt he needed to step in?

Resentment and appreciation and worry all knotted together as she searched for the best way to respond.

"I think you're just trying to make me stop work and take time off," she half accused, attempting to smile and soften the words.

"I'm trying to get more time for kisses," he admitted dryly.

Well . . . kissing was a lot better than thinking she couldn't manage to take care of herself. She laughed on a relieved whoosh. "Fair enough."

His eyes lit up, though the rest of his face remained stoic. "Is that a yes?"

"That's a yes."

He swooped down and kissed her again. "Good."

Cheeks starting to ache from all the grinning, she got into the car, waving at him as she backed out of the drive and headed out.

"What were you and Pete talking about?" Ben asked.

She glanced in the rearview mirror and smiled. "He wants to take us out to dinner tonight." She'd save Santa as a surprise. "Sound good?"

"Yeah." Then Ben closed his eyes, seeming to go back to sleep.

For the first time since even before the shop, when she was just working out of her house, Lara suddenly wished the day could speed up so she could be done with work and move on to the fun part.

She slowed to a stop behind the one or two cars going through the intersection at this hour, considering that with a dawning frown.

Maybe that wasn't such a good thing. She should be focused only on the shop right now, for the next year or two at least, and then she could worry about friends and a love life. That had been the plan. When had she lost sight of that?

Somewhere along the way, Peter had snuck in and become . . . part of everything.

Life was funny that way. Granny used to tell her that all the time. That you had to take what was thrown at you—the good, the bad, and the spectacular—adjust your plans and move on.

Was that what she needed to be doing? Adjust her plans for that love life now instead of later? Did she even have time? She could make time today, but two days in a row of not taking her work home with her—the ice cream didn't count because of their deal—would put her behind. Thank heavens she'd spent the last year, while bidding for the store and when the shop was under construction, making tons of toys. Otherwise she'd be in real trouble. Though she was already behind on the books. Finances were not her thing, and she was honestly a little terrified to look.

Her turn at the stop came, she waited, then hit the gas. She wasn't going to solve this sitting in her car. Better to get to work and try to get more done so that she could enjoy leaving early for Santa and dinner guilt free.

Inside the shop, after turning on the lights, she did a quick inspection of all the shelves, making sure they'd been restocked and set to rights from the evening before. Which they always were, but she'd been sort of rushed out of the place last night before she could do her last check.

Half an hour later a knock at the door showed Mr. Muir's weathered face at the door. He stomped his feet before coming in after she unlocked it.

"Ready for schoolwork?" he asked Ben in his rather direct, blustery way. Basically Mr. Muir was how she pictured Peter in fifty years.

A thought that had her smiling. Again.

Mr. Muir's bushy white eyebrows rose. "What's got you so happy this morning?"

"Nothing in particular."

He grunted, clearly not believing her.

"She and Pete have a date," Ben piped up.

"It's not—" She cut herself off. Because even though Ben would be with them, this was a date. Kissing, Peter had said.

Catching Mr. Muir watching her, she shrugged. "It's a family date with Ben."

"We could feed Ben dinner tonight if you want time just the two of you," he offered.

Not with Santa on the table. Lara put a hand on his arm. "You are a sweetheart."

He snorted. "No one has ever called me that before."

"Maybe not to your face. But you, Mr. Muir, are a closet romantic, and we all love you for it."

"Hmmmm," was all he said.

"But you fed Ben last night and took him sledding. Besides, Peter and I want Ben with us for this date." She thought fast for a reason. "We have to talk ice cream."

Ben gave her a long, solemn look. "No ice cream talk," he said. "You have to surprise each other with your flavors."

"What's this?" Mr. Muir wanted to know.

"Pete and Auntie Lara are having a Christmas ice cream flavor competition."

Speaking of which. "I'd better go get his first entry and put it in the case," she said. "Have fun with school."

Only when she returned, huffing and puffing as she lugged the heavy canister between the booths, they were both waiting for her. "Still here?" she asked.

"We want a taste," Mr. Muir said.

Truth be told, after hearing the flavor, so did Lara. Laughing, she led them through to the North Pole. They waited patiently while she situated the tub in the case and changed out the label. She also needed to print out a sign for people to vote. Probably easiest to do that with an app where they could go on their phones.

Scooping a single scoop into a cup for each of them, they all sat down together at the least busy ornament station table.

Lara studied her cup, frowning a little. Deep-dish apple pie. "Ben, are these chunks of actual apple pie in the ice cream?"

He nodded, eyes wide with delight. "We baked the pies first," he said.

"And the ice cream?"

"Vanilla with a little cinnamon and a caramel river."

So that's what Peter had needed with loads of sugar last night. They'd agreed he could use her stock of ingredients, because, after all, she was selling this at the store and needed to account for everything in the books appropriately, including the ingredients, regardless of who was making the ice cream.

The first bite hit Lara's tongue and she groaned. The vanilla, with only a hint of cinnamon, melted on her tongue, but the apple pie chunks were what made this amazing.

Ah-mazing.

He'd used green apples, she could tell. Her favorite kind in any kind of apple desserts because they cut the sweetness. This was like eating a tart apple pie with a big scoop of ice cream all in one delish dessert.

"That's what I thought," Mr. Muir said.

"Wow," Ben said around his bite.

"I'm going to have to up my game," Lara muttered.

Both man and boy nodded at that.

Peter let himself into the store fifteen minutes before he'd told Lara he'd pick her up. He waved at Elf Cassie, who waved back from behind the checkout counter, where she was helping a customer.

"She's in her office," she said.

He nodded his thanks and headed back, eyeing the mess that was the ornament tables. She'd want to clean that up before leaving, no doubt. Which was why he'd arrived early. He might also have paused at the ice cream counter. Looking for his flavor, he found the label and then grinned.

Would it look ridiculous to pump his fist right now?

Because Lara had run out.

All the other bins of different flavors looked barely touched. Ha! He'd known that one would work well.

With a bit of a strut, he went to find Lara. In her office, he found her staring at her computer screen, the light illuminating her face like the Ghost of Christmas Worries. Because the way her brows had scrunched together, she was definitely stressing over something.

"Hey," he said.

He'd tried to pitch his voice softly, but she startled anyway. Then, hand to her heart, smiled. "Hey."

"I see my flavor did well."

She rolled her eyes, though her lips twitched. "I think mostly because of the sign about the contest."

He'd missed that. "What sign?"

She shrugged, turning back to the screen, and her brows resumed their furrowed positions. "I set up an online poll so people can use their phones to vote."

"Good idea." He paused. "What are you working on that has you frowning that way?"

She scrunched up her nose. So damn cute. "The books." Then she sighed. "I hate the books. It's my least favorite part of the job, but I've been putting them off long enough."

Peter moved around behind her to lean his hands on her chair and study the screen. The same software system they used at the bookstore.

"What's wrong?"

"I can't get the cash drawer to reconcile from yesterday. I'm missing fifty-three dollars and twenty-six cents somewhere."

"Hmmm . . . I'm pretty good at numbers. Want me to take a look while you clean up the ornament stations?"

She glanced up at that, indecision written all over her face. Especially the pinched look around her eyes. Was she worrying that if she let him look at the books, he'd do what her ex had done?

Peter started frowning and opened his mouth to argue that point, but she beat him to it. "I shouldn't. You are already doing the ice cream and—"

"Hey. That's a competition and I'm winning." The slow build of anger leaked out of him. At least she wasn't comparing him to the ex.

"I haven't done a flavor yet," she pointed out. But the pinched look had disappeared, exactly as he intended.

"I'm still winning." He winked. "Besides, I don't want to clean up the ornaments after being glittered and superglued."

She laughed at that, then glanced at her computer. "Well . . . Since you have to wait for me anyway, if you could figure this out, I would be grateful."

"Can do." He shooed her out of the chair, dropping into it and already focusing on the screen before she'd even left the room.

Fifteen minutes later, he'd solved that problem for her. He might also have made sure to mark some of her inventory items for automatic order based on the numbers she was moving and current stock situation, as well as added a tax report to run automatically for the end of the month.

He walked into a room almost all picked up, with Lara behind the ice cream counter. "Just give me a second to clean this out," she said.

"No rush."

Their reservations were for seven thirty, although the intersection that backed up, leading into town, might slow them down a bit. It had been the usual mess when he'd headed out this way or he would have been closer to thirty minutes early. He sat down on the bench at one of the tables, elbow resting on the top, and just enjoyed the view. Especially when Lara would glance up to find him watching, her cheeks turning pinker with each peek.

"You're blushing," he pointed out shamelessly.

The pink deepened and spread. "You're staring."

"Yes, I am."

Lara stopped her cleaning and crossed her arms, giving him a side eye, the stern effect belied by twitching lips. "It's rude to stare."

"I vaguely remember my mother saying something about that."

With a laugh, she shook her head and finished up what she

was doing. "Okay," she said. "Let me grab my purse and we can go."

She disappeared for a few seconds, and when she returned, he went to stand, except his pants seemed to be stuck to the bench.

Peter frowned. "What the—"

"Oh no," Lara murmured, a hand lifting to cover her mouth, eyes wide with horror.

Peter stopped struggling to stare at her seriously now. *Please not superglue again.* "Tell me."

"Snowball spilled paint at that table today. Cassie cleaned it up. I didn't even look to see."

Paint.

Of course. Because apparently that cat had it in for him. This had to be payback for holding her so long yesterday and cutting off all her fur on one side. A long con payback but aimed at him he had no doubt.

"I didn't see anything when I sat down," he said, trying not to lose his cool.

She cut off a sound that might have been a laugh. "It was brown paint."

Which would blend in with the natural wood. "Terrific."

"Let's see how bad it is." Almost tentatively, she approached.

With her help, Peter peeled himself off the bench.

"Bend over so I can see," she said.

Which is how he found himself standing in the middle of a fake North Pole full of ice cream, candy, and ornament decorations, bent over at the waist with his hands on his knees and Lara Wolfe staring at his backside.

His backside covered in *brown* paint.

"How bad is it?" he half grumbled.

"Um."

Which meant bad.

"You might want to bring a trash bag with you to sit on in

your truck," she said. "And we should definitely go to your place so you can change before dinner. Do we have time?"

"I'll call on the way and see if they can hold our reservation."

Because going out in public looking like he'd soiled himself was not exactly a great start to an official first date.

"I'm sorry."

He shook his head as he stood up straight. "Nope, it's fine."

"If it helps . . . I think you still have skills."

He turned to find her offering a commiserating smile, but she couldn't quite hide the amusement bubbling up inside her.

Without thinking twice, he reached behind him and grabbed the first bin he touched, then dumped it over her head in a cascade of gold and silver glitter.

"Ah!" she screeched, shaking her head, sparkles flying. "What was that for?"

"So we match," he said straight-faced, containing laughter that wanted to burst from him.

"Match?" she echoed.

He caught the light of mischief in her eyes too late. Because she lunged for him, butting her head into his chest and giving it a good shake, so that basically she ground any excess glitter into the cable-knit sweater he was wearing.

Coming up laughing, she grinned like a proud child. "*Now* we match."

"Not quite," he growled playfully.

Then scooped an arm around her waist, lifting her right off the ground. He had every intention of sitting her down in the wet paint. Only she twisted in his grasp, laughing and squirming and somehow, he ended up being the one sitting down with her across his lap.

As they came to a rest, they both stilled, staring at each other for a long beat. Then a giggle escaped her, and another.

And he couldn't help it, answering chuckles tumbling out of him. What was it about this woman that made him enjoy being silly in a way that was so unlike him? Even the previous version of him.

"Good grief. What happened to you?"

Emily's voice had them both jumping in surprise. On a gasp, Lara tried to jump off his lap, but he tightened his grip on instinct, not wanting to let her go.

With no choice but to settle, she flicked him a curious glance before focusing on Emily. "Your brother sat in paint."

Emily raised her eyebrows. "So you doused yourself in glitter and sat in his lap?"

Peter snorted. "That's right."

He let them both up, brushing at the top of her head, because he could see how much was still embedded in her hair, only to get swatted at for the effort. "You're knocking it into my eyes," she complained.

"Bend over," he said, relishing that it was her turn.

Finally, after they'd both knocked as much glitter as they could to the floor, Lara went into the back to grab a broom.

As soon as she disappeared, Emily crossed her arms, giving him a stare that had him backing up a step. "What?"

"Nothing." She shook her head. "Just good to see you laughing."

Yeah. It felt good, too.

Then Emily messed it all up with, "Hurt her and you answer to me."

"Hey! I'm your flesh and blood, little sister. Where's your loyalty?"

Emily pursed her lips, unimpressed. "I have comforted more than one girl you dated and dumped in high school and even after," she pointed out.

"I would hope I've matured a little bit since then."

"Hmmm . . ." In true sisterly fashion, she made a face saying she wasn't so sure about that.

Lara appeared then and they both dropped it. He grabbed the broom from her hands and started sweeping. After all, the glitter was his fault.

Seeming happy to let him, she moved over to Emily. "Was there a reason you dropped by?"

"Oh! Yes. I know you told me to drop that whole Right Rudolph on the town forums thing, but I had already sent an email to Nan, who runs the boards."

Peter froze midsweep. Right Rudolph. That was *his* handle. Not that there couldn't be others, though he seriously doubted it. And he knew for sure he was the only one posting about The Elf Shop on the boards that Nan managed.

"Oh," Lara murmured. "And?"

"And she said she couldn't trace anything. People can put anything they want as their handle."

"I see. Well, that's that then."

With his back to them, Peter couldn't see what his sister did, but a second later, she said, "I had also asked Tilly about the bidders for the space. She said she'd check, so I imagine we'll find out something."

Peter had never been much of a praying man, but suddenly he found himself in a conversation with the Almighty. Something along the lines of begging for a way out of this. He'd told himself if they got serious, he would confess everything. This was definitely serious—he could see that now. He felt like himself around her, and it had been too long since that was true. And he *would* tell her, but if he did that right now, he'd lose her before they even started. He knew it.

Just a little more time.

"Oh no, that's okay," Lara said. "I really don't want to know."

Relief whooshed out of him on a silent exhale.

"You okay?" Emily's question had him glancing around to find them both watching him.

"Yeah."

"You were just standing there," his sister said with a frown.

"I thought of something I forgot to tell Mom," he supplied, hoping they didn't ask what.

"Uh-huh." Emily's tone said it all.

He went back to sweeping and as he finished up, Mr. Muir and Miss Tilly showed up with Ben. While Peter hustled the three of them off to change his clothes and then go have dinner with Santa, all he could think about was how the heck he was going to tell Lara the truth.

What if she hated him?

I watch from the attic window as Peter's truck heads down the long drive to the road. Meanwhile, Miss Tilly, Emily, and Mr. Muir are all walking back to the house. They were in the shops. I could have gone out with them. They'd called my name. But I knocked that paint over because a little boy pointed at my fur and laughed, and I was trying to run away. Now I'm not showing my face anywhere until my fur grows back.

Chapter 14

The knock at her front door was expected. Peter was coming over to read with Ben like he'd been doing every night. This was now routine.

Which was why she was surprised at exactly how high her heart leapt up in her throat.

Silly.

They'd been on a single date, and her six-year-old nephew had played chaperone. In fact, with the Santa time, the evening had been mostly about Ben. Which had been lovely in a funny way. And Peter had laughed. In fact, he'd smiled more these last days than she'd seen since moving here. It had become a bit of a personal challenge to see his smile or hear his laugh.

She should just go ahead and admit that Peter Diemer was turning into something . . . special.

Swinging the door open, she didn't bother to hide her smile and immediately he leaned forward and kissed her. Just a quick peck. Pulling back only a bit to smile into her eyes. Given how stingily he doled out smiles, she appreciated every single one.

"Hey there," he said softly.

Oh my. "Hey there," she echoed just as softly.

"You missed me." He waggled his eyebrows.

A flutter of nerves and something fizzy and entirely about happiness hit her right in the solar plexus. The teasing was what did it for her. That this usually gruff guy loosened up enough with her to tease.

"Meh," she teased right back, and laughed at his mock fierce scowl.

"Come in," she said, laughing.

"So . . ." he said as he took off his coat. "I was checking out the ice cream poll today. My apple pie creation still has the lead over your Scrooge Face flavor, and your eggnog from today is in last place."

She rolled her eyes playfully, but mostly because she'd also been watching the polls. "Just wait until my next one," she pointed out.

Actually, she'd gone much fancier with this last attempt. Unfortunately, she'd overestimated how many people loved eggnog as much as she did. Turned out, it was one of those love it or hate it things that split about fifty-fifty.

"Losers give excuses," he said. "Winners just win."

"Wow," she deadpanned. "That is wisdom right there."

He grinned. "I didn't get a chance to taste the Scrooge one, anyway. What exactly is in that?"

"It's a lime sherbet with sour candy hearts. You know . . . to make your face pucker."

He got that part but . . . "Hearts? For Christmas?"

"Because of his change of heart," she explained patiently.

"Right."

Lara narrowed her eyes as she studied his completely blank expression for a long beat. He looked back unblinkingly, until she burst out laughing.

"What?" he asked.

"You must be terrible at poker," she teased. "Because that blank face basically screams, *I have something to hide.*"

He scowled, which was even cuter. "It does not."

"Admit it, you're not impressed with my first flavor of-fering."

The look of guilt that crossed his face put her in mind of Snowball after she did something bad, head lowered and tail tucked, and Lara chuckled again. "Don't worry. I know I need to up my ice cream game."

He held up his hands. "You said it. I did not."

She went up on her tiptoes, offering her lips to kiss, which he did with satisfying speed.

"What was that for?" he asked.

"To make me feel better that you think my Scrooge sher-bet is inferior." She winked.

"Well, my recipe for Monday is already in the freezer," he said. "And it's a doozy."

Who knew Peter Diemer was going to get so into ice cream making? "I think ice cream making is *thawing* your grumpy ways, sir."

He groaned at the bad pun. "Just be ready, Wolfe."

"I look forward to it," she said. Then tipped her head to-ward the stairs. "Ben is already in bed."

Expecting Peter to head on up, she turned back for the kitchen, where she'd been looking up ice cream ideas for to-morrow night. She had only one more shot at this. Maybe she should get a head start tonight. Just in case.

"Actually . . ."

She paused and turned to find Peter had followed. "I wanted to talk to you about something."

"Oh?"

"So . . . I was thinking of that favor for a favor thing."

She frowned. "For helping with Ben?"

"Yeah, but now for something else."

"*You* need a favor?" Good. She liked giving favors. Get-ting them was harder.

"Well . . ." His face was doing that blank thing all over again.

Lara crossed her arms. "What?" she urged.

"So you hate doing the bookkeeping part for your shop, right?"

She nodded slowly, heart slowing to a crawl of dread, not entirely sure she liked where this was going.

"Well, I love that part."

Lara let out a sharp breath and turned her back on him, continuing to the kitchen. "You are not doing my books, Peter." That was taking favors one step too far, and she'd been down that road once. Had the tire marks to prove it.

He followed, facing her across the island. "Hear me out."

After a doubt-filled pause, she waved for him to continue.

"I'm thinking just for the rest of this month to get your system streamlined and set you up for the steadier business starting in January."

The thing was . . . she was behind in that department. And Peter wasn't her ex. "In exchange for what?"

"Our inventory of children's books is selling so well in your shop, Mom was hoping for—"

"More shelf space?" Lara perked up. The toys were selling well from that display, too. "I could give you another shelf unit beside the one you have."

"No. No. She was hoping you'd redo our children's section and maybe bring some toys to sell on consignment with them like we do in your store."

Oh. Lara thought through that, a bubble of excitement slowly inflating inside her. "I could do that."

"And also"—his voice turned sulkier—"maybe a workshop or two?"

He was giving in on that point? Squeezing in the time for all of this would be the problem, but if he could squeeze in her books, that was worth all the sleepless nights in December. Except . . . how to man the storefront? She couldn't afford to hire anyone else.

"One of us—me, or Mom, or Dad—can come work in the toy shop while you're working at our place."

He'd really thought of everything. She had to tell the suspicious voice in her head asking why to be quiet. She needed to learn to trust someone at some point.

"Are you sure?" she asked. "My books are . . ."

"Fun," he assured her.

"I was going to say a pain in the rear, but sure. Fun. We'll go with your version."

Which made Peter laugh. Deep and rich and rolling, and she might love that sound almost as much as the sound of Ben's giggle. Possibly more. It was a close call.

"Can you access your system from here?" he asked.

"Yeah."

"Let's go over what you have set up and what you want help with after I read to Ben."

"Okay. I'll start thinking about workshops for the bookstore."

He grinned as though he'd just won something bigger than traded favors, then headed upstairs. Lara stared after him, frowning a little, doubts rising up like a winter wind in his wake. Was this really something the bookstore needed? Or did he think she was so incompetent with her books that he'd come up with a scheme to "help" her?

Lance would have just let her fail and then pointed it out.

Lara shook off the thought. Just because she wanted to prove herself didn't make it right to turn down help. She hated being tied to the office and working in the systems setup to track her inventory and finances. She could do it, but if Peter could do it faster, and this was an even swap of time and effort, then she should just get over herself and her trust issues.

An hour later, he popped his head into the kitchen, where she sat at the table. And Lara could feel how she lit up at the sight of him. Like flipping on a strand of fairy lights in the dark.

This is getting serious.

For her at least. So much faster than she expected.

She nodded, then, after scooting the laptop to be between them on the counter as he took a seat at the other stool, switched the display to her financial system.

Over the next hour she explained what she could about her setup—inventory, sales, ordering, contractors, and what she struggled with most.

"Wait . . ." Peter paused them both in the middle of her covering her overall budget projections. "So I see what finances you have available personally. What about your small business loan? Shouldn't you have more to work with initially?"

Lara grimaced. She'd been hoping he wouldn't notice or ask. After all, if a bank hadn't been willing to front the money, maybe her business was doomed to failure. She was already running overbudget, and it was only a few weeks into her first month.

"I was denied a loan." She tried to be forthright, as though this wasn't a problem.

"Denied?" He blinked at her. And for a second, she swore he paled. "You're doing *all* of this with your own personal money?"

The tone of his voice was . . . off. Not anger exactly, but maybe a mix of anger and something else, though she had no idea what. She also straightened, trying hard not to bristle at how much Peter sounded like her brother and Angela.

"I told you my grandmother left me money. Not a fortune or anything, but enough for me to be able to do this without the loan. Even after finishing paying Lance back."

Peter considered her. "But it would have been easier with the loan. Am I right?"

"Much." That seemed pretty obvious to her.

"Do you know why they denied the loan?"

"I have a good idea." The debt she'd been in had gone to collectors because she hadn't known until her ex did his disappearing act. Apparently, he'd been hiding the bills from her.

He looked away from her, jaw working. Why was he getting so upset about this?

"Hey. I'm fine." She squeezed his arm. "I'm overspending a bit, but I'm also making more than I projected. If I can get through the first three years, I'll know for sure that this will work."

"Hell," Peter muttered, definitely angry. Then turned a frowning face her way. "Why didn't you go to other banks?"

Not Lance. He wasn't asking because he disapproved of her. Still, her words came out more defensive than she liked. "I did."

"And?"

"They didn't say so explicitly, but the impression I got was banks talk. At least in small towns they do. After I was rejected at one, the others didn't want to even make an appointment."

"I see."

He stared at her, gaze still hard, but something there was softening. He stayed quiet so long that she raised her eyebrows at him.

He cleared his throat. "I'm going to make sure that you don't fail," he said.

She didn't smile at that. While the offer came from what she hoped was a nice place, she didn't appreciate it. "I am the one who will make sure of that," she said as firmly as possible. "I just need help balancing the books."

"I'll help with that to start."

He wasn't hearing her. "A favor for an *equal* favor," she insisted.

"Uh-huh."

Which could mean anything. Before she could press the point, though, he was nodding at the screen. "Your marketing strategies are brilliant and definitely effective."

The tightness in her chest loosened. He believed in her. No one had done that since Granny.

"But," he continued thoughtfully, "possibly that's an area where you could save some money."

She hid a flinch, because at least he wasn't saying she should stop altogether. Maybe . . . just maybe . . . he had some points worth listening to. So long as she could set her own personal hang-ups aside. Taking a deep breath, she leaned forward. "Like what?"

Which had them bending their heads together to look at the screen.

Still, she couldn't shake the feeling that Peter had been seriously upset. Was she that terrible of a businesswoman? She knew why the banks had rejected her loan, but the main reason wasn't an issue anymore. If she tried again in a year, she was hoping they would see that.

If she survived until then.

Not for the first time, doubts crept in, sending icy tendrils through her pleasure in this adventure. Only now the ice lodged deeper, expanding and causing her foundations to crack just a little.

I am even more of a jerk than I realized.

The same thought, or variations on the theme, had been running through Peter's mind since the moment Lara said she was financing this out of her own pocket thanks to rejected loans. It hadn't let up. Not Saturday night after he'd left her house and returned to his home. Not while he'd tried to sleep. Not today when he'd tried not to think about any of it. Now, not as he sat at the four-way intersection waiting for his turn to go through on his way to Weber Haus.

Lara hadn't said his posts on the forum had anything to do with it, but he'd put objections out there. Doubts.

Was it possible his behavior had ruined her chances at a loan? It seemed that one dissenter—really very few others had chimed in to agree—would be a silly reason to deny her. He wished he could get a look at her proposal and business plan. Or even talk to George Hartwell at the bank and see if he could shed some light. But of course he couldn't, due to confidentiality and other legal reasons.

Peter had considered confessing about the posts then and there.

But if he did, then he couldn't make amends, because he was pretty sure Lara would never speak to him again. The way she insisted that she do this herself—that any help would only be accepted if she could repay the helper—she clearly had strong opinions about how she wanted this to go. All Peter could do now was help from the books side of things, win her trust that way.

Which he headed to Weber Haus to do. They'd agreed that he would come into The Elf Shop at the close of business each day and do an hour of work, however far that got him, and he'd been getting pretty far.

In exchange, she would keep track of the hours she put in on the children's section in the bookshop, as well as the workshops she was putting together, and try to balance out about the same.

Lara's insistence for a fair swap of time and effort.

Finally, he got through the intersection. The walk from the parking lot seemed to take forever, mostly because the activity at the Christmas Market, which closed on Thursday, had turned frenetic. The place was packed, but eventually he got there. Inside The Elf Shop, he found Lara at the ice cream counter scooping out what appeared to be the last of his newest flavor—hot cocoa, which was a smooth dark chocolate with a sea salt kick to it and marshmallows mixed in. Peter pointed and lifted a single eyebrow.

She laughed and tipped her head toward the back office, basically telling him to get to work.

Which only made him grin bigger.

Over an hour later, a shadow fell across the desk and he looked up to find her standing there, hands on her hips with a mock glare belied by the light in her soft gray eyes.

"We agreed to an hour a day," she reminded him. Not for the first time.

Peter shrugged, unrepentant, and around a burgeoning grin fed her the same excuse he had the other days. "Has it been an hour already?"

He'd actually figured she'd get caught up in closing the store and forget about him until she was done, giving him extra time to sneak in on what he was doing. And he'd been right. He tried not to look too smug about it, though.

"Remind me to set a timer for you," she mumbled, wiggling her phone at him. Then, with a sudden frown of trepidation that sat uneasily on her open face, asked, "How's it going?"

Peter cracked his knuckles as he shifted his gaze to the screen, satisfaction in a job well done welling up in a way he hadn't felt in a long time. Not even when he did the bookstore books, because his parents had already set up a nicely streamlined system. Very little for him to adjust. Maybe he would love the business more if he'd been in on it from the ground up?

"Come look." He beckoned her around.

When she got close enough, Peter couldn't help himself, hooking an arm around her waist to pull her onto his lap.

"That's not fair," she said, laughing.

"Fair?" he asked.

"You're trying to distract me so I don't argue with whatever you did to my books," she accused, jabbing an accusing finger at the screen.

"So you find me distracting?"

She opened her mouth on a breath, then closed it again, wrinkling her nose.

Peter leaned closer, noting the darker rims around her eyes and the way her pupils dilated. "Good. Because I find you entirely distracting."

She swallowed, not answering.

Grinning, probably looking like he'd gotten drunk on Grandma's eggnog, Peter turned their attention to the computer. Lara wasn't wrong about the distracting bit actually.

"So I added a few more expenses categories to help track certain things. Then I created a profit and loss statement that you can run anytime to see how you're trending on income versus expenses."

She nodded. "I imagine I'll be negative for a while thanks to the outlay for the building, the construction, and then the inventory."

"If you look at it from the beginning, yes. But if we start it on the date you opened, you're looking simply at how much is coming in and out for that time period. Hopefully that will reflect your marketing efforts in a more real-time way."

She nodded. "Makes sense."

Now for the hard part. "Which is why I would recommend you stop the ornament stations."

Since she was still on his lap, it was impossible to miss the way she stiffened. "But all the kids *love* that. And the parents love it because they can shop while their children are entertained."

He nodded. "I get it, but the money you're sinking into the materials is too much of a loss for the potential sales to offset."

She frowned.

"Or . . ." he suggested, "you can start charging a small fee, just to cover material cost."

The frown deepened. "I hate to do that. Especially now that the word is out that it's free."

"This is business," Peter insisted, trying to soften the words, because he knew her history with her brother and her ex. Only his naturally blunt tones didn't help much.

She stiffened again, but after a second relaxed. "Business. Right. I don't like it, but I get it. However, we're only open through Thursday before all the shops close for the holiday. I'll keep the fee thing in mind for next year. Or do something similar with Valentine's cards and try the fee thing for those."

Peter let out a silent breath he'd been holding, because he hadn't been sure, especially after some of her reactions last night, about how she was going to take that. He shouldn't be surprised that she decided to keep ignoring the advice. She was right. Christmas was nearly here.

"Okay," he gave in. "Here are a few other reports I've set up that you can look at."

And he walked her through them until she checked the clock. "Good grief, we've been at this awhile. Time to go get Ben."

School was out now, but she seemed determined to make sure Ben had fun every day, even if it wasn't with her. "Where is he today?"

"Over at Weber Haus. Something about going to the Christmas Market demonstrations today." She laughed, a sound he was coming to love. "Did you know Sophie can milk a cow?"

Peter grinned at the image in his head. "No, but I hope she didn't try that in her fancy clothes and shoes."

"Right?" She paused, clearly worrying over something. He'd figured out earlier in the week that when she went quiet, that's what she was doing. "Do you think I'll still have business after the holiday?"

"It will slow," he said. "But I think you'll find it changes to a normal pace and . . . you'll be fine. You knew this was coming and banked on it." He knew because he'd seen her planned budget.

"I hope so," she murmured.

Together they headed over to the house, letting themselves in through the back to find Ben elbow-deep in cookie dough with Emily. He grinned from ear to ear. "We took over Mrs. Bailey's kitchen, but she said it was okay because dinner is already cooked."

"Smells delicious," Lara said, moving over to take a peek in the bowl.

"They're for Snowball."

Peter laughed. "Cookies for Snowball?"

His sister plunked her hands on her hips. "That poor cat has been cowering in our room or hiding in the attic ever since you maimed her fur."

Wait. That was a while ago. They were blaming him for that fiasco? Suddenly this wasn't so funny. "I would like to point out that she rolled in superglue and cutting her fur was the fastest way to get us unstuck while she was flipping out. Look—"

He rolled back his sleeves to show the numerous scratch marks. Then looked to Lara for support, only she was hiding laughter behind her hand.

She sobered, dropping it. "It really was Snowball's fault," she said.

Peter nodded. "Exactly."

Emily hummed as though she didn't want to have to concede the point. "Well, she does get into mischief. But Ben wants to make her feel better . . . so kitty cookies."

"Do we get to eat the kitty cookies, too?" he asked.

Emily threw up her hands.

Lara edged closer to say in a low whisper. "So now you want to steal the traumatized cat's cookies?"

Peter tried not to grumble. This was a lot of effort for a cat who rolled herself in superglue, doused him in glitter, and spilled paint for him to sit in. "I want to know why I don't get cookies," he whispered back. "Maybe I'm traumatized."

She widened her eyes at him. "Because you're a grown man, and not a helpless animal."

"Ha!" Emily crowed. "Exactly."

This was not a point he was going to win. That was quite obvious now.

"Besides"—his sister smirked—"I got this recipe online and it's specific to cats. I'm pretty sure they won't be all that tasty to humans."

"Fine. No cookies for me."

For some reason, Ben found this hilarious, succumbing to a bout of giggles. "You're so silly, Pete."

A choked sound came from the woman beside him. Had this been a month ago, Peter would've glowered and probably stomped away. Instead, he found himself chuckling. "You're right, kid. *Silly* is definitely the word for all this."

He caught the odd look his sister sent his way. What?

"So . . . what have you two been doing?" Emily asked, though.

Peter jumped in, talking about the books, the things he'd done to streamline the reports, and the longer he talked the funnier his sister looked at him. Until he cut himself off. "Seriously . . . what?"

She shook her head. "I don't know. It's just . . . there's something different about you tonight."

"Different?" What was that supposed to mean?

"Yeah, I think you really enjoy doing those financial projections. You're all lit up like a . . ." She searched for a word. "Like a Christmas tree."

He opened his mouth to deny that, but paused, thinking about it.

He had to admit that being able to solve these problems now in a way that might help a burgeoning business succeed, trying to find ways to grow while sustaining a profit, was exciting. He'd had more fun tonight than he'd had in six months running the bookstore. Which was a problem he should probably deal with.

But that wasn't the reason he was so . . . happy. He slid his gaze toward the woman at his side. Lara.

Lara Wolfe had come along, with her store and her Christmas cheer, unbothered by his grumpy ways, and chipped away at the scars around his heart that had changed him so much.

That was what was different.

Jiminy Christmas, I'm in love with her.

Head over heels, Christmas miracle kind of love. His heart gave a heavy thump, and he swore that the Scrooge-like change of heart had snuck up on him. He'd somehow managed to skip the ghosts of past, present, and future.

Only, his darn heart shriveled right back up the next second thanks to a cold, hard truth. Because he still had this horrible knowledge of what he'd done to her hanging over his head.

I sniff at the plate that Emily brought up to her and Lukas's room and placed on the floor next to the bed I've been hiding under most of the day. The air-conditioner man is still around. Apparently, he had to order more equipment or something, but he's also been in the attic as well as the basement. So here I've been.

"Ben made these to make you feel better," she tells me.

I take a little nibble and perk up, feeling a tiny bit better. It was nice of Ben to worry about me.

Still . . . I refuse to come out in this terrible state. Everyone has a little pride, and cats more than most.

Chapter 15

The click of a door opening had Lara glancing over from the trunk of her car, where she'd just loaded a box full of small, carved nativity sets that she'd been working on beside her final batch of ice cream—definitely the flavor that would win this contest for her. Peter was already crossing the grass strip between them, and her immediate, whole-hearted response was . . . excitement. Like the patter of tiny reindeer feet all over her tummy.

Both nervous and eager. Emotions that came with a surge of warmth in her heart and in her cheeks because . . . well, she just liked being with him. Emotions that came with . . .

Falling in love.

I'm falling in love with Peter Diemer.

She opened her mouth to say something casual, but the discovery she'd just made lodged the sound in her throat, vocal cords refusing to work. Too soon. It was way too soon to be in love with him. Definitely way too soon to tell him. And yet, she felt as though she were bursting at the seams with the happiness of it all.

She'd found her person. She was sure of it—Christmas miracle, running down the street shouting for joy, that kind of sure.

Only the smart move was to bottle it all up and be patient. Because this was definitely too soon.

All of which resulted in her bouncing on her toes, trying to expel some of the pent-up happiness, and by the way he slowed and stared, his gaze trained on her lips, her smile was too much. Too big. Too bright.

She tried to force her face to relax and cleared her throat.

"What are you doing up so early?" she asked as he stopped near her. But not near enough. At least she managed to ask a reasonable question. Given how jumbled her head and heart were right this second, anything could have come out.

"I had a logistics epiphany."

She raised her eyebrows. "This early in the morning?"

"Actually, last night, but it was too late to call."

That late? "What's this epiphany?"

"I think you and Ben should come directly to the book-store. You have to, anyway, since it's your day to work on the children's section."

She nodded slowly. "But Ben has to get to Weber Haus," she said. "Something about ice fishing with Mr. Muir, though with the pond being used for ice skating, I don't know where."

Peter gave her a cockeyed look.

"I know." She grinned. "Mr. Muir, it turns out, despite his rather forthright manner, is a total softie and really good with Ben." Like some people she knew.

"But . . . favors?" he asked.

See. Peter got her. There was no judgment in his voice, just an understanding that she didn't like to feel as though she was taking advantage of anyone. Her brother would have—

Who cares what he would have done or said?

Lance didn't matter in this particular instance, and she wasn't going to let his voice be so loud in her head anymore.

Waiting for his approval or affection was like waiting for Santa to retire.

Peter was waiting for an answer, so she shrugged. "I still feel bad about all the time he took to tutor Ben last week. He refuses to be paid, so I am planning to surprise him with a date night for him and Miss Tilly as thanks."

"Sounds like a nice idea." Peter nodded. "Anyway, since my mother is taking over for you in the toy store today while you're at the bookstore, I figured Ben could ride there with her. Sound good?"

Actually, that saved her some commute time, especially through that darn intersection, and she could get started sooner. "Sure."

He nodded, and she expected him to walk over to his truck and she'd follow him to the store. But he didn't move.

He stayed still, gaze trailing over her features in a way that snagged the breath in her lungs like an unravelling sweater. Only really, really nice. Then something in his face . . . changed. Nothing she could have put her finger on, but almost like he'd suddenly seen her with different eyes. Eyes that softened and . . .

Her heart wanted desperately for him to have reached the same realization that she just had. That he wanted her in his life. That he loved her. A hope that sent her heart thumping so hard against her ribs, she wondered if he could hear.

He reached up a hand and tucked a strand of her hair back under her knitted hat. "I think you're awfully pretty, Lara Wolfe," he murmured. "And kind of special."

The smile she gave him came from everything inside her. "You're not so bad yourself, Peter Diemer."

"I really want to kiss you."

A glance confirmed Ben couldn't see them, blocked by her raised trunk. This was becoming a habit. A nice one. Rather than answer, she stepped into him, grabbing the front of his jacket with both hands and going up on tiptoe. She lifted her lips to his and waited, smiling.

He gave a little huff of a laugh, breath misting in the cold air and blue eyes brightening. "Where have you been all my life?"

Then he kissed her. One touch, and she didn't know if she made a sound or he did, but his arms came around her tight and she moved hers up around his neck and gave herself over to the moment. To the feel of his lips firm and yet tender against hers. To the way he sort of scooped her up against him, holding her up on her toes. To the way he smelled of winter and some kind of woodsy cologne.

But mostly to the way she felt in his arms—there weren't words. Only the loveliest sense of rightness and wonder.

He lifted his head, eyes crinkling around the corners as he smiled down at her. A smile only and ever for her. "Well . . . that's a nice start to the day."

She grinned, too happy to hide her feelings anymore.

Only Peter suddenly sobered, eyes filling with a different emotion. "Lara . . . there's something I should tell you."

Safe in her bubble of happiness, she hoped that some kind of confession of his feelings was what he wanted to share. Were they ready for that? It seemed so fast. "Okay."

He opened his mouth, only his cell phone rang. Peter grunted, but one arm still around her, he fished the device out of a pocket and checked the screen, then grunted again. "It's Mom." He showed her the phone.

Then, letting go of her, he stepped away, the winter cold replacing the warmth of him in a harsh whoosh.

After a second, he hung up. "We'd better get going. We'll talk later. Okay?"

Now she had to wait until tonight, on the edge of anticipation. *How am I going to concentrate at all?*

*　　*　　*

He was in love with Lara. But what really had him shaken was that he was pretty sure she was in love with him, too.

He'd seen it in the smile she'd offered this morning—a glow about her that was pure joy. That reached out and wrapped around his heart, and who needed a winter coat when a simple smile could warm you from the inside out like that.

And the kiss they shared . . .

And the way she'd looked at him when they'd finally come up for air.

He was having the time of his life. With her, but also with the ice cream of all things, and the books for the toy shop, and partnering with her to support her marketing ideas but in ways that made financial sense, and entertaining Ben.

He'd suddenly been able to envision a life with her, the image crystal clear, all laid out in glorious, messy, wonderful, magical detail. And he wanted that more than he'd wanted anything. Ever.

He glanced over at where she knelt on the floor in the toy shop. After working most of the day at his family's bookstore, she'd wanted to come back here to pick up Ben and take him shopping in the Christmas Market stalls. Just her and her nephew.

They'd returned from that adventure about the time Peter had come back to pick up his mother, who'd decided to stay to man the toy store. She'd taken Ben home and Peter had stayed with Lara, somehow managing to get busy restocking shelves with her. Now she knelt on the floor, organizing toys to her heart's content, head tipped sideways and a furrow between her brows as she considered whatever shelf design combination she was working on.

She glanced over and caught him watching—not the first time today—and grinned. She was *happy*.

So was he. Delirious with it.

He turned and headed outside, intending to go get the truck defrosting while Lara finished up. Only the second he was outside, Emily shoved her face through the bakery door, her expression one of angry determination.

She scowled. Hard. At him. "Peter."

"Hey." He moved toward her. Only she didn't budge.

"I need to talk to you."

"Okay. Your office?" he asked.

"No." She grabbed his hand, proceeding to drag him through the shops and booths to the edge of the "street" and then around to the other side of the building that had once been a barn, where they could be private and alone.

"Em," he said, patting her arm, "if this is about you being pregnant, I already guessed. Huge congrats by the way!" He grinned at the way she opened and closed her mouth.

Only the frown of consternation wasn't what he was expecting. "Thanks," she finally said. "But this is not about that."

"Oh." He crossed his arms. "What's it about?"

"It's about you trying to sabotage Lara's business."

His heart came screeching to a full stop, then took off at a sprinter's pace. Faster than Dasher could fly.

Emily's consternation turned into full anger. "My own brother. How could you do it, Peter?"

"I assume you're talking about the forum?"

She flung her arms out. "At least you admit it."

"I posted those things because I was angry about how the toy store owner outbid me for the space. Long before I ever knew that was Lara. And I regretted it before I did know."

Emily reared back. "Wait, *you* were who she outbid?"

"Yeah, I thought the shop had been leased by a corporation, not an individual. She way outpriced me. I mean outrageously."

In fact, he should talk to Lara about that if they got through this.

Though apparently the cat was out of the bag now. Where was Snowball when he needed her?

"But . . ." Emily shook her head. "You're *dating* her now."

Peter said nothing. What could he say?

"Am I wrong?" she asked.

Again, nothing.

"She doesn't know that her 'Right Rudolph' is you?"

"I plan to tell her."

His sister plopped her hands on her hips. "When, exactly? When you put the ring on her finger?"

If anything, panic that she was right, and he was in the middle of ruining the best thing in his life, sat like a spider inside him. Crawling through him and weaving webs impossible to escape.

Peter ran a hand through his hair, suddenly wishing for once for longer hair, which would be so much more satisfying. "I know," he said. "I've been trying to find the right time to tell her. I swear."

The disappointment on Emily's face sat like a weighted blanket over him. Crushing. And Lara's reaction would be a thousand times worse.

"I love you, big brother, but you need to set this right."

"I will. I will."

"I mean it, Peter. Either you tell her," Emily said, "or I will."

He blew out a harsh breath. "I will," he promised. "But I need time."

"How much time?"

"After the New Year?"

"What?" she squawked. "Peter—"

"I'm trying to get her books in better shape, as sort of an apology. At least let me finish that and let her enjoy the holidays. That way, if she throws me out, I'll know I've helped her in some small way. Okay?"

Emily calmed a tad at that, eyeing him with indecision. Then, "Fine. January."

He wrapped his arms around her. "Thank you."

"I'm still disappointed in you," she mumbled into his chest, but she also hugged him back.

"Believe me," he said into her hair, "I'm disappointed in me, too."

Snowball watched Emily and Peter from the attic window that faced the shops. She'd been sitting there, looking out, waiting for her fur to grow back before she showed her face anywhere.

But . . . it looked as though Emily and Peter were in a fight. Why?

She flopped down, chin on her paw, and sighed. Not that it mattered. She was still sure that she shouldn't be meddling in the humans' lives anymore. Her first two successful matches had to have been a fluke. Everything she touched turned bad.

So she stayed in her attic and let them figure it out on their own.

Chapter 16

Lara's cell phone buzzed in her pocket, but she was with a customer, so she kept smiling and ignored it. She'd just have to check it later. "This is the largest hobby horse—errr, hobby reindeer—we sell," she said, in answer to the man's question.

He frowned. "Is it possible to order something bigger?"

Lara tried to keep from letting her thoughts show on her face. The horse in question had taken her almost a year. An overly ambitious project to keep her mind off of Granny's worsening health. Eventually, it had been the inspiration for the North Pole theme of The Elf Shop. She'd fashioned it as one of Santa's flying reindeer with the fancy traces, jingle bells, and even a dusting of snow in its coat. Hand-carved, hand-painted, and set up on a sliding track for a smooth ride, she'd put it in here mostly for display. She hadn't expected anyone to actually *buy* this one—she was charging almost three thousand for it.

"Um . . . how big are you thinking?"

"About this tall and an actual horse instead of a reindeer." He put his hand out, hovering around her eyeline.

No way could she keep the surprise from her face. Or the doubt. "So the size of a real horse is what you're saying? Um . . . How old is the child this is for?"

The man broke out in a smile. "This is for my wife. Her arthritis means she can't ride her horses anymore, and as soon as I saw this, I thought . . ."

Lara's heart melted on the spot like an ice cream cone on a summer day.

"When would you need it?"

The deep voice behind her had her turning to find Peter standing there. She glanced at her phone screen. Sure enough, the end of the day when he came in for his hour was already here. Crept up on her again, although today all shops were closing earlier, so he was here earlier than usual.

The gentleman considered Peter's question. "Christmas I know would be impossible, but I was thinking maybe February, for her birthday."

February? There was no possible way. "I—"

"I'd pay extra for a rush job," he hurried to assure her.

Oh gosh. Lara bit her lip. Even if she was to only work on that one project, leaving the store in the hands of her helpers, she couldn't do a horse that size by then.

"I don't think that's doable," Peter said.

Lara stiffened so hard, she thought for a moment her muscles might snap like peanut brittle. Turning her head, she pinned him with a firm look. "*I* will handle this," she said through stiff lips.

He refused to budge, though. "How long did that one take you?"

As if she wasn't smart enough or competent enough to take that into consideration. Which hurt. He sounded just like her brother with his constant questions and objections. Granted, she signed up for a lot, but she never, ever missed deadlines, and this was just how running a brand-new brick-and-mortar business went. You did everything you could to make it successful.

"Why don't you head on back to the office," she said,

holding on to a calm tone by the skin of her teeth. Literally. They were gritted around the words.

Peter glanced at her, then at the customer, then at the reindeer. Then leaned in to murmur quietly at her. "Just don't sign up for too much, too soon. All right?"

Lara balled her hands into fists at her side, trying not to be mad. Because he was trying to take care of her. She knew that. It was sweet really, in an entirely misguided, stepping-all-over-her-toes kind of way. But Lara needed to prove that she could do this on her own. Prove it to herself, her brother, and now apparently to Peter as well. Which stung, because she'd thought he believed in her. Believed that Granny's faith in her hadn't been misplaced.

"If I wanted your opinion," she murmured back, "I would have asked."

He straightened abruptly, a slow frown descending over his features. "I was . . . just trying to help."

She forced a smile, trying to soften the situation. "I appreciate that, but I've got this. If you've got the computer stuff, that's huge."

In other words, that's all I need.

She willed him to catch the silent message. Catch it, understand it, and accept it. After another frowning beat, he gave a single jerky nod and walked away. A second later, she heard him call out, "Ben, you an ice cream man now?"

Followed by her nephew's higher-pitched voice. "Auntie Lara says I roll the best scoops."

Which made her smile as she turned back to the customer. This was the last day the shops were open. Tomorrow was Christmas Eve, Christmas the next day, and Sunday the day after for an extra day of rest. Ben had asked to help in the shop today rather than go with Lukas, who was going to take him on a holiday-themed photography expedition.

"So I'm afraid my friend was right. This one"—she waved at it—"took me over a year to do, and that was before I started this business. At the earliest, for a horse and the size you want, I'm guessing that it would be at least two years before I could finish that kind of project."

The disappointment drew the man's features down, shoulders slumping, and she hated seeing the hope just go out of him like that. "I could . . ." she offered. "I could call around. The handcrafted toy world is smaller than you would think. Maybe someone else could get something similar finished sooner."

The man brightened. "Would you? I would really appreciate it. I think she would love it."

Lara smiled. "Of course. Here . . ." She led him over to the checkout counter and handed him a card and then a pad of paper to put his contact information down.

As soon as he left, she turned with purpose to go explain to Peter in no uncertain terms that while she appreciated the sentiment, she was more than capable of making her own decisions, especially about *her* business.

"Auntie Lara, look," Ben called as she crossed over the drawbridge into the North Pole.

Pausing, she made her way to where he was standing on a stool so he could actually reach the ice cream to scoop it. He held up a cone and balanced the scoop on it very carefully, the tip of his tongue poking out of his mouth in concentration. Then handed it to the customer.

"Fantastic job," she told him with a grin.

"Why is my son *working* in your toy store?" The sound of her brother's voice, cold and angry, behind her had Lara turning slowly to face him.

"Lance?" she asked. "What are you doing here?"

His expression, which would make the real Scrooge look

like one of Santa's happier elves, didn't alter. "I asked you a question."

"Yes, you did."

He waited, brows lowering farther. "Are you going to answer it?"

Once upon a time, even as early as a year ago, she would have cowered under that look and stammered out some explanation that he wouldn't have accepted anyway.

Not today. "I don't know," she said. "I have a rule about answering questions only when they are asked nicely."

Lance did not like that, his glower building like a thunderhead. "I believe we were very clear that Ben was to be given a good time to make up for us missing much of the holiday with him."

Would it harm her business if it got out that she threw an ice cream scoop at someone's head? Probably.

"Daddy, it's okay—"

"No, Ben." Lance didn't even look at his son, staring her down. "It's not."

"But Auntie Lara—"

"We asked you to do one thing."

Seeing the sliding glances coming from a store full of customers, she reconsidered the throwing something maneuver, but she took a deep breath instead. Lara moved from around the counter. "Come with me."

"I am not leaving my son to work *your* shop on his own."

Lara marched right into her brother's space, something she'd never done in her life. Lowering her voice, she spoke as reasonably as she could. "Come with me now, Lance. I'm not asking."

Her behavior must've been enough to shock him into compliance, because he followed her back into her office. Peter was already looking up from his computer, poised as though he'd been debating getting up to check on the commotion. "Do you need my help with a testy customer or something, because I heard—"

Lance walked in behind her and Peter snapped his mouth shut.

"No," Lara said. "Just a testy brother."

Lance scowled. "I am not—"

"Sit down." She cut him off and pointed at the extra chair she had tucked into a corner of the room.

Her brother glared at her. "I will not be taken to task like a toddler."

"Someone should have a long time ago," she countered.

"I don't have to listen—"

"Peter, will you excuse us?" she asked.

He glanced between them, and given those instincts of his to take care of her, she was actually surprised when he nodded and left the room. "I'll go have fun with Ben."

Her relief followed him out the door.

Lance frowned after him. "Who is that?" Then he caught sight of the computer screen. "He's working on your *books*? I told you to get a professional accountant. Hell, Lara. Didn't you learn anything from last time?"

Lara ignored all of that. "Let's get a few things straight. Ben is helping with the ice cream today because he asked me to. He had a choice between that and going out with a photographer friend of mine to take holiday pictures."

Lance opened his mouth, but she shot up a hand before he could argue. "Ben has been sledding, and made snowmen, he's visited Santa, he's been read to every single night from a book he got to pick out, he's made Christmas cookies—" Okay, for a cat, but same thing. "He's also been shopping for gifts for you and Angela and his grandmother. We've also managed to get all his schoolwork done in between, *all while I'm running my brand-new toy store that is busy at Christmas.*"

He tried to say something, but she was on a roll now.

"You are my brother, Lance, and I will always love you. I'll also always be grateful for the help you gave me with my debt problems. But after your treatment of me since Granny died, honestly, I don't know what to do about you. To come in here and immediately start accusing me of not taking care of Ben . . . Disagreeing with the will and telling me I don't know how to run a business is one thing. But I love my nephew and I am deeply offended—*deeply* offended—that you would even think, for a second, I wouldn't do my best for him."

She paused long enough for Lance to say, "Are you finished?"

Was she? Given his forbidding expression, she had a feeling that nothing she'd said had gotten through. But no. She wasn't done.

"No, I'm not. I assume that you're here to pick up Ben, but you should have called first. I don't have him packed and we have ice skating planned for tonight."

"Do I get to speak now?"

She was tempted to tell him no, but waved at him to continue.

"I've just spent weeks dealing with Angela's mother's health and getting her home from Bermuda. And this is how you decide to treat me?"

That was it? That was all he got from that?

"I am, of course, very sorry about all of that. I'm sure that was trying," she said.

"It was."

"Then I'm sure you'll be grateful to be able to check into a hotel somewhere and just lie down for a day."

He crossed his arms, glaring. "I don't want to lie down. I want to go home."

She didn't bother to hide her disappointed sigh. "You are Ben's father, so that's your call. But you will break that little boy's heart. He's been looking forward to this since he got here. Is that really what you want?"

That at least made him visibly pause. As much of a hard line as he drew with her, he was a total softie for his son. She'd give her brother that much. He blew out a harsh breath. "He really wants to do this thing tonight?"

"Yes."

Lance shook his head, obviously not liking his plans to be interrupted. "Fine. I'll go check into a hotel and get some work—"

"And then go pack up Ben's things at my house. I'll give you a key."

"Can't you do it—"

"No. If you had called ahead, I could have maybe figured it out, but giving me zero advanced warning was your choice. I have a business to run, and it's only a few days till Christmas."

Something her brother had clearly forgotten or dismissed. The latter was more likely.

His jaw worked for a second. "When is the ice skating tonight?"

"The shops close early today. We were going to eat dinner at six and then head over to the pond. It's on this property. There's a map in a clear bin near the parking lot. If you would like to join us, I'm sure Ben would love that. You can either join us for dinner as well or meet us at the rink around seven."

He shook his head. "I'll take Ben with me now."

Good grief, her brother could be so myopic. "I'm not sure packing and then sitting around your hotel room would be all that entertaining for a six-year-old."

Seeing the descending scowl, she tacked on sweetly, "After all, you're so concerned about his holiday fun."

Which made him frown harder, but what could he say to that, given his blowup a moment ago? Lara paused a moment to relish being on this side of an argument with Lance. A little petty, but it felt good.

"He's welcome to stay here if he wants," she offered. "Why don't you ask him?"

After a moment of consideration—reluctant consideration—he nodded.

She followed her brother out, immediately making eye contact with Peter. "You okay?" he mouthed.

She nodded and, while he didn't exactly stop bristling, tracking Lance with a hard stare, he also didn't say anything. After a quick conversation, Ben chose to stay with her at the shop and Lance, none too happy but resigned, left.

"Am I a horrible person that I got a little satisfaction that Ben wanted to stay with me?" she whispered to Peter as they watched her brother's retreat.

She felt as though she'd just won a huge battle and could conquer anything.

Not that Lance had admitted in any way he was wrong, but still . . . she'd won. She'd proven that he didn't have the kind of power over her life that she'd let him have up until now.

"I heard most of what he said to you out there," Peter admitted. "*I* was ready to punch him in the face."

Lara snorted a laugh. As much as she'd needed to fight her own battle, that would have been something to see. "Thanks for letting me handle it."

He shrugged. "I don't have to learn a lesson twice."

"Good to know." She grinned.

Then stilled, because he was looking at her that way again. The way she'd caught him looking at her more and more. A way that sent her heart tripping over itself.

He lifted his hands to frame her face, but she put a hand to his chest, stopping him. "We're in public."

He grinned, eyes crinkling with it. "And they're all jealous," he said. Then kissed her anyway.

Kissed her softly, lingering over it a tad, but nothing shocking for the kids, and she sighed into the touch. Into him.

He lifted his head. "Ready to close up shop?"

She pulled out her phone to check the time and wrinkled her nose. Sure enough, five o'clock had come and gone while she'd been busy with her brother. "Never enough hours in the day."

But somehow, today at least, that didn't come with anxiety. The holiday was here, she had a three-day break, and they had a fun evening planned. The last with Ben apparently, which made her heart ache in an unexpected way to have to let him go. Christmas was so close, and she'd been looking forward to spending it with him. Watching his joy as he opened gifts and getting three whole days with the shop closed to spend together.

Still, he'd be much happier in his own home with his parents. She'd just have to enjoy this little time they had left.

Maybe Peter was right about that. She needed to take time for herself here and there, or the business would suffer and so would she. Though she had no intention of telling him that and encouraging more "caring" interference. Still nice to know someone out there cared.

I've found a new hiding place. It's under the fancy, scrolly, really uncomfortable couch in the formal living room at the front of the house. Miss Tilly calls it a settee, though I don't know why. Either way, not a ton of people sit on it, and where it's positioned, I can see all the humans coming and going without them seeing me or my raggedy coat.

Which is where I am when the door opens and a man strides in very purposefully.

All it takes is one look at his face, and I think I know who this is. Ben's dad. He's basically just a larger-scale version of Ben. Or Ben's a smaller-scale version of the dad. Either way, Lara doesn't look a thing like either one of them with their sandy hair that's closer to brown than blond and eyes a darker brown.

Sophie looks up from the front desk, where she just happens to be standing, and smiles. "May I help you?"

"I would like to check in."

I see the way she blinks, as though slightly confused. "Do you have a reservation?"

Ah. That's why. Because Sophie makes a point to be there for check-in for every guest in the inn portion of the property. "No."

"I see." She starts to fiddle with the new computer that she talked Miss Tilly into using to manage the reservations. "You must be lucky today. Usually at Christmas we are booked solid. But we happened to have a cancellation."

"Excellent." Lara's brother pulls out a credit card and shoves it at her.

But she's still fiddling with the computer and doesn't see. "It will be a queen-sized bed on the second floor in our new hotel wing."

She looks up in time to catch his frown. "I would prefer to stay in the house," he says.

"I'm sorry, but—"

"My name is Lance Wolfe."

Sophie looks back at him blankly.

"My sister is Lara Wolfe, who owns the toy shop here," he says. "I assume that helps."

Wow. We get some arrogant types coming to stay with us, but I have to say Lara's brother sounds pretty bad to me.

Sophie assumes her professional "dealing with a difficult customer" expression that I'm pretty sure she doesn't realize she does every time she runs into one. It involves a smile, but her eyes go all hard.

"We love Lara so much," she says. "Her shop was a perfect addition to the Weber Haus stores, and it's doing so well."

"Uh-huh." Lance Wolfe looks unimpressed.

"Unfortunately, every room in the house is booked through New Year's. We're lucky that this hotel room opened up."

Lance makes a face. "I see. I guess it will have to do."

Wow again. That hotel wing is brand-new and was modeled to match the interior of the Victorian house itself. Daniel and his crew did all the work last year. It's gorgeous. Maybe Lara's brother is just having a very bad day. Miss Tilly, and Sophie, too, actually, are always talking about giving people the benefit of the doubt. I guess I should try that.

"I expect to check out tomorrow anyway," he says next. "I'm taking Ben back home with me."

Sophie makes a sympathetic moue and nods. "Ben is a sweetheart. I'm sure he'll be thrilled to be home with you to celebrate Christmas."

Lance nods, and then raises his credit card again, clearly expecting her to get him checked in immediately, no time for chitchat. Seeing his impatience, Sophie gets him all settled as quickly as she can and, without a word of thanks, he leaves to find his room.

"You're welcome," Sophie mutters under her breath.

I don't blame her. I can't say I'm all that impressed with Lara's brother. He speaks to people in a way that is not nice, scowls like a polar bear, and stalks around like a tornado whipping through things without care or concern.

But I'm not worried about him. I'm thinking about Ben.

I like Ben. Some kids are hard on cats, too rough or too timid. But he's one of my favorite tiny humans so far. He gives great snuggles.

And now he's leaving. Tomorrow.

My fur isn't going to be grown out by then. I sigh and lay my chin down on my paws. Now I won't get to say goodbye to him.

Squawk.

I wince at the sound of those darn birds. It's almost as though they are taunting my disappointment. I stay where I am.

Chapter 17

"Do you see my daddy?" Ben asked, craning his neck to look and then wobbling on his skates.

Luckily, Peter had a good grip on his hand, holding him up. Though, given his own precarious balance on metal edges, the likelihood of them both going down was high.

"Not yet," Peter said, tugging on the boy's beanie, which had skewed lopsided.

The weather was about as brisk as it got around here in winter. He kept trying to think of that as a good thing, because it meant the large pond at Weber Haus had frozen thick enough to allow ice skating this early in winter. It didn't always do that by this time of year, but when it did, the property set up a proper skating rink, including strung lights, a hot chocolate stand, skate rentals, benches and rubber matting around the edges, music through a sound system, and tickets allowing only so many on the ice at a time.

They'd been skating for about twenty minutes so far, and Lara's brother Lance had yet to show or answer any of her texts.

Peter adjusted his grip on the flimsy cardboard cup of hot chocolate he held in his other hand. If he squeezed any harder, he'd pop the thing. Still, after being a jerk about Lara taking care of his kid, Lance showing up at least a half hour late wasn't impressing Peter at all.

The fixer in him wanted to step in. Track down the guy and drag him here if he had to. But after the way Lara had looked at him today with that customer—the same way he imagined she'd look if he'd deliberately kicked Snowball—he was trying darn hard to let her handle it.

"Let's scoot to the side," Lara said.

With her grip on Ben's other hand, she guided them through the moving tangle of skaters of all speeds and abilities until they got to the edge. "I'm going to call Weber Haus and check on him."

"Is that where he's staying?"

She nodded. "They had a cancellation and he got lucky." She made a face but didn't elaborate.

Peter had no idea what to think about that.

"Sophie?" she asked into the phone before he could ask. "I'm sorry to bother you with this, but my brother is staying at the inn tonight . . ."

She paused, listening, and Peter couldn't hear what Sophie was saying thanks to the holiday music piping through temporary speakers loud enough to blow Santa's beard off.

"I see," she said. "When did he leave?" Another pause. A nod. "Thanks, Sophie."

Lara hung up and looked at him. "He left about ten minutes ago. He should be here any second, I imagine."

It wasn't that far a walk, the path clearly marked.

"Yeah." *Give the guy the benefit of the doubt*, he told himself. *He just underestimated getting here.*

Lara smiled at Ben, the expression almost too chipper. "Let's keep going," she said. "He'll find us."

"Lara!" The sound of her name being yelled from a distance was like ten drummers drumming in unison. A pop of sound. Looking around, they discovered Lance standing on the edge of the pond on the other side, mouth flat and white around the edges.

What exactly did he have to be angry about?

Luckily, going the direction of all the skaters brought them to him quickly, rather than having to make a full circle.

As soon as they got within hearing distance, Lance was speaking. More like snarling. "I can't believe you didn't wait for me."

Lara blinked. "We did," she told him. "For thirty minutes. In the freezing cold."

"It's not *that* cold," Lance snapped.

"It's eighteen degrees," Peter pointed out in a dry voice.

Only to have Lance shoot him an irritated frown. But Lara . . . Lara hid her amusement behind her hand.

Getting ahold of herself, she cleared her throat. "The rink closes in forty-five minutes from now. I tried calling and texting you."

"You know damn well the reception here is terrible."

It probably wouldn't impress her if Peter decked the guy, but he really wanted to. Because if any one of his brothers—Max or Paul or Oscar—had ever spoken to Emily that way, that's what he would have done.

To her credit, Lara took a deep breath. "Well, we still have forty-five minutes, and Ben is so excited to skate with you. Go get a ticket and get your skates on. We can wait here."

"For that small amount of time?" Lance grumbled. "I might as well not bother."

Nope. Lara might kill him, but Peter wasn't letting this slide. Not with the expression that just crossed Ben's face. Was Lance really that selfishly oblivious?

"Tell you what," Peter said. "I'll come with you. I need to throw this away anyway."

He ignored Lara's searching glance. Lance, meanwhile, looked him up and down. "Fine."

Rather than remove his skates, Peter skated over to where the rentals booth was set up, then hobbled along the rubber mats to meet Lance there. After getting the guy skates, they sat together on one of the benches so he could put them on.

"I have a younger sister, too," Peter said.

Lance glanced at him, then continued lacing up his skates.

"Three brothers, though," he continued. "So a bit of a different dynamic."

"Yeah?"

"Yeah, but if any one of them talked to her the way you just did to your sister, I'd take him out back and punch him in the face."

Lance reared back at that. "You have no right—"

"No, I don't. But neither do you."

"I'm her brother—"

"Not so anyone else would notice."

"What's she been saying to you?"

"Nothing. This is entirely based on *your* behavior. While you've been dealing with your mother-in-law, which is a stressful situation and I understand that . . . But meanwhile, your little sister has been killing herself trying to keep *your* child—the same child you just said you don't care if you skate with or not after he's been talking about nothing else since you arrived—educated and giving him the best holiday ever while trying to run a brand-new business in the height of the busiest season of the year. She's done this with little to no communication from you or your wife. And instead of being grateful, you've done nothing but throw accusations at her and complain when *you* were thirty minutes late." He paused. "Also, I would never . . . *never* . . . do to Lara what her ex did to her."

It was worth saying.

Through that entire speech, Lance turned an alarming shade of eggplant, a vein pulsing at one temple. "I don't have to listen to this. I should take Ben and leave if this is how—"

Peter surged to his feet, not to hit the guy, but definitely to tower over him, and Lance flinched. A bully with no backbone, basically. "Feel free to be pissed at me. But as Ben's father, I suggest you sit here and calm down. Because if you ruin this for him, that's on you, man."

With that, Peter skated away—well, hobbled awkwardly, then tried to skate and almost lost his balance. Lara passed him a worried look when he got to her and Ben. He glanced at the kid significantly and shook his head. He'd confess what he'd told her brother later, and probably weather another of those angry-disappointed looks. Worth it. But he wasn't going to upset Ben's night in the process.

A few minutes later, Lance joined them on the ice as well. He took Ben's hand and, Ben radiating happiness like a bonfire, father and son skated away together.

"What did you say to him?" Lara asked the instant they were out of earshot. "Lance looked like he was going to blow a vein."

"Yeah," Peter admitted grimly. "Your brother's a—"

He cut himself off and shook his head. Because the way he felt about Lara, that jerk could be related to him someday.

"It's not your fight," Lara said, keeping her voice low, but obviously angry.

"I kept all my comments to my opinions only. Nothing about you."

She slowed on her skates. "What exactly did you say?"

Peter repeated the conversation as word for word as he could recall. He had enough secrets from her. He wasn't going to keep more.

Lara stayed silent for a full trip around the rink while the song on the speakers rang out joyfully about winter wonderlands. Finally, she pulled her shoulders back. "Part of me is really touched that you care enough to stand up for me."

Peter skated around in front of her, stopping them both. "I lo—I care about you, Lara Wolfe. Don't ever doubt that."

Pink surged into her cheeks that he was hoping had nothing to do with the cold, and she nodded. "But I don't want you fighting my battles for me."

Right. "I figured that out earlier with that customer."

"So why'd you—"

"This wasn't fighting your battle, but mine. I would have said the same thing to any guy treating his sister the way he's treated you. I kept my comments only to what I'd observed. Nothing you've mentioned or assumptions I built. This was one guy telling another guy not to be a jerk. Okay?"

Only not okay, because she pinned him with a hard, searching gaze. "So this wasn't about thinking I couldn't handle my brother myself?"

"No." He was being totally honest about that. He'd caught a good chunk of her discussion with Lance in her office earlier today. "I know you can."

"Then why did you feel the need?"

"Because I've been up against guys like that my entire life, especially in my previous career. They don't listen, especially not to people close to them. But to a stranger who calls them out . . ." He shrugged.

Lara narrowed her eyes, but the way her shoulders dropped, he could tell she'd accepted that explanation. "Well . . . then thank you."

"Yeah?" he asked. "We're good?"

Her slow smile was a thing of beauty, but even better, she wrapped her arms around him, laying her head against his thick jacket. "We're good." She breathed in as she let go and scooted back. "It's nice to know someone has my back."

"Always." He held out his hand, and smile widening, she took it. Together they started slowly back around the rink.

"Auntie Lara," Ben called from behind them.

They turned to find they'd been lapped.

Ben was grinning from ear to ear. Lance, at least, rather

than scowling, was watching his son with smiling affection. "I can do it on my own," Ben announced. "Watch."

He let go of his father's hand and, legs wobbling and shuffling more than gliding, scooted forward by himself a few feet.

"See?" He looked over his shoulder and lost his balance, arms flailing.

Lance got there a beat before Peter did and scooped his kid up. "That was great, buddy!" he said, sounding sincere, and actually smiling.

Peter considered the other man. At least he could be a decent father. Maybe he'd been upset about being late because he knew Ben would be upset and then taken it out on Lara. Not that that was cool, but at least Peter could understand it a little.

"Let's go." Ben tugged at his dad's hand.

Together they all set off.

Luckily, the rest of the evening was enjoyed without incident. Except for the fact that every time Peter looked at Lara, all he could think about was that, as soon as they were alone, he needed to tell her everything. And hope Christmas magic did its thing and helped her forgive him.

The next afternoon, Peter sat in Lara's office, the glow of the computer illuminating everything, just staring at the screen.

Ben was leaving any minute. Lance had had to work this morning, so they weren't leaving until the afternoon. He had promised to bring his son by the shop one last time to say goodbye to Lara before they left. Which meant that Peter would have her undivided attention tonight after work.

Time to confess and let her make her choices.

The Peter who'd written those posts had been bitter. Not just at losing out on the storefront, but at his life. At the turn it had taken and how he knew he should be grateful to be alive and happy to have such a terrific fallback plan. But really, he hadn't been any of that.

Until now.

He could hardly remember what he'd written in those posts, actually. It would probably be good to remind himself for certain before he made his confession. Because in his mind, they were pretty awful. His hand was clicking and typing before he'd even consciously made the decision, logging into the forum and bringing up his profile, which displayed all his posts.

Peter read the first one and felt marginally better. Not bad. Just asking a question. But the next one had him frowning. By the sixth one down, he leaned back, staring at the words. Again, nothing that was a direct or personal attack, but the bitterness and blame were there in every nuance, every phrase.

How had he let himself become that guy?

No wonder Emily had looked at him as though she didn't know him anymore when she'd confronted him about this. He didn't know this version of himself, either. Not anymore. And he had Lara to thank for that. Something about her . . . the same qualities that made him fall in love with her . . . had brought him out of that dark place he'd been in.

"Hey," her voice broke into his thoughts, and Peter quickly clicked away from the website before she could see it.

"Hey," he said back.

"Ben is here to say goodbye."

"Right." He was up and around the desk following her out into the shop.

In the North Pole, Ben was waiting, Lance standing behind him, hand on his son's shoulder. Ben held up the book they'd been reading together. "I'll make sure to finish it."

"Me too." Peter dropped down to one knee in front of

the boy. "Great story. But it won't be the same, reading it
on my own."

"Yeah." Ben wrapped his spindly, little-boy arms around
Peter's neck and squeezed so tight Peter grunted.

"I hope you'll come visit your auntie Lara often, and then
I can see you again."

Ben grinned at that. "That would be cool." He glanced
over his shoulder. "Can we do that, Daddy?"

Lance glanced first at Peter, then at Lara, and Peter got the
sudden impression the other man was running through their
altercation last night in his head. Had opening his big mouth
destroyed Lara's chance to see her nephew?

"We'll see," Lance said.

"I'd love for him to visit anytime," Lara murmured. Then
smiled tentatively at her brother. "You and Angela, too."

Lance's eyebrows lifted slowly. Then, he almost seemed to
soften a bit before he nodded.

Peter had a feeling that was the best they'd get from the
guy. Lara stepped forward and hugged her nephew, whispering in his ear about how much she'd loved having him, and
then hugged her brother briefly.

Together, they walked them out to their car and waved as
they drove away.

Beside him Lara heaved a heavy sigh.

"You okay?" he asked.

She huffed a small laugh. "You know, when Angela called
asking me to take Ben, all I could think of was how I didn't
have time. But then he got here and . . ."

"And you miss him already?"

She glanced up at him with a crooked smile. "Something
like that."

"Yeah." Him too. "I'd better go finish up."

They returned to her office. Him to work, her to grab
more cards for the front counter. "Hey . . ." he said, scooting

his chair in closer to the desk. "Dinner tonight? There's something I want to talk to you about."

He'd told Emily January, but he didn't want to have this hanging over them anymore. The shop was closing for the holiday, so if he hurt her, she'd at least have a little time to lick her wounds before dealing with the store again.

Or maybe he was being selfish and should wait. This entire situation had him second-guessing himself.

She paused and smiled at him. In the same instance, Snowball, out of nowhere, jumped up on the desktop with a soft *prrr-rrrup*.

"Snowball," Lara crooned, coming over to pat her. "Finally decided to come out of the house, huh? We've been worried about you."

Only as Snowball arched into Lara's touch, she somehow stepped on the computer mouse. "How about over here?" He scooped the cat up and deposited her on the other side of the L-shaped desk.

"What is this?" Lara asked.

Peter glanced at the cat, then around on the desk for anything out of place. "What?"

"On the screen." Her voice sounded tight.

And an odd preemptive dread sank a pit through his gut even as he turned his head to look in the same direction Lara was. Then he closed his eyes. Snowball had not only woken the computer up but clicked over to his profile on the forum.

"Peter?" Her voice had taken on a shake.

Peter reached for her, but she jerked away.

"I can explain," he said.

"Explain?" She flung a pointed finger in the direction of the screen. "That was *you*? You're Right Rudolph?"

"I didn't know . . ." He was rushing this. Messing this up. "I was the person you outbid for this space and didn't know it was you when I posted those things."

"And that makes it all right? To attack someone else's business?"

"No, I was . . . angry. All the time. Something to do with effects of brain trauma and a coma, and . . ." This was all wrong. "Not that it's an excuse."

She put a hand over her mouth. "You . . . you made me think . . . You *kissed* me."

"I fell in l—"

"Don't." The word came out so harshly guttural, she might as well have punched him. "Don't you dare . . ."

She was shaking her head now, backing up, bumping into the wall and then the doorjamb as she went, and he tried to follow while not crowding her. But as soon as they were in the storage room, she pointed. "Get out."

"Lara—"

"No." She wrapped her arms around her middle as though protecting herself from a physical blow. "I don't want to hear it. Please go."

"Lara—"

"Please, Peter," she whispered through white lips, and wrapped her arms around her middle so protectively that it physically hurt him to see it, like barbed wire wrapped around his heart.

So he listened. What else could he do?

"I'm . . . sorry," he said in a low voice. Not wanting to pile onto her pain with his own. Because he did this. This was his fault. So he walked away.

I did this.

I got so cooped up in that house, I just couldn't stand it anymore, but when Ben came to tell me goodbye I still hid. Then I felt awful because I could hear in his voice how upset he was that he couldn't find me. Ben really loves me. Not that my forever family don't, but kids are just . . . different.

So I hurried all the way to the shop to try to get to him before he left.

But he was already gone. He just . . . left. I messed up again, and then I made it worse with whatever I just did to Peter.

I run after him, trying to bring him back. I manage to get out of the store, and now I'm slipping and sliding my way across the cobblestones—the snow must've melted a bit and frozen over again while I've been hiding. Finally, I reach the grass and I hop up on the fence post as I go along.

I pause, searching for Peter. He should be easy to find. He's taller than most of the humans around here.

There he is!

Only he's not going to his car. He's heading toward the woods. Why? What could a human possibly need to do in the woods? They don't hunt or burrow or hibernate or anything. And it's cold outside. I glance at the gray skies threatening more snow. He shouldn't be out there.

As he tromps away, a rustle of movement near where he's walking catches my eye.

And then I see him. Sleek black coat, sparking green eyes, and all. Only the boy cat isn't alone. A girl cat is with him. Common tabby, but a pretty shade of orange with white ears. Their tails are practically twined as they walk slowly, side by side, into the forest along our border not far from where Peter just disappeared.

My heart cracks like a glass ornament I've knocked off a Christmas tree. Nothing is right, and it's all my fault.

Chapter 18

Lara dropped into the seat behind her desk, staring at the screen still all lit up with the evidence.

If Peter had told her as soon as he knew she was the owner, while it would have stung, she could have accepted his posts as a difference of opinion—sour grapes, like Emily had said—and moved on.

Only you wouldn't have learned what his kisses taste like.

She swallowed hard and reached for what she was feeling. An emotion. Any emotion. But she was numb. Logic told her that wasn't good. She'd felt this way twice before in her life. Once . . . when she'd learned just how badly off her ex had left her. And the other time . . . when Granny died.

She'd gone through all the motions of organizing the funeral, and burying her beloved grandmother, and settling the will, and selling the house. Even dealing with Lance and Angela. Months of numb only to have the avalanche that had been hanging over the precipice finally tumble over. The day she'd locked the door of that house, where she'd grown up and felt loved and laughed and cried, for the last time.

Her emotions had barreled through her, leveling her. She'd gotten into her car and just driven and driven and driven. Until she'd seen the lights of Weber Haus and stopped.

And met Peter the first time.

Lara closed her eyes, trying to shut it all out. But she kept seeing the screen with his name and that handle and those awful posts.

How could he hide this from her?

Not that the posts had been mean or nasty . . . just enough to give her confidence a good knocking, especially after her brother. Although all that bidding . . . He'd helped drive up the price on the space. Though that was just how business worked. But still . . .

Oh God. Those kisses.

Kisses she'd thought were real. That they meant something. Kisses that had her thinking she might make room in her life just for him, to give whatever was between them a chance.

She scoffed, the sound painful in her throat.

A chance.

What a joke.

The worst part was, despite his overly helpful moments, she thought he believed in her. The way he'd praised her marketing skills, and the toys. The way he'd assured her the store would succeed. Had he believed in none of that? Had he been secretly judging her?

That was worse than Lance. At least her brother was up front with her about his doubts and worries. Even if it hurt her to know she didn't have his support, she knew that and could deal with it accordingly.

But Peter . . .

Yeah, the joke was on her. She dropped her chin to her chest, the weight of everything making it impossible to hold up.

Then a thought hit and she jerked her head back up. Her financial systems.

Lara scooted into the computer and quickly brought up everything he'd been working on. But honestly her head was such a mess right now, she had no idea what to look for. The totals all looked fine. He didn't have access to her bank account info.

Peter wouldn't steal from me.

She mentally swatted that small voice away. Because how did she know that for sure? How could she trust anything about him?

You know him, that voice insisted. After all, the posts had stopped before the store even opened. In fact, the very last one had been concern for her when she'd had to close early to go pick up Ben.

But I don't know him. Not really. Because the man she thought she knew would have been honest with her about it.

Lara surged to her feet.

She couldn't figure this out right now. Couldn't process anything sitting here and she had a shop to run.

Taking a deep breath, she left her office and moved into the heart of her toy shop. Her dream. Her feet kept moving of their own accord, through the North Pole, onto the main shop floor, past the empty front counter. Then she walked outside, took a right, and let herself into the bakery. It was closed, like all the other shops today, but she'd heard someone moving around in there and had assumed it was Emily.

She'd been right.

Emily glanced up with a smile that froze as she caught sight of Lara's face. She opened her mouth, probably to ask what was wrong, but Lara beat her to it.

"Did you know?"

Emily frowned. "Know?"

"That Peter was 'Right Rudolph.' Did you know?"

The other woman—a woman she'd thought was her friend—stilled in a way that told Lara everything.

Lara shook her head. "I don't even know what to say."

"I only just found out," Emily rushed to assure her. "I told him to tell you or I would, and he said he would. I guess he . . . did."

How could Lara trust that was the truth, either? Peter was Emily's brother. Of course she should take his side.

"He didn't tell me. I saw him logged onto the account. On *my* computer . . ."

Emily winced. "I'm so sorry. What did he say?"

"I don't care what he would have said. I told him to leave, and he left."

"Oh, Lara . . ." Emily started around the counter. "Don't you think—"

"No." Lara jerked back a step. "I don't want to think about this right now. I just . . . I had to know if you knew."

"I'm sorry," Emily whispered, mouth pulling into a stricken grimace.

Right.

Maybe even more numb than she'd been before she came in here, Lara turned, shaking her head, and left. She'd get through Christmas first and deal with all of this later. She had a three-day break to get her head on straight and tell her heart to stop breaking over a man she shouldn't have fallen for in the first place.

Hopefully before the numb wore off and buried her.

I wait for Mrs. Bailey to let me into the house, scratching at the door halfheartedly. How could everything I thought was true have been so wrong?

I thought I'd helped Emily and Lukas find each other and me. I thought I'd helped Daniel and Sophie find forever love. I thought I was special, but Peter and Lara are fighting, and Ben is gone without saying goodbye, and Mr. Muir and his birds are moving in forever, and that boy cat . . .

My instincts are all wrong. All . . . wrong.

"There you are, Snowball," Mrs. Bailey says as she opens the door. She closes the door behind me and tutt-tutts her way back to the counter, where she is no doubt working on dinner. "Emily just came in here looking for Peter," she says.

I pause at the foot of the narrow back stairs. Emily was? Why?

"It sounds like he and Lara had a fight."

That I already know.

"Someone should help those two work it out. They're too perfect together to let whatever has come between them end things."

A few weeks ago I would think she was talking to me. But not now.

With a sigh I hop up the stairs until I reach the top landing. I'm planning on going all the way up to the attic, but voices draw me down the hall to Miss Tilly's room. I sit outside the door listening to Miss Tilly and Mr. Muir talking to Emily.

"I don't know where he went," Emily is saying. "But he needs to fix this. You should have seen her face."

I don't want to hear it. I've messed things up so badly, I shouldn't try to fix it. I'll probably only make it worse.

Instead, I go up to the next level. As I near Mr. Muir's room, a terrible squawking starts up. Not the taunting kind those birds always throw at me. Instead, this is . . . terrible. They're afraid.

I don't even think about it, I rush right to the door. I get lucky this time, that it's cracked open a tiny bit. Just enough that I manage to push my way inside.

The turtledoves are in their cage and they're flapping and screeching, a wild look in their eyes. But why?

I look around, and then I see it. A huge black rat is stalking them.

There are no rats in Weber Haus. If anyone would know, it's me. But . . . the man working in the basement . . . he must've disturbed the rat's hiding place. Tilly will be horrified it's in the house at all, but I don't have time to think about that.

The rat has already made its way up to the armchair next to the chest of drawers where their cage sits.

Kitty instinct overrides my own fear—because he really is a big one. In two bounds, using my claws on the velvet of the chair for leverage, I leap at him and pounce. The rat and I struggle, falling to the floor as we thrash around. His sharp teeth glint in the lamp light, and the birds are squawking and I'm growling and the rat is squeaking. Until I manage to end the fight.

I won't tell you how.

But as I stand over it, making sure the threat is gone, making sure it doesn't move again, Mr. Muir rushes into the room.

"Snowball, no!" he shouts.

What? But I just—

He scoops me up and shoves me in Miss Tilly's arms before rushing toward the bird cage. "My babies," he coos at them. "Did the mean kitty scare you?"

Mean kitty? I just saved those ungrateful feathered friends from a terrible fate.

Miss Tilly suddenly gasps. "Oh my goodness. John—"

"Hold on, Matilda. Let me just—"

"John, look!"

He stops at the urgency in her voice and she's pointing at the rat on the floor.

Mr. Muir turns and stills, staring. Then he lifts his weathered gaze to me, staring at me as though he doesn't really know me.

"She saved them," he says to Tilly.

She nods.

"She saved my babies," he repeats.

She nods again, only this time a slow smile spreads over her face, and she's petting my fur and cuddling me close. "They may be your babies, but Snowball is mine," she says. "I think it's time to start trusting her."

It is?

Mr. Muir steps closer, then reaches out a shaking hand and runs it gently over my ruined fur. "Thank you for saving them," he whispers.

Something in my heart unlocks. The gratefulness in this older gentleman's gaze, directed at me when he usually stares at me with such mistrust . . . I give a tiny rumble of a purr, just to let him know that maybe we can be friends now.

"She really is something," he says to Tilly.

"I know." She cuddles me close, rubbing her cheek against my mangled fur as though it doesn't matter that it's bristly in parts. Maybe it doesn't matter.

I want to stay here with them and bask in the love that I've been missing these last few weeks. But now that my own world feels as though it's righting itself, I've started thinking. Thinking hard about Peter and Lara.

Emily is right. So is Mrs. Bailey.

What Lara and Peter could have is *special*. It doesn't come along every day. Believe me, I watch people come in and out of the inn, and now the hotel and the shops, too. The kind of connection they have is important and worth fighting for.

Yes, I've made some mistakes lately, but they shouldn't suffer because of that.

I need to help them.

Purpose puffs my chest out. If I can save a pair of stupid birds, I can definitely fix the situation with Peter and Lara.

As all that hits me, I give myself a shake, all the way down to the tip of my fluffy tail, and in my head, I make a plan. Because this romance is going to take more than kitty magic. I left them on their own too long, which is on me. This is going to take extra help.

I twist in her hold until I can put my paws on Miss Tilly's face. Then I meow my little heart out until they listen to me and follow.

* * *

Peter sat at the ice-skating pond watching kids and parents gliding around, all happy and laughing. Except one little girl too scared to let go of her mother's hand. *She* didn't look happy. But the rest of the people . . .

Maybe sitting here surrounded by holiday cheer had been a bad idea.

Everything was wrong. He'd left Lara intending to go home and think. Instead he'd found himself first walking through the woods and then circling back around to the rink. They'd just been here last night, laughing and happy just like the skaters today.

He'd messed all that up. Him. By not telling her sooner. Maybe they could have gotten around the posts eventually if he'd been up front to begin with.

So fix it.

"*Meow.*"

He glanced down to find Snowball sitting at his feet, tail wrapped primly around her paws. The look in her eyes—he would swear right to Santa's face—was one of apology. And worry.

Peter sighed. "I'm not angry at you, Snowball. It's all my fault. Not yours."

"*Meow.*" The tenor changed, and he interpreted that as, "*True.*"

He patted the bench beside him, and without hesitation she jumped up and turned so she sat facing the same way he was, watching the skaters, too. Petting her soft fur, he stopped when he reached the patch that had been cut.

"Sorry about that business, runt," he said.

After all, if he was apologizing, he might as well cover his bases.

"*Prrrup,*" was Snowball's reply.

He toasted her with his lukewarm hot chocolate, which

he'd sort of wished he'd sweetened with whiskey, but he didn't exactly carry the stuff around.

"I really messed up," he said, more to himself than her.

"Then fix it, son."

Peter glanced off to the side to find Miss Tilly and Mr. Muir slowly making their way toward him across the snowy ground, their feet crunching in the fresh layer of snow. Then he glanced at Snowball, having the actual thought of, *"Did she bring them?"*

And damned if the cat didn't nod at him like, *"You should listen to their wisdom."*

Then she hopped down as though making room for the older couple and pranced away toward the little girl who was now crying at the edge of the rink.

"I don't know how to fix it," Peter finally said.

Mr. Muir helped Tilly to sit, then dropped to the bench himself, forcing Peter to scoot over. "I can't tell you how. That is going to depend on what you did and how you did it."

Great. Not helpful.

"But I will say this . . . You know my story with Tilly. I walked away and she didn't want to follow. And while I had a wonderful life that I can't regret, I do regret not trying harder. Only a week away from her and I knew I should come right back. Beg her. Convince her. But I didn't want to put my heart out there again to get it smashed. To endure that hurt or even the humiliation."

Mr. Muir faced his sweetheart, taking her aged hand in his and looking at her the way a child looked at the tree and presents on Christmas morning. "The older, wiser me now would tell my younger self that that small prick of pride is worth it. That sacrificing what I want in that moment, if it means we stay together, is worth it. That doing everything I can to be with that one person who makes me feel the way she does . . . that's worth it."

Peter watched the two together and his heart ached for them, both for the years they'd lost and for the love they'd renewed now.

Mr. Muir dragged his gaze away from Miss Tilly. "So learn from an old man, son. Ask yourself if she's worth it. If the answer is yes, go fall on that sword."

"She doesn't want to hear anything I have to say."

"So you make a gesture," Tilly said. "And then another. And then another. And you don't stop until she hears you out. Respectfully, of course. Don't be scary." She waved a hand at that. "If after that she still says no, then that's her choice."

Peter slowly stood up, mind buzzing. Because the older couple was right. And he intended to start by telling Lara that he'd give her space for a little bit, but that they needed to talk this out. That he'd wait for her to be ready, no matter how long that took.

In a jerking motion, he looked at them.

"Go," Tilly urged.

Peter took off and forgot about being dignified about it. He needed to get to Lara. He ran all the way back to the shops, ignoring the curious looks of the people he passed, and had the door of The Elf Shop open when Emily stuck her head out of the bakery.

"Where have you been?" she snapped. "We've been worried."

"Sorry, Em. Can't stop. I need to talk to Lara."

The door was closing behind him when his sister called out, "She's not there."

He whipped back around to find her waiting outside. "What do you mean?"

"She left. After coming to see me, she went back into the shop and two minutes later came back out with her purse. Said she couldn't do this, got in her car, and drove away."

No.

Which was the exact moment when the weight of what he'd done struck with all the force of a winter superstorm that would've delayed Santa and his reindeer by a week, regardless of Rudolph's nose.

"Where?" he managed to force from his lips.

"I don't know."

"When?"

"About twenty minutes ago."

"Did you see which way she went?"

She shook her head.

"*Mrrrooowwww.*" Snowball suddenly was at his feet, winding around his ankles, almost as though offering comfort.

Only when he absently reached out to pet her, she trotted a few feet away, then meowed again.

Peter frowned.

The others had told him tales of this cat leading them to the person they were looking for. Honestly, he hadn't really believed it. Except that he could swear she wanted him to follow her now.

"Do you know where Lara is?" he asked.

She meowed again and trotted farther.

Peter glanced at Emily, who shrugged. "It's worth a try."

Right. He took a few steps and sure enough she kept going, turning every so often to make certain he was still with her. She led him all the way to his truck.

Peter stared at his truck, then at her.

"I can't believe I'm doing this," he muttered under his breath. What if he lost Lara while he was playing cat whisperer?

Even so, he scooped Snowball up and got in.

Before he started the engine he made a call to Emily, letting her know he'd bring Snowball back later. And then he took minutes—minutes where the cat pawed at him urgently—as he did one more thing on his phone, hoping like heck it was the right thing to do.

Finally, he put down his phone and started the truck. "All right, runt. Where to?"

"*Meow.*"

She might understand human, but he didn't understand cat. He'd have to make this call himself.

"Right. Home it is."

Chapter 19

Lara tried not to look back at her house as she drove away. It had taken her all of five seconds back in the shop to realize that she couldn't possibly finish working. Not in the state she was in. So she'd snatched up her purse and left.

After that, the rest was a blur. Getting home. The relief that Peter's truck wasn't parked out front. Packing quickly. Relief again that he hadn't returned while she'd been doing that. Then heading out. Feeling all the while as though she was in the wrong, like she was the one sneaking away.

At least she knew where she was going.

To Lance's house. Not that she'd probably be all that welcome, but maybe if she offered to help look after Angela's mother, who was staying with them while she healed, they wouldn't mind. At least then she'd get to spend her holiday with Ben . . . and not completely alone.

Who knew she'd ever look at her brother as an escape from her problems?

Not exactly a Christmas miracle. After all, she was basically counting on both Lance and Angela to fill her head with so much noise that they drowned out her own thoughts. But still . . . better than nothing.

As she hit the end of town, a snowflake hit her windshield

and she wrinkled her nose, leaning forward a bit to look up at the sky.

"Santa, if ever I needed something for Christmas, snow is not it," she muttered.

Right now the roads were clear and dry. Hopefully they'd stay that way.

Another snowflake on her windshield seeming to laugh in her face. With a sigh, Lara kept going. Only the closer she got to Weber Haus, and her store . . . and Peter . . . the worse the ache in her heart got. This was so wrong. All of it. And maybe she would be handling things better if she hadn't fallen in love with him.

Her mind wanted to replay every moment, every glance, every word since the day she moved in next to him until now. How had she not known, not realized?

Oh God . . . she'd made him play Santa. That grouchy thing he'd been doing that day hadn't just been Peter, that had been him not wanting to help the store that he'd been hoping would fail. No wonder he'd acted that way. Except then he'd . . . changed . . . helped with Ben, and helped with the books, and helped with the ice cream.

And kissed me.

And she was so confused, her head was starting to hurt, the ache setting up right behind her eyes.

A little time. Just the three days the holiday was giving her. After that she'd go home and get on with her life.

She sighed as she hit the four-way stop with its usual lines of backed-up cars. Tapping her fingernail against the steering wheel, she stopped and went and stopped and went all the way up to the sign, taking careful note of the order things were moving so that she knew when to take her turn.

Only when she tried to take that turn, the guy across the street tried to go, too. They both stopped and looked at each other.

"My turn, buddy," she muttered. And hit the gas.

Only he did, too, at the same time.

And they both stopped. Again.

"Go then." She waved.

He waved.

She went.

He went.

She stopped.

He stopped.

The person to her right got sick of it and went.

"Oh, good grief." Lara threw up her hands. All she wanted to do was get out of town.

Peter was in the four-way stop line trying not to lose it. The backup was even worse than it usually was. As he pulled up to the stop sign, Snowball, who had been sitting nicely beside him, suddenly jumped onto the dash.

"Hey! Get down." He reached for the little cat.

But she pranced out of his way and started meowing and pawing at the windshield.

"Snowball! Get—"

He happened to look to his left in the direction Snowball was pawing and cut off everything with a grunt as he recognized the little blue car with an irritated woman waving politely, but slightly aggressively, at the man across from him and to her left.

Without thinking about anything except getting to Lara, Peter put his truck in park and was out the door and walking through the intersection toward her.

Lara's gaze moved from the man she was in a wave battle with and landed on Peter, and even in the dim of the car, and shadows of the gloomy, overcast day, he could see how she paled. As he walked, she started to shake her head.

But he wasn't going to stop. Not until she'd heard him out.

Apparently, she realized this, too, because she made a disgruntled face and rolled her window down.

Peter bent over the car, hands on the top, to look her in the eyes.

She took a visible breath, then, lips pinched, stared straight back at him. "You're holding up traffic—"

"I love you."

Her hands curled around the steering wheel, knuckles turning white. "I don't believe you."

Then she frowned, gaze moving over his shoulder, and waved an impatient hand at the guy who apparently wanted to go.

"I love you," Peter repeated, pulling her gaze back to him. "All I ask is that you hear me out—"

"How can I trust anything you have to say?"

"Just listen," he pleaded. "And let me show you something."

Her lips compressed in a mulish expression. "I don't—"

A car horn honked from somewhere in the four lines backing up. Peter ignored it. "Please." He held up his cell phone. "Just look. If you don't want to hear me out after that, I'll accept it."

For now. Until he could find another way to try to show her how sorry he was.

Lara stared at the device in his hand and suddenly her eyes welled up, a tear slipping down her cheek, and Peter had to lean over, because "gutted" didn't cover it. He did that. He made her cry.

"Peter," she whispered.

Another car honked.

She blew out a breath. "We're holding everyone up."

"This is more important," he insisted.

She closed her eyes, giving her head a shake. Then, with a small huff of a breath, held out her hand. "Fine."

That was something. He'd take it. He'd take any small amount of willingness to listen that she'd give him.

Please, God, let this convince her. Because he wasn't sure what else he could do.

"First, you should know that I was in a bad place, angry all the time. I had my heart set on your location and was so invested in that bidding war. I was sure I was going to win. But when I didn't, it hit me hard. I know what I did was wrong. I think I even knew it then. I've been trying to fix it."

"I don't see how you can—"

He pulled up the screen of what he wanted her to see and handed her the phone.

Only she took one glance at it and shoved it right back out the window at him. "I'm not reading those posts again."

"Please." He'd go down on his knees and beg if he had to.

Honking was coming from multiple cars now.

Since they were blocking two lanes, he was vaguely aware that two were going at least. He ignored it all. But Lara looked around and frowned again. "Is that . . . Is Snowball in your truck?"

He offered a sheepish shrug. "She wanted me to come find you."

Lara blinked, then moved her gaze back to his face, seeming to search for something there. Peter stared right back, hoping like hell that she saw what she needed to see. His heart beat a rapid tattoo against the inside of his ribs, his stomach trying to push heart and lungs up his throat.

Lara bit her lip and pulled the phone back inside to look at the screen.

At first, her expression remained doubtful. After a second, she brought the screen closer to her face as though she couldn't quite believe what she was reading. Then her brows furrowed.

And Peter stood there, snow softly falling all around him, Snowball in his truck, and cars honking as he waited for the woman he loved more than anything to decide if he was worthy of forgiveness.

* * *

Lara stared at the phone screen in front of her, and it took her more than a couple tries to focus on the words.

Peter standing right there didn't help. Neither did the honking.

But then she caught the drift of the post he'd written. A new post by Right Rudolph on the town forum. Only the words made her heart tremble in an entirely new way than every previous post of his.

He'd confessed who he was and why he'd posted those things. He apologized to her, and to the town, but more than that were the words that came after. Words about how the toy shop was a magical place for adults and children alike. Words about how much the town needed that store as well as her. About how brilliant she was at making such a wonderful place and how the town should support her.

Everything else fell away as she read his post, and then read it again, and again until the tears blurring her eyes wouldn't let her read it anymore.

She lifted her gaze to the man standing outside her window, his expression almost painfully hopeful.

He offered her another of those crooked, self-deprecating smiles. "I left something out of that post that's personal . . ." He swallowed, Adam's apple bobbing up and down over the top of his scarf. "I am so in love with you that my heart aches a little when you're not around. I didn't want that to make people think I was only posting because of my feelings. So I left out the part about how much *I* need you. Way more than this town needs you and The Elf Shop."

He leaned closer, close enough to see the small scar between his brows and the slightly hazel ring around his pupils.

Peter searched her gaze. "I think the day you dragged me into your store to be your Santa was the best day of my entire life."

Something inside Lara gave. Not an avalanche this time.

Not destructive like that. This waterfall of emotions was more like the snow softly falling over the landscape right now, making everything fresh and pristine, covering all manner of sins.

Maybe that's what forgiveness was.

Relief and love swelled inside her, melting the ice that had formed around her heart, and she gave a watery laugh.

His crooked grin stretched wider, a desperate, unmistakable kind of hope in his eyes.

On a sob of emotions—too many to name and number—she scrambled to release her seat belt and clamber out of the car, throwing her arms around his neck on a laugh.

He hugged her so tight, she could hardly breathe. "Thank God," he whispered. "I'm glad I listened to that darn cat."

Lara looked up on a laugh, and her heart tumbled over itself at the look in Peter's eyes. No one had ever looked at her that way except maybe Granny. As though she was his center, the most precious person in his life.

"You really do love me?" she asked.

He nodded.

She lifted a hand to his jaw, the rasp of his scruff rough against her palm. "I believe you."

He grunted, as if those words were both painful and perfect. To soothe the pain, she went up on her tiptoes and placed her lips to his. Kissing him long and lingering. Trying to put every ounce of the forgiveness fizzing through her into the touch. Taking away the pain for them both.

All around them cheering broke out, along with a lot of honking. They broke apart to find that several people had gotten out of their cars.

"Good for you!" the overly polite man across from her called out. "But you might want to find another place to do more kissing."

She and Peter both laughed.

"Follow me?" he asked.

She nodded, cheeks flaming with heat, and hurried back into her car. Rather than turn for home, though, Peter swung his truck around and headed in the direction of Weber Haus.

Blinking a little, she shrugged and followed, and blushed at every person who waved and smiled at her as she drove past the long line of cars they'd been holding up.

All the way to Weber Haus Lara played the words of Peter's post over and over in her head, heart lifting a little more with each moment.

In the parking lot, she swung her car next to his. By the time she got out he was around to her side, pulling her right back into his arms where he kissed her, and kissed her, and kissed her, until they both needed to come up for air.

Peter put his forehead to hers and breathed out. "I was so scared," he said. "Terrified I'd messed this up before we ever got started."

Her big, burly, apparently not that reluctant Santa had been scared? Too cute.

"Where were you going?" he asks.

"To spend Christmas with Ben."

He winced. "At your brother's?"

She nodded.

"You must have been desperate."

"You broke my heart," she whispered.

Peter flinched against her, true regret in his eyes. "I knew I should have told you sooner," he said. "I just couldn't figure out how, and I didn't want to lose you, and the longer I waited the worse it got."

"Was this what you wanted to talk to me about tonight, and the other day?"

He nodded.

And another small worry released, melting away.

But still she frowned. "You had to have meant at least a little of what you posted on the forums," she said. "I need you to be honest now."

Peter stilled against her, and she knew she'd been right to ask.

Deliberately she took a step back, letting her arms fall to her side. "I mean it," she said. "I need to know."

What if he told her what Lance had been telling her all along? That she wasn't meant to run a business. That she was great with toy making but crap with finance. That she was going to squander all of Granny's hard-earned money and bankrupt herself.

Could she really stay with a man who didn't believe in her dreams, no matter how much she loved him?

Peter took a deep breath, turning so solemn, fear rushed into all the holes her own self-doubt had left inside her.

"At first, I thought that you had made some potentially costly decisions that might be a problem for you."

She swallowed back a knee-jerk reaction of wanting to defend herself and forced herself to listen.

"Outbidding me that way." She opened her mouth, but he held up a hand, stopping her. "I drove up that price as much as you did," he admitted. "But then there was elaborate setup of the store and not recouping costs like the ornaments."

Each new thing she'd done wrong made her want to argue, but she waited. Because something in his tone told her it was worth waiting for.

"Then I saw your income, and I have to say that not only do you make wonderful toys that kids love, but you have a terrific marketing mind."

He may as well have taken her up in Santa's sleigh, the extreme from down to up like whooshing into the sky.

"You think so?" she asked. "Really?"

"Really."

"But the books . . ." she pointed out. "You've done all those things to help me cut back my spending." As though he thought he could fix the problems he saw by going around her.

Except Peter shook his head. "Every business can cut back somewhere. But those were all small suggestions to maximize your income. Things I'm sure you would have thought of yourself if you weren't run off your feet trying to get the store going."

Lara looked at him, and what she saw looking back was total sincerity. And thinking through things, not only did she see what he meant about finding small ways to maximize income, but she saw other things in his behavior, too. He'd stopped badgering her about getting enough sleep and just stepped in to help, letting her make those decisions for herself. He'd trusted the way she'd handled Ben, only offering help, but never altering her plans. And after the Santa incident—which he still did nicely, though in full Peter fashion—every action he'd taken had been to help her. *Nothing* like her ex. Real help. And not just with the store, but with Ben.

He really did believe in her.

And she would have seen it if she hadn't been letting her own fears and her past with her ex and her brother's doubts hold her back.

"I suppose . . ." she said slowly. "That now would be a good time to tell you that I've fallen in love with you, too—"

The breath punched from her along with anything else she might have said as he yanked her right back into his arms.

"Now I know why Scrooge changed his ways. Love. Because that's the best Christmas present I've ever had . . . or could have ever asked for . . ." he whispered against her lips and kissed her breathless all over again.

Until a small little meow pulled them apart. Still holding on to each other, they looked down to find Snowball prancing around their feet.

"Maybe you should thank Snowball," Lara murmured.

At his huff of a laugh, she lifted her head and grinned at him. "After all," she pointed out, "she's the reason you played Santa for me in the first place."

The little cat meowed again, as though in agreement.

Peter shook his head, but even so, he scooped the cat up between them. "Thank you, Snowball."

Immediately Snowball put both paws on the sides of his face, as though making sure she had his attention. After a long look, she leaned forward and butted her head into his chin, an impossibly loud purr erupting from her tiny body.

Lara laughed. "I think you're right. She really does speak human."

Taking Peter's hand—still stunned that less than an hour ago she'd been figuring out how to live her life without him and now here she was, willing to give this all another chance—together they walked toward the house where they'd met, where they'd fallen in love, where they'd almost messed that up, and now, where they looked forward to a future together.

She sighed, for once letting her happiness silence any lingering doubts. Deep down inside she knew they'd work through any other obstacles together. Peter had proven that over and over the last weeks, and that was while he resented her at the beginning of things, looking for ways she was messing up.

Just think of how they'd be with him entirely on her side.

Darkness had fallen while they'd been gone, and right on time, the lights of the house and shops blinked on, illuminating the white siding and making the place glow, the snow glittering and glinting . . . a magical winter wonderland. Santa's real North Pole home couldn't be better than this.

And now she would get to spend Christmas here with the man she'd given every ounce of her heart to—a holiday humbug who managed to learn to love.

Epilogue

The following summer . . .

Music floats over the warm summer breeze from the direction that Emily is carrying me. Lukas was going to carry me, but apparently that would mean getting white fur all over his dark suit. I'm not sure why that's a problem, but I don't mind either way.

Today is special, and I'm so happy to be right at the center of it.

Emily rounds the corner of the house and I can see now all the white chairs set up on the lawn out front for a wedding. Weber Haus hosts lots of weddings, but this is the most important one. The chairs are filled with people who are turned around to watch us walk toward them. There is a narrow aisle down the center and at the end of it a groom is waiting for his bride.

He is so handsome in a dark gray suit with a pink tie. They'd argued about the pink, but the bride had won that one in the end. And she'd been right. It looks fantastic against his white hair.

Beside Mr. Muir, Lukas stands as best man. And Emily is

the matron of honor. And I . . . I am the most important one
here.

I am the ring bearer.

The rings are tied to my collar with a pink silk ribbon and
a bell, so you can hear them tinkle as I walk. As soon as she
reaches the "aisle" Emily sets me down, which is a little awkward. Her baby bump makes bending hard. The baby is due
any day now.

By the way, Emily is not the only one with a baby. Near
the house a flash of movement catches my attention. The
tomcat and his tabby are walking around the corner with a
trail of three tiny kittens rolling and tripping and bouncing
along behind them. Seems soon to me for them to be having
babies.

I think I had a narrow escape with that one.

Emily reaches the end of the aisle and turns and smiles at
me. That's my signal.

Head raised high, I prance and preen down the aisle, enjoying every *ooh* and *aah* that follows me along.

I go right to Lukas, who is waiting with a treat, which I
nibble right out of his hand. Then he unties the ribbon and
takes the rings before picking me up gently and settling me
into Ben's arms. He's sitting beside Lara and Peter, his parents seated farther back. Peter and Lara have joined forces.
He runs the business side of both the toy shop and the bookstore now. He hired another man to take over the running of
the front of the bookstore, and Lara focuses on making toys
and running the front of the toy shop. Peter is in charge of ice
cream, though.

I also saw the ring he's been hiding. He's going to propose
tonight at the reception. He told me so!

We are seated next to Sophie and Daniel, who reaches over
and pats me on the head, and I bat at his hand with my paw.

Then, the music changes, and all the humans stand up and turn.

It takes a few minutes before I see her, and if I was human, I would cry at how beautiful she looks. Miss Tilly is wearing a gown of satin covered in lace. The top is light pink with three-quarter-length sleeves, and the floor-length skirt with a small train is a darker pink. A glittering belt at her waist matches the pink diamonds sparkling in her ears and the bigger one in her engagement ring.

But what makes her the most beautiful bride in the world is the way she glows with true, deep happiness. A happiness reflected at her by the groom, who I turn my head to watch as he sees his bride. The woman he pined for most of his life.

I sigh in blissful contentment.

Then I glance at the display of flowers set up behind where the minister is standing. An unusual arrangement that incorporates a golden bird cage.

Mr. Muir's turtledoves look out over the ceremony, watching our happy humans, the closest things to smiles that my new feathered housemates can manage, given the beaks, wreathed across their faces.

I sigh again.

We may never be *best* friends, but we get along when we have to. Mr. Muir is part of my forever family now, living in Weber Haus with all of us. Everything is going to be all right.

Tilly reaches her groom's side and takes his hands, and as we all sit back down, I start to purr. This really is a wonderful life.

Acknowledgments

I get to do what I love surrounded by the people I love—a blessing that I thank God for every single day. Writing and publishing a book doesn't happen without the support and help from a host of incredible people.

To my fantastic romance readers: Thank you for going on these journeys with me, for your kindness, your support, and generally being awesome. Peter and Lara's story started in my head the second they were on the page (ever so briefly) in *Snowball's Christmas*. I love a good grumpy hero with a squishy middle, and a toy shop owner was just purrfect for him! I hope you fell in love with these characters and their story as much as I did. If you have a free second, please think about leaving a review. Also, I love to connect with my readers, so I hope you'll drop a line and say "Howdy" on any of my social media!

To my editor, John Scognamiglio: Thank you for your continued love of Snowball and her antics and a shared love of classic holiday movies for inspiration for the next one!

To my agent, Evan Marshall: Thank you for your belief in me and constant, steady guidance. You are my rock.

To the team at Kensington: I know how much work goes into each and every book, a ton of which authors never see. I thank you so much for making this book the best it could be!

To Nicole and Courtney, who jumped in and helped me figure out the conflict resulting in such a fun story!

To my support team of writing buddies, readers, reviewers, friends, and family (you know who you are): I know I say this every time, but I mean it . . . my stories wouldn't come alive the way they do if I didn't have the wonderful experiences and support that I do. And that's all because of you.

Finally, to my husband, I love you so much. You are why I know what a good man is and how he acts in this world, which means I found my hero. And to our amazing kids, you are my light, my laughter, and my love.